BARBECUE & BROOMS

A Southern Charms Cozy Mystery

BELLA FALLS

Evermore Press

ISBN-10: 1799298450

ISBN-13: 978-1799298458

Cover by Victoria Cooper

❀ Created with Vellum

Also by Bella Falls

A Southern Charms Cozy Mystery Series

Moonshine & Magic: Book 1

Lemonade & Love Potions (Southern Charms Cozy Short)

Fried Chicken & Fangs: Book 2

Sweet Tea & Spells: Book 3

Barbecue & Brooms: Book 4

Collards & Cauldrons: Book 5

Cornbread & Crossroads: Book 6 (Coming Soon)

*All audiobooks available are narrated by the wonderful and talented Johanna Parker

For a FREE exclusive copy of the prequel Chess Pie & Choices, sign up for my newsletter!

https://dl.bookfunnel.com/opbg5ghpyb

Share recipes, talk about Southern Charms and all things cozy mysteries, and connect with me by joining my reader group Southern Charms Cozy Companions!

https://www.facebook.com/
groups/southerncharmscozycompanions/

CONTENTS

For all my Southern Charmers—Thanks for giving me encouragement, barbecue team names, and your patience while you waited for this book!

Preface

In *Barbecue & Brooms*, I had some fun with Lucky the leprechaun and his true origins. In creating his own original tale, I took liberties with real mythology and stories of the origins of the fae and all its kind, so some of Lucky's story may not match the history books if you go searching for him. But I hope you like finding out our friend may be a little more than he seems.

Chapter One

Drinking sweet tea. Bugging my brother Matt. Baking the tastiest chess pie. Gobbling up all the good food Nana makes, like this morning's buttermilk biscuits with fried country ham and grape jelly. Finding things for people. My brain shuffled through all the stuff I excelled at on a regular basis. So why couldn't flying on a broomstick be on that list?

I squeezed my thighs around the skinny length of wood, trying my hardest not to fall out of the sky. Mason had patiently given me multiple lessons over the past two months, but for the life of me, I still couldn't get the hang of it. Today's was all about increasing my speed to a respectable rate. But zooming faster somehow made the rest of my lessons leak out my ears.

When I copied Mason's movements, I could almost

believe that I might master being on a broom. But when he switched places, putting me in the lead, I figured the only place a broom should exist was in my hands, sweeping dust.

"You need to direct yourself right or left, up or down. Flying in a straight line is only going to work for so long," Mason called out while soaring slightly behind me to my left. I'd bet a pound of unicorn manure he wasn't sweating at all.

I let go of the wooden handle long enough to wipe a drop off my brow. "I got this," I gritted through my teeth at the man. *I got nothin'*, I admitted to myself.

The far edge of Tipper's land, which now belonged to my brother, loomed ahead. Right. Left. Up. All good choices my body couldn't figure out how to execute in order not to crash into the trees.

"Just lean a little to your left," instructed Mason. "No, not your right, your left." He motioned the correct direction with a jerk of his head.

Somewhere inside of me existed the knowledge of how to maneuver my exasperating flying contraption, but the fear of knocking myself out shadowed any ability to recollect how.

"I can't!" I exclaimed, holding my arm up to shield my face from the imminent impact into the protruding forest.

"Charli!" Mason zipped to my side and nudged me off course.

I dropped underneath the incoming branch at the last second. Instead of the hard impact of wood knocking me out, tendrils of Spanish moss tickled my forehead.

In a panic, I aimed my body toward the ground and forgot

to slow down for the descent. The second my heels touched earth, I tumbled over the front of the handle and somersaulted a couple of times until I lay splayed out on my back, staring up into the afternoon sky. It wasn't the first time I'd fallen off my broom and I doubted it would be the last.

When my senses and brain caught up to my body, I remembered why I needed to land. "Mason," I cried out, "You okay?"

Like a pro, the detective landed next to me without so much as a mark in the dirt. "I'm more worried about your noggin'," he joked, holding out a hand to help me up.

Accepting his offer, I allowed him to hoist me onto my feet. My eyes lit on a few scratches on his face, and I touched the pink lines with my fingertips. He reached up and held my hand against his cheek, leaning into my touch. His eyes went soft with a familiar warmth.

Biddy's dark form fluttered down next to us, and she squawked a few times. No, it sounded more like cackling with bird amusement. Her interruption dashed cold water on the moment between the detective and me.

"No more leftover biscuits on the porch for you, missy," I taunted the bird, slipping my hand out from under Mason's. I jutted my bottom lip out to pout, "I'm never gonna get the hang of this dang blasted thing." For good measure, I kicked the bristles of the broom.

Mason chuckled and sighed. "Well, I don't think we'll be signing you up for the amateur race this weekend, that's for sure. But you are getting faster. That's something."

I shot Biddy a sideways glance for her sarcastic caws. "Faster, maybe. But my goal is still at the level of a toddler's."

Mason shook his head. "That's not true. I think Big Willie's youngest can out-fly you."

Life was not fair if the little hairy sasquatch could soar through the air better than me, an experienced witch. "That's because he's using one of Lee's special spellcasted brooms," I defended my poor abilities.

Mason threw his arm around my shoulder. "Or maybe flying can be more of a hobby for you, much like knitting or painting. At least that way it will be safer."

"But I don't do either of those." I frowned in confusion.

The detective's eyes sparkled with too much glee. "Exactly."

His comment earned him a quick punch and a shove away from me. The genuine smile on my lips reminded me how much I enjoyed my time with Mason when there wasn't so much pressure on defining who we were to each other. He never pushed too hard, and for that I was grateful. But I knew time was running out for my avoidance of emotional definitions, whatever they might be.

"You are signed up to race, though, aren't you?" I asked.

Mason lifted his eyebrow with rare cockiness. "At least one. It'll be fun to stretch my proverbial wings again. I've forgotten how much fun it is to compete, plus there may be a few dollars on the line as well."

I gasped and covered my mouth in fake shock, putting on

my best Scarlett O'Hara imitation. "Why, Detective, you're bettin' on yourself?"

"Who better to place my faith in?" He shrugged his shoulders. "Now, why don't you let me show you a little of what it'll be like when I take control of the stick?"

We'd flown together a few times, tethering our magic and connecting on a very intimate level. Usually after one of those occasions, we came mighty close to taking the intimacy between us to a new level.

My cheeks heated under his gaze. "I don't know if we have time for a long shared ride before tonight's town hall meeting," I countered, taking no pleasure in the lie.

We had time for a short tandem flight, but I wasn't prepared right now to deal with what came after. Sometimes I craved the exhilaration of hurtling through the air with his body pressed against my back and his arms wrapped around me to hold on, but I didn't know what to do after our feet touched solid ground again.

A slight wrinkle appeared in between the detective's eyebrows, and I knew my lack of enthusiasm frustrated him. Unable to help myself, I reached up with my finger and tried to smooth the crease out. "I'm sorry, Mason," I whispered.

He relaxed a little. "I told you I wouldn't push things between us and I meant it. Being your friend is important to me."

Before I could reply, Mason placed a finger over my lips. "You don't have to say anything. Even though I move fast on a broom, slow and steady is my normal pace. As long as the door is still open, I'm good."

Doubt seeped into my heart, but I did my best to ignore it and changed the subject. "I wish I could experience what you do when you race."

Mason's eyes brightened. "You can if you're willing to trust me. We've already shared magic before, so it shouldn't be that hard."

"What are you talking about?"

He took a step closer to me. "You can borrow a piece of my magic for a short amount of time. Use it to fly at least one lap around this field. I know we've got time for this."

Fear and excitement mixed in my stomach. "Isn't that dangerous?" With my new job not keeping me as busy as I'd like and a lack of murders to investigate, I kind of missed the adrenaline rush. But using big magic always came with a price, and Nana had instilled in me a goodly amount of caution.

Still...frosted fairy wings, I couldn't let the sheriff's hairy offspring best me. Besides, when one has the opportunity to capture a unicorn even for a brief moment, one shouldn't turn it down, right?

Mason thrust the handle of his broom into my hands. "Trust me."

With a nod and a willful ignoring of a Nana-type voice blaring a warning in my head, I agreed. "I do. Now how do we do this?"

He stood in front of me and took both my hands, his thumbs stroking my skin. "This might feel a bit weird at first, and you won't have much time. Try to keep to the edge of the field and don't go beyond the border of the field."

"But what if I lose control and the trees threaten to smack my witchy behind back down to Earth?" For goodness sakes, I still had grass stains and bruises on my rump.

Mason shook his head. "I won't let you get hurt. If something happens, I should be able to steer you out of the way."

My eyebrows raised in alarm. "You mean, this would give you control over me?"

The detective pondered my slightly freaked out inquiry. "Yes and no. That's why you have to trust me not to take advantage. I'll let you use my skills but won't overpower you. You up for it?"

Nana's powerful voice echoed too loud for me to ignore in the back of my mind, "Birdy, don't you *dare* do it!"

But my curiosity and immediate desires drowned out her sensible advice. "I'm ready."

The corners of his lips curved up in gleeful satisfaction. "Right. I'm going take a page out of your spellbook, so to speak. Here we go." He closed his eyes and squeezed my hands.

I took the unguarded opportunity to gawk at him, marveling at his intense sincerity in wanting to share so much with me. My fingers itched to scratch the slight stubble he allowed to grow out because he knew how much I liked the bad boy vibe it gave him. Too caught up in my scrutiny of the man in front of me, I almost forgot to throw up a wall of protection. Without one, I risked his magic short circuiting me. Closing my eyes, I focused on keeping us both safe.

Mason spoke with a clear tone. *"In this time and in this hour, let us share our magic power. Into her body, my powers pour and let her take the broom to soar. This special skill I give for free. As I will it, so mote it be."*

The traditional end of his spell surprised me, and my eyes flew open only to find him smirking at me.

The cheeky detective winked and finished his spell in a little more my style. *"With my magic, let Charli fly, and give her confidence that she won't die."*

Power tingled in my hands and jolted up my arms. I drew in a breath and closed my eyes again, trying hard not to pass out from the sudden sensation. After a few moments of concentration, I let my guard down and relaxed. The foreign yet familiar magic settled down and flowed inside my body until it filled me to the brim.

With relief that I didn't faint, I blinked my eyes open to find Mason staring with concern. Determined for him to stop seeing me as weak, I licked my lips and snickered. "Mmm. Kind of tastes like chocolate."

The tension from Mason's shoulders dropped. "Good, but you better take advantage fast. I'm not sure how long the spell will hold," he reminded, tapping the wooden handle.

Following the instructions he'd given me since day one with a broom, I kicked off the ground with more grace than I'd ever known. Leaning forward, I willed the flying instrument to go, and it bounded off like a rocket. Instead of normal fear coursing through my veins, adrenaline pumped excitement through, fueling pure joy inside me.

No longer struggling to control the simplest maneuver, I loosened my grip and allowed myself to enjoy the ride. Testing my limits, I leaned forward and pushed faster.

Biddy dropped out of the sky and joined me on my left flank, her wings spread wide enough for her dark feathers to almost brush my arm. The first time I flew together with Mason, we'd allowed her to guide us. I sent a silent wish, hoping she'd rise to the challenge. With a slight cock of her head, the crow banked a hard left, and I dove with ease right behind her.

A loud whoop escaped my throat as I zigged and zagged right behind her feathery figure. She tested my ability to keep up with a few dips and climbs that would have stumped me before, but with the borrowed magic I tapped into, it felt like child's play.

"What else you got?" I dared with a grin.

Sensing my newfound skills, Biddy let out a defiant caw and led me closer to the woods at the far border of the property. I dodged outreaching branches with ease, no longer acting out of fear at the threat of one of them knocking me out. Effervescent giggles bubbled up and burst out of my mouth at the thrill of the ride. If someone could fly like this, why would they ever want to walk on the ground again?

Without thinking, I performed a barrel roll in the air, much to Biddy's and my own shock. Maybe I could talk Mason into doing this again and letting me enter one of the races after all. Wouldn't it knock the socks off of all my friends and shut down my brother's teasing for good?

My vision blurred and my ability to see Biddy faltered. The broom lost a little altitude, and I shook my head to try and clear it. The taste of sweet chocolate in my mouth turned bitter by the second, and my confidence evaporated into concern.

Instead of coasting through the air with ease, it took a considerable effort for me to turn in Mason's direction and head back. I needed his assurance that everything was okay, but seeing him doubled over and breathing hard freaked me out. Another wave of unsteadiness hit me, and the broom shook underneath my thighs. I struggled to shake it off, but an overwhelming exhaustion weighed on top of me and my eyelids drooped.

"Charli, stay with me," called out Mason.

A little more power zinged through me, and I gripped the handle tighter. My shaky descent slowed with considerable effort on my part as I struggled to stay upright. My legs and feet dropped down in preparation for the landing even though I hadn't intended for that to happen.

"I've got you," reassured Mason, his outstretched hands glowing with power as he assisted me.

The second I hit the ground, my body crumpled against his. "What's...happening?" I struggled to catch my breath.

The detective pulled me into a sweaty embrace. "I guess we pushed it a little too far," he managed. "Maybe next time we need to put a time limit on things. Or eat a full meal first."

Even a fool like me understood there shouldn't be a next time if it affected both of us this way. If I had pushed any harder or been further away, the whole experience could have put us both in serious jeopardy.

Mason plucked a strand of hair stuck to my face and curled it behind my ear with a gentle touch. "I can't wait for the others to hear about your incredible flying talents."

"Yeah, I could shut them all up with the shock and awe of it all." I smiled at first, but the realization of them not believing me and then asking more questions erased my amusement. "Wait, you're not gonna tell, are you?"

My friends finding out that Mason and I had a habit of sharing magic the way we did didn't stress me out as much as what Nana would do if she heard.

"Why not? You were really good up there." He nudged me with his hip. "Your grandmother would be proud."

I freaked out at the mere possibility. "Holy unicorn horn, you're not thinking of letting my grandmother know what we just did?"

He winced at the volume of my panic. "What, fly together? I think she knows about that."

"No, about how you helped me do it on my own." I raised my eyebrows, willing him to get my gist.

"O-o-h, that." Mason tapped his chin in mock thoughtfulness. "And what will you offer to keep my mouth shut?"

My jaw dropped. "Are you kidding?"

The detective broke into chuckles. "You should see your

face right now. Charli, your grandmother will have many other things to worry about than you this weekend."

"Doubt that," I muttered under my breath. Nana always had time to worry about me. A thought dawned on me, and I snapped my fingers. "How about you promise you won't say a word and I will share some of Nana's homemade chicken and dumplin's, a goodly amount of creamy mac and cheese, and a heapin' of collards?"

Mason took his time in answering me, amusement dancing in his eyes as he watched me squirm. Finally, he put me out of my misery with a slight nod. "I can do that."

I squinted at him. "S-o-o, I feed you and we keep what happened just between us."

"That's the agreement. Besides, I kind of like having something that's just between you and me. Maybe I need to cast a spell on you more often." He took a step closer.

I stuck out my hand, stopping his progress and squaring things properly. "Let's shake on it. Deal?"

Mason took my hand in his. "Deal."

Without any more hesitation, he pulled me into his body and planted his warm lips on mine.

Chapter Two

My head floated in the clouds from the second Mason's lips had left mine. Although the intimate contact had only lasted for a brief moment with no follow up or further acknowledgment, the kiss had me so catawampus I wouldn't be able to decide whether to scratch my watch or wind my behind if my life depended on it.

I didn't know how affected I was until I found myself on Main Street, standing on the sidewalk outside of my office. Coming out of my fog of elation and confusion, I quickly checked to make sure I hadn't made the trip to town *nekkid* as the day is long, as Uncle Tipper had been a few times he'd tippled a bit too much moonshine.

Relieved to find myself fully clothed, I let myself relax and marvel at the window to my business. The sunflowers that framed my etched logo reflected golden in the amber rays of the late afternoon sun. A warm shiver prickled over my skin, and for a second I could swear that my parents were here with me, one on each side. I wondered what they would think of Mason and his sudden boldness?

Someone called out my name, and with regret, I stopped searching the glass for the reflections of my dearly-departed parents. Voices echoed off the buildings on Main Street and broke through my fog as most of the citizens of Honeysuckle Hollow headed to the town hall for tonight's very important meeting. A loud whistle shattered the last of my nostalgia, and I turned on my heels just in time to say hey to a few familiar faces walking by and to acknowledge Henry with a wave.

My self-proclaimed assistant pushed his way through a group sauntering down the middle of the street. "Y'all know they made sidewalks for a reason. Move out of the way, old man comin' through," he grumbled, holding up two cups with straws to keep them from being knocked out of his hands. When he made it across, he handed me one of them. "Here. A little fuel to help you celebrate another successful day at the office, boss."

"I told you not to call me that," I insisted, accepting the sweet tea with gratitude. "And I say again, you should really consider doing something more valuable with your time than pretending to be secretary to a business that has no clients."

"Nuts to that," scoffed Henry. "What else do I have to do with my time? Besides, I have one word for you—gremlins."

I chuckled at the joke at first, but a sliver of fear rippled through me at the realization he might be serious based on the mischievous glint in his eyes. "I will not be drumming up any business using nefarious methods, Henry. Gremlins are nasty little creatures. Haven't you seen the movies? Things can get out of control very fast. I don't think either one of us wants to explain to my grandmother why or how we started an infestation of those troublesome critters in Honeysuckle."

Henry shrugged. "It was just a suggestion. Anyway, I gotta go meet up with the fellas before the meeting to make sure everything's in order for our entry." He gave me a brief genuine smile with a wink before replacing his traditional smirk on his face so no one else would know how sweet he really could be.

He hadn't declared which team he was on for this weekend's barbecue contest, but I thanked my lucky stars Henry remained on my personal team—even if he wanted to stoop so low as to suggest the use of gremlins so people would seek out my services.

Taking a much-needed long sip of the gifted drink, I followed the crowd and greeted everyone with politeness and a quick nod with a smile, relishing the quiet normalcy of our special small town. Maybe peace and quiet ranked higher than constant drama, and if all it took was a simple kiss to raise my adrenaline, then I would choose to do that over and over again.

My fingertips brushed my bottom lip at the memory, and I forgot to watch which way my feet took me. With my usual lack of grace, I bumped into a tall figure, barely managing not to spill my drink on him. "Oops, I am so sorry."

Raif, the vampire who had been one of the reasons my best friend and I were almost killed, looked down his nose at me. "It is quite all right, Miss Charlotte. I fear you would be the one hurt more than me."

His tone held none of the old haughtiness I expected. Instead, the vampire sounded tired and a little defeated. Maybe even a touch bit humble, which creeped me out.

A bunch of conflicting emotions fought inside me. On the one hand, his actions with the town council election brought in one of the most dangerous villains I'd ever met. On the other, he too had been a victim since he'd been blackmailed into some bad decisions. Raif had returned to Honeysuckle a little while ago, and in a way, I admired his bravery to come back and face the consequences of his own actions in order to live in a place he liked. How long did he need to pay penance to be forgiven?

Deciding to give him another shot, I allowed a genuine smile to spread on my face. "Are you participating in the barbecue event this weekend?"

Raif's stoic expression relaxed a tiny fraction, and he answered me with a faint grin of his own. "I am indeed. A group of us vampires have joined forces and will be entering together."

My eyebrows lifted so high, my eyes hurt from not blinking. "Which team?"

Raif's lips curled into a deeper smile, revealing his fangs.

"There are a few of us who have pooled our resources to purchase the finest and the highest-rated smoker available. In addition, we managed to procure one of the most lauded barbecue masters this side of the Mississippi." The crafty vampire licked his lips in anticipation of my next question.

"Who?"

He leaned in closer and put a hand up to his mouth. "Sam Ayden," he whispered.

I gasped. "Sam Ayden? Of the Skybird Inn over yonder in Jonesville? How in the world did you score him?"

Everyone in the supernatural *and* human world knew Sam's name and his barbecue joint's reputation. People traveled from all over just to get one of his plates with heapin' scoops of chopped pork smothered in sauce, collards, and a crumbly square of cornbread on top.

The tall vampire relished my shocked reaction. "We share more in common now, and I convinced him that our small event here in Honeysuckle would be worth it." The proud glint in Raif's eyes reminded me a little of his old self.

However, I couldn't begrudge the vampire his smugness when he brought in a major player for the contest, especially since he saw it as good for our little town.

I patted him on his cold arm. "Good for you. I hope your team has fun." I started to walk away but turned around when a question dawned on me. "Out of curiosity, what is it you have in common?"

Raif brought a finger to his lips and opened his mouth, tapping one of his pointed fangs. "He's one of us now. His recipes that have been handed down for generations will last for an eternity. But don't let me interrupt you. I am sure you are meeting some of your friends. Please give them my regards, especially young Blythe." He nodded in dismissal.

I stood on the steps to the entrance, a little dumbfounded from the complete change in him. Sure, he was attempting to make up for his past transgressions, but to want me to pass on any type of salutations to my friends stunned me. A big part of me that had anticipated a verbal sparring with him remained skeptical. But this was Honeysuckle Hollow, and strange things happened every day.

Perhaps I would pass on his greetings to help his campaign of change, but probably would skip saying anything to my best friend. Even with the vampire Lady Eveline counted as one of her closest companions, I didn't think Blythe would ever truly forgive Raif in the long run.

"Hey, girl," called out Lily. "Why are you standing out here with your mouth open like you're trying to catch flies? Shouldn't we go inside?"

Her cousin followed right behind with too much mischief sparkling in her eyes. Lavender pointed above my head. "Why is your aura so bright and twinkly with pink and red?"

My friend's psychic ability to read moods and figure out hidden truths panicked me, and I shut my mouth tight. Although she could probably detect that something in the heart department had gone down recently, I needed to keep Mason's kiss secret at least for now. "I don't know what you're talking about. Come on, let's go find Alison Kate."

Lily tugged on my arm and narrowed her eyes. "That's fine, but since we're all staying at your place this weekend, you know you're gonna have to spill your guts at some point." She raised an eyebrow and beckoned her cousin to follow her inside.

Lavender giggled. "I bet whatever she has to tell us is juicy. And it probably involves a certain somebody who she's been hanging out with lately, too."

"My grandmother?" I asked, following behind them.

Lavender turned so I could watch her roll her eyes. "Nope."

"Matt? TJ? Charli Junior?" I proposed.

She shook her head. "Your niece is still cooking in your sister-in-law's belly. And while I know you love your family, that flavor of emotion shows up more as a purple hue. This has a more...romantic tint."

She tittered behind her hand, and a few heads turned in our direction. We made our way to the row of seats next to Alison Kate, who beckoned us to hurry up.

I grabbed Lavender's hand before she joined her cousin. "Listen, Lav. I'm not ready." To think about my future with the detective. To make it real by telling others. To do anything else other than enjoy things in the moment.

She squeezed me and let me go. "I know. Lily likes to stir up trouble, but I'm just so pleased to see your life going in the direction that it is, that's all. You'll tell us when you're ready." She shuffled down the row of seats.

Before I joined my friends, a warm hand touched my arm.

My cousin Clementine greeted me with a light hug and a friendly smile.

"Hey, Clem. You nervous for tonight?" I asked.

She nodded, her eyes widening a bit. "I've done my best to encourage Tucker, and I know he'll do great."

"He will," I reassured her. After everything that had happened to him, he carried the heavy burden of trying to redeem himself and his family name.

My cousin nodded, but a small frown remained on her lips. "Clarice chose not to be here. She said she wanted to go visit Hollis, but I think she couldn't handle that he's not on the council anymore." A tinge of bitterness flavored her words. It didn't take a psychic to pick up how she felt about her mother-in-law.

"Well, I'm rooting for him." The truth of my statement both surprised and satisfied me.

Despite the fact that Tucker had given my name to Duke, he did so out of desperation and blackmail. After taking a deal in order to give information about the dead man's dealings to both WOW and the IMP agents, he'd dedicated himself to doing right by our town. But it would be a long time before people forgot the scandal of his father's crime of murder.

Moisture rimmed Clementine's eyes and she dashed a finger at the corners of them. "It means a lot to me that the two of you can get along." With a sniff, she straightened herself. "And I hope that you'll come over again some time."

Honoring the memory of my mother and knowing her

wishes for the rift in the family to be repaired, I'd visited once for afternoon tea. I think it surprised Clem and me how much we were starting to like each other.

"I'd be happy to." It would be worth it to enjoy how much it irritated both my Aunt Nora and Clarice as well as. "But you'd better get to your seat. It looks like things are about to start."

The members of the town council walked onto the stage and found their places, Nana taking her position of high seat of the council. Flint sat to my grandmother's right, but it shocked me to see Tucker flanking her on her left. Aunt Nora situated herself next to her son-in-law, her normal resting witch face a little more puckered. She no longer had a ready ally to plot with since Tucker would be wary of following in his father's missteps.

Tucker kept a stoic, almost regal countenance on his face that reminded me too much of Hollis, who now resided in a magical holding facility outside of Charleston. But Tucker's eyes betrayed his nerves. He caught sight of Clementine making her way to her seat in the front. I strained to see her wiggling her fingers at him. The newest council member's expression relaxed, and he shuffled the papers he held in his hand, looking a little more comfortable than before.

The auditorium buzzed with excitement, but when Nana called the meeting to order, the audience quieted with immediate respect. "Before we get started, I want to thank each and every one of you who've stepped up in some way or another to make this whole event possible. All my life, I've felt it a great privilege to live in such a strong community, and you continue to renew my faith in it."

The room erupted into applause and cheers. Someone in the back shouted, "You're welcome."

Nana chuckled along with everyone else. "But that's enough with the sentimental histrionics. I know some of y'all got to get back to attending your smokers full of what I know will become award-winning barbecue."

"That's right," piped up Henry from the back. "Lucky's Seven are gonna take home the prize."

"Oh, I do not know about that." Raif's British accent rang out clear and true. "I think our Fiery Fangs team has an ace up our sleeve."

Lucky spoke out, his Irish accent a bit thicker than usual. "To be sure, we've all heard about your secret weapon. I would put it to the judges to look in ta how you chancers managed your advantage."

My assistant piped up, "We want to know if it's against the rules that they might have turned Sam Ayden just for the competition." His accusation gained a little support from those sitting near him.

"Oh, quiet Henry," Steve scolded, shocking the rest of us in the auditorium by uttering anything. The cafe owner continued, "We all have our own secret advantages. It's why our barbecue competition will be the most interesting with all of the magic being used to win. I wouldn't complain unless you wanted some of your own secrets revealed."

"On that note," Nana interrupted the two teammates,

"there are actually some rules to what you can and cannot use. I think I'll let Tucker give his explanation since the event has been his baby all along."

The new member of the town council stared at the papers in his shaking hands for a second. He took a deep breath and straightened himself. At first, his words came out with a hint of nerves, but once he got deeper into the rules, he commanded everyone's attention.

The more he talked, the more I had to admit to myself how much Tucker took to his newfound authority. Although it hadn't been that long, what he brought to the leadership of our town had been not just good but also beneficial. Perhaps he wanted to make up for his father's mistakes.

Lavender 's sharp elbow startled me out of my thoughts. "What?"

My friend pointed at the stage, and I caught Nana glaring down at me. "If my granddaughter was paying attention, she would stand up and wave at all y'all so you would know who to check in with if you're entering any of the contests. And make sure y'all spread the word that she'll be coming around the smokers and checking every team in, so everyone can be on the lookout for her tonight."

With my cheeks flaming, I stood up and waved at the laughing audience before crashing into my seat as fast as possible, failing to hide my embarrassment. Flint took over from my grandmother to explain how the magic of our town extended out further to include the large field prepared for all the events just beyond our normal border. When he got to the part about beefing up security, he called Mason to the stage.

My heart beat a fast rhythm at the sight of the detective, and once again, my fingers brushed over my lips, invoking the intimate memory of our kiss. Mason's eyes roamed over the entire crowd until he found me, and I swear he smoldered when he stared.

Pixie poop, the man was right. It was delicious to have something that existed just between us.

"Would you like to know the color of *his* aura?" teased Lavender into my ear.

I shook my head a little too hard and strained to pay attention to what the man at center stage was saying instead of how cute he looked being in charge.

All too soon, my grandmother dismissed him. "And now comes the fun part. We have many thanks to give for the whole reason why we'll be attracting so many to our small event, making it extra special by putting together incredible days of broom racing. Please give a warm welcome to former champion, Mr. Billy Ray Dobber."

Lee exploded out of his chair a few seats down from me, whistling and hollering the loudest. Several people stood up in front of me, blocking my view of the retired broom racer walking up to the front of the stage. I shifted from side to side until I could see him and caught the short and stocky celebrity winking at my grandmother. Danged if the old woman didn't blush and bow her head in embarrassment.

"Um, Lav, can you tell what color Nana's aura is right now?" I asked, mortified to guess the answer.

My friend giggled beside me, but Billy Ray stirred up the crowd into a roaring frenzy when he introduced his friends. "It's been a pleasure getting to know all of you, and I want to thank you for the kindness you've shown me since I've moved here. And there are a few others I've convinced to come this weekend that deserve your praise as well. Please put your hands together again for my fellow racers, starting Mr. Larger-than-life himself, Roddy 'Big Mouth' Bass."

A man almost as tall as Mason, but as round in the belly as my troll friend Horatio, waddled up the stairs to take the stage. He wiped sweat from his brow and waved at the crowd. "Now, I heard a couple of your teams squabblin' over how they think they're gonna win. They don't call me Big Mouth for nothin', and I'm here to tell ya that I brought my own team all the way from Texas to burn the competition. Y'all heard it from me first." He took off his cowboy hat and waved it around, pointing at a group in the back who'd started singing, "Deep In The Heart of Texas."

Billy Ray patted the robust racer on the shoulder and moved him over. "We'll have to see about that, buddy. You might get some stiff competition from our other friend who came to us all the way from Kansas City, Mr. Franklin 'Fireball' Irving."

A shorter but cocky man strutted to stand next to Big Mouth. "I know I might get drummed out of town when I say this, but I also brought a barbecue team with me, and our KC sauce will put all of you to shame."

"Boys, boys, let's not start a fight," said Billy Ray, stepping in between them. "We've got one more person to introduce, and let me tell you, it took a lot of convincing to get this gem of a racer to travel all the way here. The biggest champion of them all with a record-breaking number of wins under belt as well as a trailblazer in her own right, y'all better stay on your feet for the lady, Ms. Rita Ryder."

An older woman with silver gray hair cut in a fashionable short style joined the other retired racers. I waited for her to say something sassy, but she only grinned and offered a curt wave.

"Whew, girl, it's been a hot minute since I've seen you," declared Roddy.

Billy Ray addressed all of us, pointing at the collection of racers. "Y'all, it's been a long time since all of us have been together in one place. The years have been kinder to some of us than others."

"Much kinder," agreed Rita, daring to pat Roddy's bulbous stomach.

He opened his big mouth and uttered a booming laugh. "You'll still eat my dust when we race, darlin'."

Rita narrowed her eyes. "Aw, you're gettin' old and dotty in the head. I forget, which one of us has more trophies?"

Franklin stepped out of the way of the arguing two and took out a flask from his pocket, sipping from it while he watched the verbal sparring. Nana joined all the racers at the front of the stage, holding up her hands to stop the trash talking.

"Now, now, save the competition for the actual competition." She waited for the noise to stop, giving one of her famous glares to Mr. Bass, who shut his mouth with a snap. "And for those of you entering the amateur races, we've decided that the winner of the field will get an automatic entry into the professional exhibition race at the very end. Who knows, one of our very own might take home a trophy."

Franklin pocketed his flask and clapped politely while Billy Ray leaned in and spoke into my grandmother's ear. My own jaw dropped, and I watched with suspicion when she whispered something back to the racer, making him turn a shade of pink.

"He's flirting with her," I accused out loud.

Lavender patted my arm. "Looks like she's givin' just as good as she's gettin'."

I wrinkled my nose. "I don't even want to think about the double meaning of that." If only I didn't have to make the rounds to check in all the barbecue teams, I could corner my grandmother and find out what in Sam Hill was going on.

Nana held up her hands. "We all know how important it is for this weekend to go well. Let's do our very best to give people a good time and have fun while doin' it." She dismissed the meeting with the slam of her gavel.

I wanted to make my way to the stage, but several others had the same idea, trying to get close to the racers for autographs and pictures. Lee pushed me back into my seat when he scooted by with barely an apology, too excited for the chance to talk to some of his heroes.

Not wanting to get caught up in the chaos, I followed the girls outside to wait. "Now, who all's staying with me?"

Lily, Lavender, and Alison Kate raised their hands at once.

Ooh, if my baker friend had changed her mind to bunk at my place, we were gonna get to eat some good treats. "You're not staying at Lee's?"

Alison Kate clucked her tongue. "And attempt to put up with all that?" She pointed inside. "I don't know whether to be embarrassed by my man's enthusiasm or happy for him. With all the racers here this weekend, I'm not sure our own wedding will be able to compete on the same level."

"Don't worry, Ali Kat. He'll forget all about brooms and racing the second he lays eyes on you in your wedding dress," I reassured her. "Plus, I think we'll have a lot of fun with all of us bunking at my place. Y'all know there's plenty of room."

Mason appeared at the top of the stairs, glancing around until he found me. He nodded at the girls and pointed at his watch, reminding me of my duty.

"I gotta go check in the teams. I'll come home after that," I promised.

Lily nudged her cousin. "And then you'll explain to us why you've got a goofy grin on your face and what it has to do with the detective."

I gaped at her in surprise. "I do not have a grin on my face."

My friend pointed behind me. "Mason's waving at you."

My head whipped around to check, but the detective was talking to Zeke and definitely not waving. All of my girlfriends broke into laughter at my expense.

"See," snickered Lily. "Goofy grin."

Without a second thought, I aimed a stinging hex at her hiney and let it loose. She squealed and rubbed the spot, still laughing at me. "That right there proves I'm right."

Lavender grabbed her cousin and Alison Kate. "Have fun," she sang out, leading them away.

My heart fluttered at the thought of what kind of fun the detective might have in mind if we managed to have another private moment later. Shaking my head, I did my best to ignore my giddiness and get down to business.

Chapter Three

N ames of teams and their members filled my clipboard of forms, and I still had two more rows to register.

"Tucker's outdone himself with this event," I admitted under my breath. A small bit of pride for my cousin's husband rose in my chest.

Mason stopped talking to one of the team captains and joined me. "What was that?"

I showed him the copious entry forms and full pages of names I'd collected. "I'm admitting that what we thought was going to be a small event might end up being a bigger success."

"Which is good on one hand," the detective agreed.

His response caught my attention. "And on the other?"

Mason's brow furrowed. "Bigger event, bigger problems,

or at least the potential for something to go wrong increases. I'm glad we added a few extra volunteers to the patrols. And I should get Flint to add more people at the entrance." He took out his spell phone and typed out a quick message to the gnome.

A loud boom that shook the ground interrupted us and a fiery ball lit up the sky followed by a ton of whoops and hollers. We hurried over to the next row, working our way through the gathered crowd of laughing idiots.

"What happened?" Mason asked.

Roddy Bass guffawed even louder. "Now you done did it. You got the lawman's feathers all ruffled, Fireball. Guess they didn't know you lived up to your nickname in more ways than just speed." The boisterous racer clapped the smaller one on the back.

After witnessing what he could do with his magic, I couldn't call the ex-racer Franklin anymore. Fireball Irving cackled loud and long, waving a bottle of alcohol around. "My deepest apologies, but my old friend here claimed I couldn't even light a candle anymore. I showed everybody I ain't down and out yet." He winked at me. "Care to taste a little Fireball, young lady?"

Mason shouted in protective alarm, but I took care of myself, understanding what the harmless inebriated man meant. "No thanks, I'm not a huge fan of cinnamon whiskey."

The bigger racer snatched the bottle from the other. "Why not? It tastes like Christmas." He took a long swig, swallowed it, and started singing "Jingle Bells" at the top of his lungs, getting louder until a few watching the spectacle joined in at his insistence.

I shook my head. "Not very convincing, Mr. Bass. Now, who here is on your team?"

"Call me Big Mouth. Everybody does. And those four idiots are part of Team Texas Hexes, the makers of the best brisket that'll make you wanna slap yo' mama." He gestured his pudgy finger at a group of quieter men surrounding a crackling campfire while wiggling his eyebrows at me.

Mason frowned again but stepped away to get the rest of the crowd to disperse, and I picked up the entry form and registered all the names for the rowdy group from Texas. It took great effort to finish my job with all of the bad jokes the retired racers kept exchanging.

"I thought you two were enemies," I said. "At least that's how it looked when you were on stage."

Fireball took the bottle back and swallowed another sip. "It's all for show. That's what the people expect of us. But me and Big Mouth go way back. While we're old rivals, we've been great friends all this time. But I mean every word of smack talk when I say that our Kansas City barbecue will make the rest of you weep."

"And what about Ms. Ryder? Does she have a team entering the competition, too?" I asked.

Both men slapped each other on the back and tried to catch their breath from too much laughter. Big Mouth hit Fireball so hard drops of whiskey splashed out of the bottle.

"The woman is a nomad with no hometown anything. She

wouldn't know good barbecue from bad," the bigger racer exclaimed.

Fireball's expression sobered. "Plus, the only team Rita's on is her own. She never did go in for much socializing back in the day. Heck, neither one of us have heard or seen hide nor tail of her for years. Mud Dobber's got some mighty strong pull to get her here."

At the mention of Billy Ray's nickname, I recalled the urgency to find out just what was going on with him and Nana. But judging on their unsteady sway as they hugged each other around the shoulders and sang an old country song out of tune, I wouldn't get any good information from the pair in front of me anyway.

"Good luck to both of you," I called out, finding Mason and working my way to another campsite.

Mason remained tight lipped and watchful while I picked up registrations, but he didn't leave my side. I couldn't take too much of his silence and sullen mood, so I bumped him with my hip. "What's wrong with you?"

He raked his fingers through his hair and blew out a breath. "I know you can take care of yourself. I know it, but I can't help but feel protective. And I don't want to go all caveman on you. You're a strong woman, Charli. It's one of the things I lo—I mean, I like about you."

His admission stunned me. I took his hand and pulled him over to a more private and inconspicuous spot where we couldn't be seen. "You know, sometimes I forget you didn't grow up in the South, being trained as a gentleman to believe that we women are wilting flowers in need of a man's strength."

"You are no wilting flower." Mason took my hand in his. "It's not easy letting someone talk to you like that."

"But you let me handle it anyway, which means you made an effort against your instincts. That's kind of..." I trailed off.

"Sweet?"

I shook my head. "No, hot." I stood on my tiptoes and brushed my lips against his once. Twice.

With a muffled grunt, Mason grabbed me around my hips and pulled me against his body, crushing his mouth against mine.

A loud explosion and a bright light burst behind my closed eyes. Whoa, he must be one heckuva kisser to ignite that kind of fire.

The detective pulled away with a regretful groan. "Seriously, I may have to restrain Fireball if he can't stop doing that." He grumbled something under his breath that sounded like a very nasty curse if he'd put any intent into it.

The moment was well and truly over, and I patted him on the arm in sympathy for the both of us. "Why don't you go give them an official warning, and I'll try and finish registering the last few teams."

"All right. And then I'll walk you back to your place." Mason's tone held the authority of a warden in it.

I didn't want him to forget what had made me kiss him in the first place. "You can accompany me on my way to my house because I so desire it, not because I need you to escort me, right?"

He picked up on my hint and shot me a sexy side grin. "Absolutely. See you in a few." Leaving me alone, he walked off in the direction of the retired racers' row. I may or may not have taken a few seconds to admire his backside as he went.

I did my best not to fangirl too hard over Sam Ayden. No doubt my vampire roommate would give me no amounts of heck over my eagerness to meet the barbecue master when I officially registered the Fiery Fangs. Then again, if he gave me too much grief, I'd remind Beau that I didn't have to let him back into the house after this weekend, since he'd given up his room for my girlfriend sleepover while he stayed with one of his teammates.

Lee jumped up from his rickety chair to give me a hasty hug when I arrived at our other home team's area. "Charli, can you believe it? The Mud Dobber is gonna let me be on his pit crew this weekend."

"That's great," I exclaimed, a little more concerned that Alison Kate's worry about whether or not her engagement could stand up to her fiancé's excitement over the racers was warranted. "Ali Kat will be so proud of you."

My talented friend's eyes widened. "Sweet honeysuckle iced tea, I forgot to call her."

"Well, get on that spell phone of yours lickety-split. She's staying with me, in case you've forgotten about everything else going on," I chided.

Lee bit his lip in humility. "I know, I know. I promise to

do better." His eyes lit up when Alison Kate answered. "Hey, sweetums. You'll never guess what's going on." He walked away from me, and I thanked my lucky stars I didn't have to hear any make up mushiness.

The rest of Lucky's team greeted me by yelling my name in unison, making me feel like a minor celebrity. The leprechaun offered me a tall frothy pint of beer. "On the house, darlin' girl."

With regret, I turned him down. "Since I'm a part of the event committee, I can't accept a free gift from one of the teams. It might look like a bribe when you guys take home the prize for first place."

Henry stood up and cheered, offering me an enthusiastic but a little tipsy high five. Steve pulled him back down to his seat. Horatio closed the lid of the smoker and ambled over. "Greetings and salutations."

I freely hugged the massive troll. "What in the world are you doin' here?"

Lucky raised his glass in honor of his friend. "You'd be more than surprised how much knowledge our friend here brings to our team. He's given us more of an advantage than you might think."

Horatio bent his head in embarrassment, letting his shaggy hair fall across his face. "'Tis only a few special ingredients of which I may have enlightened my fellow grilling enthusiasts."

"Magical ingredients?" I goaded.

The troll had been the one to introduce William

Shakespeare to the real faerie royalty of Titania and Oberon, allowing the playwright a glimpse into the magical world. No doubt there were great depths to the knowledge swimming around in Horatio's giant noggin.

Flint's brother Clint held up a hand to stop the troll from revealing anything more. "Now, that would be telling and spoiling our advantage.

Lucky pulled the registration sheet from his pocket and handed it to me. I wrote down the names of those enjoying many gulps of the leprechaun's brew. "So, Lucky's Seven. I've got six names here."

"The last one will be mine." Billy Ray appeared at the edge of the circle. "I figured if the others were entering their own teams, then I'd better follow suit."

"You always were one to join things," accused the woman standing next to him. Rita Ryder surveyed the group. "Although between the two local teams, I think this might be your best bet."

"Because I'm not a vampire?" Billy Ray asked.

Rita allowed herself to smile. "No, because I'm betting that this team will come out on top." She earned a loud cheer from each member of Lucky's Seven. The leprechaun thrust a glass of beer into her hand for the compliment.

She took a couple of sips but handed it back. "Good luck to all of you."

"You're not staying?" Lucky asked.

Rita shook her head. "Unlike some of my former rivals,

I've always liked to get a good night's sleep when I'm about to compete."

A bit of pride bloomed in my chest for the female broom racer. "Probably why you won so much."

She turned her attention to me and smiled with genuine pleasure. "Exactly. Goodnight." With a quick nod of her head, she departed.

Billy Ray chuckled. "She always was business first."

Seeing an opportunity to ask him about my grandmother, I opened my mouth, but Lee jumped in front of me and talked a mile a minute about brooms and spellcrafting one to go faster to the retired racer.

"Son, let the man breathe," insisted Leland Chalmers, Sr. "He's already letting you crew for him. Don't make me kick you out of our team area."

Mason sidled up beside me. "Is someone giving you problems, Mr. Chalmers?"

"Nah, Detective. It's all good. Your shift has to be coming to an end. Why don't you pull up a chair and have a drink?" my friend's father offered.

Mason placed a hand at the small of my back. "I'm going to go with Charli to help her finish registering the teams. Maybe another time."

Our friends gave us a friendly goodbye but descended into snickers and whispers when we walked away. I rolled my eyes. "Those men are bigger gossips than the ladies of Honeysuckle."

"Sorry about putting my hand on you. I didn't think," Mason apologized.

I took the detective's hand in mine. "This is a small town, which means there really aren't any secrets. I'd bet dollars to donuts they already knew something about the two of us." I linked my fingers through his and walked to the very last group on the edge of the field closest to the tree line.

"If you don't listen to me, you'll ruin the meat," a young woman's voice rose and floated in the air.

It pleased me that a girl seemed to be in charge of one of the teams, and I hurried a little faster to register her. I dragged Mason with me into the light of their campsite and uttered a brief greeting. The sight of one of the members of the team staring back at me stopped me cold.

Dash Channing looked up at me from his camping chair. He glanced between me and Mason, and settled a challenging gaze on me. "Evenin', Charli."

Chapter Four

Words jumbled around in my head, but not one coherent phrase floated to the top. Where had Dash been? Why didn't I know he was back? Why had he been gone so long? With so many questions I wanted answers to, I couldn't figure out which one to ask first.

"Dash," acknowledged Mason beside me, his grip tightening around my fingers.

The slight pain alerted me to my current surroundings. I winced and drew in a breath. The detective let go but kept his eyes on the wolf shifter.

"Detective." Dash flashed his gaze to Mason for a brief second, nodding at the warden.

A younger woman bounced over to me. "Are you the one we give the registration to?" She handed me the paper and giggled. "We're the Lexington Boo-B-Q team. I came up with the name."

"We are not going with Boo-B-Q. I thought we discussed this," complained a handsome young man from a seated position behind the campfire, popping the top of a can with a hiss.

"Shut up, Davis. That's his name." The cute and chaotic girl pointed at my clipboard. "Write down Davis Channing. And mine's Ginny Whitaker. Well, technically, it's Virginia, but I don't like my full name. You can call me Ginny or even Jinx. And I guess Dash called you Charli? It's nice to meet you officially, Charli. Why aren't you writing anything down?"

I clutched the clipboard to my chest, still trying to process everything. Dash's unexpected return. Mason's caveman instincts turned up to an eleven. The chatty female trying to get my attention. It all overwhelmed me.

Mason's demeanor changed to one of serious authority. He tore his attention from the wolf shifter and turned to face me. "I think I should brief Zeke to what I've observed tonight. I'll give you some time." He nodded his chin once to punctuate his efforts to walk away and not escalate the situation, giving me the space to figure things out. "Call me when you want to leave."

"Mason," I uttered with cloudy regret, but the detective hurried away.

The feisty young woman reached her hands out to take the list from me. "Here, I'll write down the names for you."

"Let the woman do her job, Ginny. And I told you, we're

not calling you Jinx, especially not this weekend. You know words have power. Hey, I'm Georgia Whitaker." The new person approaching me smelled a little like wood smoke, and I recognized her voice as the one in charge. She held out her hand to shake mine. "And we're sticking with the Lexington Boo-B-Q team name, right Dash?"

At the mention of his name, my heart jumped, and I frowned in frustration at my reaction. When I caught him staring at me again, heat rose in my cheeks.

"Whatever you say, G. You're the team captain since you're the one communicating with your grandpappy's spirit." The familiar yet foreign sound of the wolf shifter's gravelly voice beat against my heart like crashing waves.

Georgia protested. "Don't give away how we're going to win. I'm sorry," she apologized to me. "It's not really a secret that I can see and talk with ghosts, but it can kind of freak people out. After they accept the possibility it's true, they want to know if there are any spirits around them, which can be upsetting." She glanced at the space to my left and right.

I took a step back. "I've got ghosts around me?"

"See?" she said. "It would probably spook you to know you've got two strong ones with you right now."

"G," warned Dash.

A sudden desire to show my strength to the formerly absent man overwhelmed me. With one bold step forward, I faced the situation with my head held high. "No, it wouldn't. My guess is it's my mom and dad. I sensed their presence with me earlier today at sunset."

"Ha!" Georgia flipped her middle finger at Dash. "I like a woman who doesn't mind a little haunting. Do you want to stay and have some of the liquor I brought from my family's distillery? It's got a bit of a kick in the alcoholic and magical sense, enhancing our normal behaviors. Which is why she's a Chatty Cathy, why I'm the smartest cookie of the bunch, and why Dash is grumpier than usual. He's always broody these days."

Dash growled out, "Georgia."

"So, he hasn't changed at all," I accused with a little too much venom.

The young man who'd been quietly watching all of us talk with a little too much amusement leaned forward. "Wait a minute. Your name is Charli?" he piped up, waving his beer can at me, clearly choosing not to drink the alcohol. "Are you *the* Charli? The witch my brother can't stop talking about?"

Dash's intense eyes flashed golden and he snarled. "Everyone shut their mouths right now."

I jumped a bit at his abruptness and busied myself, writing down their names at the end of the last page. "Okay, you're officially checked in. Good luck this weekend." Dash's short-tempered fuse was the last thing I wanted to witness.

"Hold on." Georgia held up her hand to stop me. Something about her plea made me stay.

She approached Dash and leaned down to say something, reaching out to hold him in place until she finished. When she was done, she backed away and gestured for him to get out of his chair. Her foot tapped the ground while she waited with her hands on her hips.

With a grunt, the wolf shifter put down his drink and pushed himself up. A pang of jealousy rippled through me at his obedience. Who was she to him that he listened to her?

Dash approached with heavy steps, his head hanging down so his longer than usual hair hid his face. "Will you take a walk with me?"

My mixed emotions battled it out with each other. A part of me wanted to hug him because I'd missed him, but my more pissed-off violent side wanted to beat that part of me to a pulp and then throw some punches at the shifter.

More than anything, I didn't think he deserved much more than watching me walk away. "I have to turn in all the forms. Good luck and all that."

Georgia rushed over and separated us like a parent scolding two children on the playground. Turning to me, she flashed a very insistent smile. "Here, give me your clipboard. I promise to keep it safe while you two talk." She held out her hand and waited with the same patience as before.

A heated debate exploded in my head. If I gave in and talked to him now, I might forgive him for all of his transgressions way faster than he deserved. Then again, I wanted answers to my many questions. But if I did spend time with Dash, how would that make Mason feel? And how did I feel about the detective's feelings versus the automatic stirring of emotions for the wolf shifter?

"You two should talk. Give him a chance to explain,"

whispered Georgia to me. "I promise, whatever the outcome, you'll feel better. And you won't be alone." She nodded in acknowledgment of the spirits surrounding me.

Knowing my parents were by my side sparked my courage. With resolve to maintain a level of control and distance, I handed over my clipboard and narrowed my eyes at Dash. "Let's go." Without a word, I conjured a light ball and let it float in front of me, stomping toward the space between the edge of the field and the dark line of trees.

Once my feet got going, I didn't want to slow down for the wolf shifter to catch up. It felt good to push myself ahead, letting my blood pump and fuel my anger. My chest rose and fell with heavy breaths under the slight exertion and the fury boiling right under the surface.

Dash stayed behind me, his footsteps following mine. At first, I relished his silence since he hadn't done anything to earn my attention yet. But after several minutes of quiet and no attempts to explain anything, I spun on my heels to face him. His body crashed into mine at the sudden turn.

"Shit," he exclaimed, placing a hand on each of my arms to steady himself.

His light embrace sparked a rush of heat through my body, which ignited my anger to full blast. I placed my hands against his chest and pushed him away. "You don't get to touch me."

"Charli, before you bite my head off, can you give me a chance to explain?" Dash held up his hands in surrender.

I poked him in his rock-hard chest. "Oh, you want to talk

now? Not like you had a spell phone and could call at any time. Not like you weren't talking to Lee but refusing to talk to me. Not like you didn't tell *him* you were coming back more than two. Dang. Months. Ago." For good measure, I shoved him again.

Dash kept his hands in the air. "I know, Charli. You've got a lot of reasons to be mad at me."

My mouth hung open, too many things I could say right now fighting to break out. My eyes watered and my bottom lip quivered. Large tears ran down my cheeks, making me more irritated at my emotional outburst, which only made me cry a little harder.

Dash dropped his hands and reached out to wipe the wetness from my cheek. "Oh, Charli."

I batted his hand away. "I'm not crying because of you, you idiot. I'm crying because...because..." I couldn't come up with a reason other than how much his staying away and not talking to me actually hurt.

My chest ached so hard I thought it might crumble in on itself. Acknowledging that pain threatened to cause even more tears to spill. I raised my head to the sky in a failed attempt to force the tears to roll back.

"Frosted fairy wings," I swore at myself. With the palms of my hands, I wiped the moisture from my cheeks. "Ugh, fine. I'm crying because I am mad. I'm mad at you for staying away. And I'm angry at me for caring so dang much."

The concern on Dash's face broke when he chuckled. His amusement did the trick and cured my bout of tears.

"You find this funny?" I squeaked in indignation.

He shook his shaggy head. "A little, but not for the reasons you think. If you think I stayed away from you to intentionally hurt you, then you never knew me at all."

With that one statement, he put me on the defensive. My hackles raised. "I didn't say you did it deliberately. And you never gave me much of a chance to get to know you in the first place. I'd get a glimpse of who you were and then you'd throw up barriers, telling me how much trouble you would be. And right after what happened with Damien, you decided you had to leave. So, you know what? I guess I'm justified in not knowing you that well."

I bumped him away from me with my shoulder and headed back to where his brother and friends waited to get the clipboard. No way did I need to hear any explanations from a man who ran away when things got tough and then had the audacity to try and turn things on me.

A warm hand gripped my arm. "Charli, wait. That's not what I meant."

Misunderstandings defined our relationship, and I paused not because he wanted me to but because I figured I didn't have to make a choice between Dash or Mason. Who wouldn't want the guy who broke down the walls between me and him? Why would I ever choose someone who made great efforts to keep cementing brick after brick of a barrier between us.

"It's okay, Dash. I get it. I'm glad you're safe and that you have a nice girlfriend to take care of you now. Don't worry about me." Keeping my gaze as far away from his eyes as possible, I peeled his fingers off my skin. "I truly wish you all the best."

"Wait, what? What girlfriend? I don't have anyone but...I have no one." His surprise rang out into the darkness.

Thanks to my incessant curiosity, I turned, allowing my floating ball of light to hover between us. "That woman who's running your barbecue team. Georgia. Aren't you with her?"

Loud laughter pealed out of his mouth and his shoulders shook. "She would be mortified if she heard you say that. She's ended up being a good friend after everything that happened." Reminded of his recent past, he sobered up and cleared his throat. "I should tell you who she is to me. She and her sisters. Why I couldn't call you even though I wanted to. Every day. Every damn minute." He stepped closer to me. The wind blew his hair aside, giving me a clearer view of him.

I took one long look at his bearded face and gasped. My fingers flew to the long raw scars scratched across the left side of his cheek. "Oh, Dash. What happened?" I didn't even attempt to stop the renewed flow of tears.

He winced as my fingertip brushed the edge of one of the scars and grasped my hand to stop me. "It really is a long story. But my brother Kash made sure I would never forget how hard it was to fight him. Or how important it was to win."

"When did you get hurt?" I counted the months since I'd seen him last in my head.

Dash snorted. "My brother always did fight dirty. He hired

a couple of witches to help him. These," he pointed at the gashes in his face, "were made with his claws that were dipped in a potion mixture of wolfsbane and atomized silver. Georgia's older sister Caro has worked hard to get me to look this good." He attempted a wry smile.

The wolf shifter was right. We did have a lot more to talk about. I set aside my anger for the moment in order to ask him more important questions. But a loud explosion shook the ground underneath us, and an inferno of fire blasted into the night sky, lighting everything up.

Would I go to jail if I strangled a retired racer? Thanks to him, I might never hear Dash's story. "That's gotta be Franklin 'Fireball' Irving. He's been showing off his actual fire magic while drinking. I'll bet he gets more than a warning of being disqualified," I explained with a sigh.

Dash sniffed the air and stiffened, his eyes wide in high alert. "No, I don't think whatever's happened is quite as harmless. Look. The blaze is still roaring."

Alarmed shouts rose in the air, and my stomach clenched. Both of us took off running toward the chaos, but Dash's shifter abilities allowed him to arrive faster. My orb of light vanished in my panic, and I did my best not to trip and fall until I made it to the edge of the gathered crowd.

Heat emanated from flames that shot up into the night sky. I pushed my way to the front, unsure of how I could help, and stood next to Dash. There was already a group of people surrounding a body on the ground.

"He didn't mean to do it," shouted Big Mouth Bass, pointing at a person rolling on the ground.

"Who is it?" I asked.

"It's Fireball Irving," a voice across from us answered.

Dash's brother Davis broke through the crowd and wrapped a blanket around Fireball. "I think he's out," he assured us. "He'll need some minor medical attention, but he'll be fine."

Dash leaned into me. "My brother worked for the fire department before." Pride dripped through his words.

"I'll get Doc Andrews," shouted a voice I recognized from Honeysuckle.

An unknown witch stepped forward and raised his hands at the smoker still filled with roaring flames. "I'm going to cast a water spell," he informed us.

"Don't," yelled out Henry. "You do that, we could all go up in flames. I didn't serve on the volunteer fire department for four decades for nothing. Everyone move back."

Without hesitation, he cast a spell that encased the blazing smoker and contained everything within it. Straining, he concentrated and mumbled something under his breath. "Gotta get the air out," he gritted.

"I'll help." Steve stepped up next to his friend and extended his hands out as well.

The quiet cook added his magic to the mix, and the spelled pocket of air keeping the fire contained shimmered with more power. Checking with his friend, Steve counted down from three. Both men concentrated, and the flames of the fire dwindled until they flickered and went out. They kept up the spell until smoke dissipated inside the containment. Coordinating together, Steve and Henry released the spell, and the crowd erupted with applause.

Doc arrived with Nana in tow, and they moved others out of the way to check on Fireball. Mason, assisted by Zeke and my brother, moved the crowd back, trying to disperse everyone. He looked over and found me standing next to Dash, and my stomach dropped. But he turned his attention back to the task at hand, ignoring me. Add him as another man to the list of people I needed to have a long talk with.

Someone tapped me on my arm, and I jerked it back in surprise. Flint's brother Clint put a finger to his lips and gestured for me to follow him. I left the scene a little perturbed at not being able to find out all the details. The gnome picked his way through another team's campsite over to the row where Lucky's Seven were settled.

"What does he want?" Dash asked, startling me.

"I don't know. That's why I'm following him," I hissed. "Why are *you* coming with me?"

The shifter raised his eyebrow. "Because trouble tends to find you."

"I can take care of myself," I insisted.

"Hey," Clint interrupted in his squeaky voice. "I asked you to be quiet so you don't draw any attention to the situation."

I scrunched up my nose and apologized. "Sorry, Clint. What's going on?"

Horatio stepped into the light of their campfire. "I am

afraid we are in desperate need of your services tonight, Holmes."

When my troll friend called me by his special nickname, invoking the famous fictional detective, it meant nothing good was about to happen. "Why?"

Horatio looked at Clint and then back at me. "Because I fear that we have lost our leprechaun. Lucky has vanished."

Chapter Five

Frosted fairy wings, why did Horatio and the other team members want to involve me? The whole thing could be a very minor problem that would solve itself as soon as Lucky returned from doing whatever he was doing.

Dash shook his head. "He's probably in the crowd checking out the aftermath of the explosion." I nodded my head in vehement agreement.

"No, he's not." Clint frowned in frustration. "I quietly checked with Steve and Henry. We'd left Lucky behind tending our own smoker when Fireball got out of control."

Something tugged at my gut, but I didn't want to listen if not for any other reason than I had enough to deal with on my plate tonight. "Maybe he went into town to get something or found some other friends to drink with."

Horatio shook his massive head at me. "Please, Charli. Listen." He patted the gnome's shoulder to continue.

Clint stumbled forward at the troll's heavy-handed touch. "I came back to get him because I knew he wouldn't want to miss out on what was happening. But when I got here, the lid to the smoker was left open."

I waited for further explanation but got nothing back but eager gazes. Confused, I prompted for more information. "And that's a bad thing?"

"Yes," all of the men, including Dash, replied in unison.

"Once the meat's on the grill, you only open it to baste or to briefly check on the progress. You never leave the lid completely open for any significant amount of time. If you do, you'll lose all the heat and smoke," explained the wolf shifter.

I shrugged my shoulders. "Okay, he left the lid open. That doesn't necessarily mean that he's disappeared."

"But I found a half-drunk glass of beer." Clint walked over to a table by the smoker and picked up the glass half-full with an amber liquid. "Lucky would *never* leave any drink he poured for himself. Especially not this brew."

Dash crossed his arms. "Is there something special about your beer?"

All of the present teammates glanced at each other. "That's not the point," said Clint.

The sinking feeling in the pit of my stomach grew. "Okay, you might be right. But what do you want me to do about it? Shouldn't you be talking to one of the wardens?"

Horatio stepped forward, holding up a piece of fabric. "I

found this located on the ground near the smoker. Perhaps you could use your talents to help locate our friend."

I accepted the rag, which felt slightly damp. Wrinkling my nose, I lifted it up to try and figure out why it was wet.

Dash stopped me. "Are you seriously going to stick that near your face without knowing what could be on it? What if someone dosed it with some form of chemical to knock Lucky out?"

"Do your supersonic senses pick up anything?" I snapped at him, even though he wasn't wrong.

"That's not the point," he argued. "But no, I don't detect anything artificial. It could be enchanted though."

The fabric didn't have the tingle of a lingering spell still hanging on it. "Honestly, I think it might just be water. Or maybe his sweat." The more I thought about it, the more I agreed with the latter possibility since it made sense he might have wiped his brow while working near the hot smoker.

"Do you detect his presence from it, Holmes?" Horatio asked.

"With this?" I held the fabric by the tips of my fingers and curled up my lip. "Hold on. Let me try." I'd have to grasp the rag hard to make a connection. Ignoring the source of the dampness, I closed my eyes and concentrated.

Nothing. No tremor of magic. No slight tug of direction. The fabric felt like a blank object in my hands.

"That's weird," I said louder than I meant to. "But a leprechaun is a type of fae."

"Why would that matter?" asked Dash.

A low voice penetrated our group. "Because some of the fae's powers act differently and are harder for Charli to detect. What I want to know is, what are you trying to find?" Mason joined us, standing directly on the other side of me.

"There are reasons that make us believe that Lucky's disappeared somehow. They want me to find him using this rag." I waved the fabric at him. "But I can't pick up anything."

"Did you spellcast at all?" the detective asked.

Lowering my voice so not everyone would be privy to my methods, I spoke out of the corner of my mouth. "You know I haven't had to do that in a while."

"But I also know that finding objects over people is the easier task for you," Mason countered.

"If you gave her a little room to do her thing, she might have already picked up on Lucky's trail." Dash loomed a little closer to me, staring the detective down.

Mason took the shifter's words as a challenge and closed the distance as well, trapping me between the two of them. "I don't think she needs your help." His chest puffed out a little more, and I found myself sandwiched between an awkward situation and disaster.

"Guys." I attempted to separate them without much success. "How about you both give me some space."

Despite the strength I used to push them away from each other, it took the two men an extra beat to comply. Once I got the requested space, I rolled my shoulders back to relax and focus.

Closing my eyes, I did my best to initiate my magic. "*In case our friend has gotten lost, I cast this spell on the fabric tossed. Where oh where has Lucky gone? Help me find the leprechaun.*"

I released my will and felt a light tingle of magic flicker to life and roll down my arms into the rag. I waited for the familiar connection. As seconds ticked by, I felt an odd pressure creeping me out. I opened one eye and found the lot of them watching me with nervous anticipation.

"Anything?" asked Clint.

Still nothing. There was absolutely no thread of connection or anything there for me to catch. I furrowed my brow and spoke the dreaded truth. "No."

"We're wasting time. I should get the other wardens involved and set up a search party if you think something's happened to Lucky." Mason took out his spell phone.

I stopped him from texting or calling anyone by reminding him in a lower voice of the town council's wishes. "Nana wants things to go as smoothly as possible this weekend. It's not even the first full day of the event, and you want to alert everyone that we have a missing person?"

Dash uncrossed his arms and held out his hand, wiggling his fingers. "Give it here."

Mason scoffed. "I'm not giving you my phone."

"Not your phone," Dash sneered. "Give me the rag."

"Why?" Mason and I both asked.

"Stop delaying. Give. It. Here." Dash reached out for the fabric and plucked it from my grasp. He brought it up to his nose and took in a deep whiff, his nostrils flaring. "Yep, this definitely belonged to Lucky. I recognize his...odor."

"Can you find him from that?" I quirked an eyebrow at the shifter.

Mason smirked. "I thought most werewolves didn't like using their scenting abilities like bloodhounds."

I cringed at the clear insult and elbowed him hard enough in his side to make him grunt. Mason had his reasons not to like Dash, but in this situation, he needed to find a way to get along with the shifter.

"I will do what it takes to help a friend. More than what you seem to be willing to do right now, Detective," Dash spit out.

"I'm the warden here. I should have the evidence." Mason snatched the rag out of the shifter's hand.

Unimpressed with their childish behavior, I blew out an exasperated breath. I cocked my head to the side and asked him, "And what are you going to do with it?"

The detective's arrogance fumbled when he recognized my displeased tone. "I'm not sure, but...hold on." He closed his eyes for a brief moment. Opening them again, he held the fabric up and gazed at it. "I don't think Lucky's that far away."

"How do you know?" I made no effort to hide my doubt.

"I don't know, it's just a feeling." Mason pointed behind the team's area. "I think he went that way."

"So now you're the bloodhound?" Dash teased. "We'll see about that." He took long strides in the direction Mason had indicated.

The detective ignored the rest of us and hurried behind him, leaving me dumbfounded and stock still where I stood.

"Your party is departing without you, Holmes," encouraged Horatio.

The troll's repeated nickname for me startled me out of my surprise, and I stumbled forward. It didn't take long for me to catch up to the two bickering boys scanning the edge of the mowed field.

"I'm telling you, he's back here to the right." Mason's anger outweighed the authority he attempted to throw around.

"And I say that we should get in the brush and look around. That's where his scent is strongest," argued Dash with a growl.

I cast a dim light ball, and the two stopped facing off with each other and gave me their attention. "You two put aside your egos. If Lucky's hurt and we're delayed getting to him because you can't work together, I will—"

"Hex our hineys," Mason completed.

"Seven ways to Sunday," uttered Dash with a sheepish expression. "Sorry, Charli."

We didn't have time for arguments and apologies. If neither of them could get it together, then I needed to take the lead. I pointed at the shifter. "Why do you want to search in the brush?"

Dash took careful steps into the tall grass. "There's an indent here in the weeds as if someone trampled them. And it definitely has Lucky's scent all over it." He crouched down, taking in deep breaths through his nose. "The good news is that I don't smell any blood."

I sighed in relief. What he said made sense, so I questioned the detective next. "And why do you think we need to search further down?"

Mason held up the rag and grimaced at it. "I can't tell you why. I just know that Lucky isn't here. He's somewhere down there." He pointed again in a direction away from us.

Thinking quickly, I came up with a plan. "Dash, you stay here and see if you can find anything useful. And if you pick up any other scents, let us know. Mason, take me to where you think we should be looking." I held up my hand to stop the wolf from starting another argument with protests. "We won't be that far away. And if you need us to come back, you can text my spell phone. If you still have my number."

He winced at my intentional jab. "I've got it."

Feeling a little like a witch with a capital *B*, I took Mason by the arm. "Take the lead, Detective."

The ball of light bounced in front of us, giving out enough illumination to guide us safely but not shining so bright that it might attract attention. The further we got away from Dash, the more Mason relaxed.

He put a hand over mine. "I hope you know that finding Lucky is a high priority for me."

No way would he got off that easily. I let go of his arm, slipping my hand out from under his. "Really? Because it looked like you were about to come to blows with Dash instead of doing your job."

"That's not fair. You've got to know it's not easy for me to see you with him. It took everything I had in me to walk away when we came across his campsite, but I did it because I knew you needed to talk to him." His voice rose loud enough to scare the chirping cicadas into silence.

"I know," I acknowledged. "But we can't focus on that right now." Nor could I pester him about why he had a gut feeling of where the leprechaun was. Or the big fat fact that I didn't.

Mason stopped, his body stiff on high alert. "Take a few steps back," he instructed.

Obeying, I held onto him to make sure we didn't fall over. Inch by inch, he turned his body counter clockwise until he faced the side of the field. "I think he's somewhere close."

My spell phone pinged and vibrated in my pocket. Taking it out, I read the message. *"Headed your way."* So, the wolf shifter did know how to use his own technology to get in touch with me after all.

"Let's wait for Dash," I suggested and ignored Mason's automatic grunt of displeasure.

Without the sound of pounding footsteps any normal human would make, Dash approached us using his shifter stealth. "There's a faint trail away from that area." He lifted his head and sniffed the air. "And I can smell Lucky again. Only stronger this time."

"Do you detect anyone else with him?" Mason asked, his detective instincts beating out his jealousy.

Dash concentrated. "No, no one else but you two." He gestured for the warden to plunge into the bush. "After you."

"No, your senses might be able to pinpoint the leprechaun more accurately. I'll follow you." Mason nodded his head with professional resolution.

I rolled my eyes at both of them trying to make a good impression in front of me. "Someone go or I will, and I know how both of you hate when I find the body."

Pixie poop. Saying those words made me realize that although Dash could sense Lucky being close, there was a real chance we might not find him alive. "Hurry, please," I begged.

Dash entered carefully into the brush lining the field, using his shifter sight to find his way. Mason followed behind. He stopped and turned, holding out his hand for me. I waved him off, determined to walk on my own.

"Detective." Dash's sharp voice pierced the darkness. "Get over here."

Mason crashed through the tall weeds with me right behind him. When we got to where the shifter crouched, my ball of light illuminated the leprechaun's face.

"Is he...?" I couldn't finish the question.

Dash put two fingers on the leprechaun's throat to check for a pulse. Tense seconds ticked by, increasing the agony waiting for an answer to the question I couldn't finish.

Lucky groaned, and I almost screamed in fear and relief. He tried to open his eyes, but it took him a couple of attempts.

With pained effort he leaned up from the ground on his elbows. "What are ye three doin' here, staring down at me?" His hand flashed to the back of his head. "Oh, me noggin'. I feel completely banjaxed. Where am I?"

"Try not to move too much until we can assess your injuries," instructed Mason.

Dash stood up and backed away, allowing the warden to do his job. I took the wolf shifter's place in front of my friend and held his hand. "Are you okay, Lucky?"

"I'm not sure yet, but by the looks on your faces, especially this lass goin' all soft, I'd say ye thought I might not be amongst the livin'." Against Mason's instructions, the leprechaun sat up. He groaned and clutched the side of his head.

My concern grew and the light orb brightened. I squeezed Lucky's hand. "Do you know what happened?"

His jaw went slack. "You don't know why I'm here?"

I shook my head. "We only knew what Clint told us. That you stayed behind to tend your barbecue when the big explosion went off. When he came back, you weren't there."

Panic spread over the leprechaun's face. "What explosion?" He looked between Mason and me. "What did I miss?"

"You don't remember the ground shaking and the big ball of fire erupting into the sky?" Dash asked from behind me.

"Are ye daft? I think I would remember if someone blew somethin' up. Wouldn't I?" His eyes pleaded with me, and it broke my heart to see such a strong friend of mine weak and afraid.

I patted Lucky's hand and let him go. "I think it's time."

"For what?" Mason asked.

Standing up, I turned to Dash, hoping he would understand my request. "To find my grandmother."

Chapter Six

By the time Dash brought Nana to us, we'd made it out of the brush. Despite our protests, the leprechaun refused to be coddled, and he'd taken great pains to walk himself. In agreement about not wanting too much attention, the only thing he allowed was to be examined on the edge of the field right behind his team's campsite.

Doc Andrews flashed a conjured pinpoint of light in and out of Lucky's eyes. "Well, I don't think you've suffered any major damage that I can tell while examining you here in the dark."

Nana touched our town doctor and healer on the shoulder. "Less griping and more assessment, Wilbur."

"What about this lump on me head?" Lucky rubbed the

spot and winced. "And the fact that I was knocked out or that I cannot remember much of what happened right before?"

Doc Andrews nodded in consideration. "You may have a concussion and will need to be watched. I'd feel better if you came back with me to my office so I could give you a more thorough once over."

"But me team—" Lucky protested.

"Will be fine without you tonight," interrupted my grandmother.

Dash stepped forward. "So will mine. Georgia has to do most of the work anyway, so I can help you with Lucky, Doc, and then I can stay with him afterwards to make sure he's okay."

His willingness to help surprised me. "Why?" The question burst out of my mouth before I thought better of it.

The shifter stroked his beard, bringing attention to his scarred face. "Because I'm well acquainted with taking care of injuries."

"Begging your most gracious pardon." Horatio joined us. "But I have taken the liberty and contacted my fair Juniper. She has arrived with great expedience and is willing to open a pathway to wherever you may need to take our most unfortunate friend."

Nana contemplated the offer. "After the warning we got from that IMP agent about using the fairy path too often, I'm not too keen on taking her up on her offer." She paused and then sighed in resignation. "Then again, I've been deep in talks with a most interested party of representatives from both the regional council and our *friends* in Charleston." She wrinkled her brow at the mere mention of them.

"Spies, you mean?" I hated the political fight my grandmother was in the middle of, shouldering most of the battles herself.

Nana harrumphed in agitation. "Some of them are legitimately attending because they enjoy barbecue and broom racing. But there are some key people here with whom I'd rather not arouse suspicion. Horatio, would you please fetch your lady friend to assist us?"

Dash raised his hand and waited for my grandmother to call on him. "If you don't mind, ma'am, I'll head on to Doc's office on my own. I'll meet you there," he addressed the doctor.

"Ye need not come at all. I appreciate the sentiment." Lucky stuck out his hand.

Dash shook it but stood his ground. "No, you need someone looking out for you tonight, and nobody will be suspicious if I disappear. Plus, I've traveled the fairy path. It doesn't particularly care for my kind." His eyes darted to me.

It didn't take much to remember the time he carried me through the path to Nana's house and how much he struggled to stay on it. More conflicting emotions reared their ugly heads inside me, but in the company I was keeping, I didn't have time to wrestle with them.

"I just need to let my brother and the Whitaker sisters know where I'm headed. Charli, I'll bring you back the clipboard you left with Georgia, and then I'll join you at Doc's," Dash finished, nodding at the leprechaun.

Doc pulled out his spell phone. "I'll call Queenie and have her prep an exam room."

Nana's watchful gaze bore into me, and I kept my head down, inspecting the tops of my shoes. Call me a coward, but my grandmother always saw too much. There were definitely some things I didn't want her prying into.

Mason kept a lookout to make sure no curious straggler found us. After Juniper joined us, she opened a door with a blue-green tint on the edges of it, and we watched Lucky and Doc walk through. The fairy followed behind them to make sure they made it without any problems at my grandmother's request.

Dash rushed back with my clipboard in tow. He tilted his head to the side, silently asking me to step away from the others.

Despite risking Mason's displeasure, I wanted the brief privacy. "Thank you for getting this for me." I took the clipboard from him.

"Georgia promised she didn't look through it although she couldn't vouch for her sister. Charli, I want a chance to talk to you. A real chance with just you and me. Do you think you might be able to find time this weekend?" His low voice held a lot of emotions despite his attempt to hold them back.

"I want to talk to you, too," I admitted. "There are things to say on both our ends, I would guess."

Dash's eyes lifted to look at Mason. "It seems that there may be. Just text me when you're ready."

Oh, the irony in his request. My natural snark bubbled to the surface, but pointing out his lack of use of his spell phone over the past few months wouldn't move us forward. "I will."

His hand moved as if to take mine, but he clenched it into a fist instead. "See you soon."

My heart ached to watch him walk away, and I acknowledged the automatic fear that he might not return that flipped my stomach. With a breath, I tried to convince myself I was being silly and that I could see him again in the morning.

Ready to face the firing squad, I rejoined my grandmother and Mason only to find her grilling him. "Nobody can nail down the exact time Lucky disappeared?" she asked.

"We have an approximate timeline, but his loss of memory doesn't help." Mason took out his notepad and wrote down some things.

Nana acknowledged my presence with a sharp question. "And how long did it take you to find him?"

I bit my lip. "I didn't. Dash and Mason did. Well, Mason's detective instincts did."

Her eyebrows raised. "You didn't do anything to help?"

"She tried, Ms. Goodwin." The detective jumped to my defense a little too fast, and he grimaced at his mistake.

"I've told you before to call me Vivian, Detective."

Uh-oh. Her syrupy tone meant nothing good was about to happen. I looked about, praying someone would come interrupt us. Our attempts at secrecy were working too darn well.

"Now, explain to me exactly how you found Lucky." Nana held Mason and I in her gaze. No amount of hemming or hawing would get us out of doing exactly what she asked.

After I gave her a brief description, she made the detective recount his perspective. When he tried to describe how his gut knew where to look, he faltered. "I'm just glad we found him when we did."

Nana shrugged. "It's more than probable the fool drank too much of his own beer and stumbled out there on his own, bumping his head in the process. But the possibility that someone attacked him still exists, so I won't dismiss it. Detective, I appreciate you keeping this matter to yourself for the moment."

"Even from Big Willie?" Mason did nothing to hide his displeasure at the request.

"Definitely from him. For the moment. Trust me on this, the quieter we can keep the matter, the better it will be for our futures. Please." Nana's many talents included making a request sound like an order that couldn't be defied.

"I'll agree not to say anything to the sheriff for tonight. Tomorrow, I want to try harder to figure out what happened," conceded Mason. "Charli, are you ready to go back to your place?"

Nana hooked her right arm through mine. "My granddaughter is going to give me the pleasure of her company for a little while longer, Detective. I'll make sure she makes it home quite safely, thank you." With a curt nod, she dismissed the detective. "Come along, Birdy, you and I need to have a discussion away from prying eyes or ears."

I mouthed, "Help," at Mason, but he raised his hands in the air in defeat. We both knew there was nothing either one of us could do.

My grandmother dragged me a few feet from where we were standing and stopped so suddenly, I lurched forward. Flourishing her fingers, she cast a bubble around us.

"Seriously, Nana? A sound-proof spell?" My stomach churned with nerves, and I knew for sure I would never be prepared for the barrage of questions about to be aimed at me.

"What did Mason mean by *you tried*?" she started with.

So, deep end of the pool first. "I did what I always do. You know finding people is my biggest struggle."

"I do, but the detective made it sound like you tried...and failed."

I kicked a rock on the ground with the toe of my shoe. "I did. When I cast my spell, I literally couldn't find any thread of connection." Recalling the incident and lack of what normally happened, it made me feel empty.

Nana glared at me for a second, and then cleared her throat and cheered up. "Okay," she chimed.

"Okay?"

"Yes. Okay." Her lips curled into a smile as sweet as iced tea.

Pixie poop, it was worse than I thought. I hoped for her

to release the spell but braced for maximum impact when it remained hovering around us.

"So, tell me, Birdy, what's been going on between you and the detective." She batted her eyes at me.

Now she'd filled the pool I was barely treading water in with sharks. I blinked back at her. "We've been hanging out together just the same as we have these past few months."

"And that's all?" Nana placed an impatient hand on her hip. "Nothing more than just being together. Nothing of note at all."

The more the woman picked at me, the more I wanted to clam up. "Nope. Nothing to tell," I lied and prepared to redirect a shark at her. "And since you've been so kind as to inquire about my relationship, perhaps I could ask you the same thing?"

She blinked in innocence. "You want to know if I've been doing anything with the detective?"

The woman was too savvy for her own good. "No, not with Mason. How about a certain retired racer who moved to Honeysuckle Hollow not too long ago? Anything about you two you'd like to share with me?"

Caught by surprise, Nana's interrogation faltered. With immediate haste, she burst the spelled bubble around us. "Nope. Glad we had this chat."

I smiled in triumph. "Me, too."

"You need me to find someone to take you home?"

"No, I can make it on my own," I assured her.

"Good. Talk to you tomorrow, Charlotte." Nana scuttled away from me like the guilty person she was.

I clutched my stomach, giving in to shaking laughter at her avoidance and use of my real name. My turning tables on her must have really thrown her off balance. The celebration in my unexpected victory stopped with a gasp when I connected the dots. If I had avoided telling her about the kiss between Mason and me, then that meant that she and Billy Ray...nope. A whole bucketful of nope's existed down that pathway of thinking.

"Ew, ew, ew, ew, ew." I wiped my hands down my front as if I needed to clean them off.

Trudging back to say my goodbyes to Lucky's team, I let them know discreetly where he was before taking all the registrations and names to the administration tent and dropping them off. Every few seconds, I shivered in disgust as my brain couldn't stop thinking about Nana and Billy Ray. Nothing but nightmares waited for me back home and for the rest of the night.

Chapter Seven

The sweet scent of baked goods wafted up the stairs, waking me up from only a few hours of decent sleep. When I'd gotten back home last night, I was surprised by an impromptu pajama party thrown by my closest girlfriends. With everything that had happened at the event site, it had slipped my mind they were staying with me.

The door to my room creaked open, and two heads popped through the entrance. With a smile and a stifled giggle, I pulled the quilt over my head.

"Wakey, wakey, eggs and bakey," Lavender sang.

Lily snorted. "Come on, Charli. We let you sleep as late as possible and did all the work for breakfast."

I lowered the quilt and found Lavender's head twisting to look up at her cousin's face. "You so did not do any of the work in the kitchen."

"I laid the table," Lily countered.

"Ooh, like that took a whole lot of effort." Lavender stuck her tongue out at her cousin.

I tossed a pillow at the two of them. "Where's the snooze button for this bickering alarm?"

Lily took my comment as an invitation to enter my bedroom. She whipped the pillow right back at me. "You know, if you let Mason or Dash see you looking like that when you wake up, you might not have a man problem."

"I do not have a man problem." My hands flew to my hair, feeling the chaos of tangles. With a groan, I got out of bed, approached my two friends with a smirk, and waited for them to move out of the way. "I just have one who kissed me and one who hasn't yet told me where he's been for months."

Lily waved a hand in front of her face. "Phew, you definitely have a bad breath problem. Go brush your teeth, girl."

"I was already headed that way." I marched past them and closed the bathroom door, shutting them out in the hallway.

The wooden barrier muffled Lavender's voice. "If she brushes her teeth, the orange juice will taste funny."

"If she doesn't brush her teeth, we might all die before we get to eat," joked Lily.

"I heard that," I yelled at both of the cousins.

When I got downstairs, my mouth watered at the delectable smells. No doubt Alison Kate had been having fun in my kitchen making some tasty goodies. I rubbed my hands together and followed the cacophony of voices into the dining room.

A spread that could rival Nana's awaited me, as did three smiling faces. My stomach growled, and I took inventory of a quiche that looked too perfect to eat, fluffy biscuits piled high on a platter, a tray of gooey cinnamon rolls dripping with icing, muffins with big chunks of berries nestled in a basket, and a large plate loaded with greasy bacon.

Without a word, I rushed over and hugged my baker friend tight. Letting her go, I got down on one knee and held her hand. "Alison Kate Johnston, will you marry me?"

We all laughed, and my friend gazed down at me with sheer joy in her eyes. "While I love you and you're one of my bestest friends in the world, I have to say no."

I pushed my bottom lip out in a mock pout and got off the floor. "Why?"

Alison Kate held up the back of her left hand and wiggled her fingers at me, pointing at the decent-sized rock that sat on her finger. "Because my man already put a ring on it."

I shrugged. "Fair enough, I won't fight for you. But I think Lee should lend you to me once a month to make sure I'm well-fed."

We all took a place at the table and began passing our plates around so those closest to the dishes could serve up the goodies. I put a little scoop of eggs on a plate and slid it under the table where Peaches rubbed against my legs, begging for food.

"Speaking of your being engaged," Lavender said while

licking the frosting from her lips, "when are you gonna come in and start choosing your flowers?"

Alison Kate stopped mid-bite of a piece of bacon. "I know, I'm way behind on things. But the bakery's been incredibly busy these days with more and more people coming to Honeysuckle, especially on the weekends. Also, Lee's been a little..."

The rest of us stopped eating and waited for her to finish her thought. We'd all talked about it amongst our group, but none of us wanted to say anything directly to our most sensitive friend. Ever since coming back from making his deal with the spell phones and starting his own spellcasting consulting company in an old barn he'd renovated with the money he'd made, Lee had talked more about the exciting new ideas he and a few new employees were coming up with and spent less time cherishing his fiancée.

"You could come out with me today," I suggested, going back to eating to try and take away some of the tension in the room. "I'm sure Lee will want to show off the work he's doing with Billy Ray's equipment."

A dark shadow of doubt passed over my friend's face, but Alison Kate shook off her concern with a sigh and finished her slice of bacon. "I know he loves racing, too. I just hope he loves me a little bit more."

Lily's chair scraped on the floor as she pushed herself away from the table. She approached Alison Kate and threw her arms around our friend's neck.

"He does love you. He's just got a lot more going on in his

life." She planted a kiss on Alison Kate's cheek. "But you just say the word, and I promise that all of us girls will hex him so hard he confirms a date then and there."

Our friend sniffed back the tears that threatened to spill and patted Lily's arm, letting her go back to her seat. "I know I'm being silly." She looked around the table at all of us. "And I haven't even asked you girls to be my bridesmaids yet."

The front door slammed shut and Blythe yelled out her greetings. Without saying anything else, she picked up a plate and reached over in front of me, snagging the largest cinnamon roll. She took a massive bite and chewed on it while we all stared at her.

"Y'all, it's been a heckuva morning, and it's not even past ten yet," she explained, taking another big mouthful. When she finally noticed the heavy silence, she stopped. "What?"

"We were just about to accept being Alison Kate's bridesmaids," I stated in a calm but very purposeful tone.

"Oh-h-h, sorry. Sure, I'm up for it." Blythe reached across me again and grabbed a piece of bacon.

Alison Kate giggled. "It's fine, y'all. I promise I won't make you wear anything too poofy or ridiculous. Blythe, tell us what has your feathers ruffled."

Our busy friend regaled us with her troubles of making sure guests were situated in the volunteered houses across Honeysuckle. She assured the two Blackwood cousins that the group staying in their place was perfectly lovely. But there had already been more than a few calls to handle small problems this morning.

"There's a gang of male witches I'm not so fond of. Turns out a couple of them are staying at the Turner place, but a bigger and more unpleasant part of their group are sleeping in an RV out at the event site. But that didn't stop them from coming into town and doing a little damage in the backyard." Blythe stopped long enough to gulp down her entire glass of fresh orange juice.

"You should delegate to someone else," I suggested. "You can't take on something that big all by yourself."

Blythe nodded. "I'm way ahead of you. I'd ask Eveline to help, but she's been wanting to spend time with Raif's barbecue team. I suspect the newest member and master of the grill has piqued her interest."

"Who're you going to ask?" Lily buttered her biscuit, missing Blythe's innocent smile aimed in her direction.

"Hello, friend. Would you mind helping me manage the housing situation for the weekend?" Blythe blinked her eyes at Lily.

Before the grumpier cousin could reply, Lavender clapped her hands. "We'd be glad to help you. As long as we get some time off to watch some of the races."

"I'd help, too, but I've got to man the tent of baked goods with Sprinkle and Twinkle." Alison Kate shrugged.

Blythe turned her greedy gaze in my direction, and I concentrated on cutting a perfect portion of the quiche with my knife and fork. Nana had directed those involved in last night's debacle to keep it to themselves for now. The more people that knew, the less of a chance we could keep it quiet.

"I already know why you can't help me," my best friend teased.

Realizing I'd misinterpreted her attention, I carefully chewed on my flavorful portion. "Hmm?"

"It's a small town. What, did you really think you could keep it a secret?" Blythe smirked.

Nana would not be happy if rumors about Lucky were already spreading. "I have no idea what y'all are flapping your jaws about."

"Ooh, what do you know?" Lavender asked. "We only got out of her that Mason kissed her yesterday."

"Lav!" I opened my eyes wide to try to get her to shut up.

Blythe stopped eating. "You got kissed by the detective? No way. Was it good? Where were you? Is it just the one time or has this been going on for a while? Are you two a thing?"

I pushed my plate out of the way and banged my head against the table while my other three friends filled her in on the little I'd shared with them the night before.

"Hey, wait. That kind of complicates things, doesn't it?" Blythe pulled on the back of my hair, making me sit up straight. "What about Dash? I heard you went on a long walk with him. Did he kiss you too, or is he dating one of those girls on the mountain barbecue team?"

Sweet honeysuckle iced tea, I did not need my girlfriends jumping into the very confused mix of things.

Lily crossed her arms and flashed me a smug smile from across the table. "See, I told you so. Man problems."

My spell phone dinged several times in a row. Saved by the

technological bell. I checked it and cringed reading Nana's message first.

"We still need to have a longer conversation today, Birdy. I'll give you an answer to your question if you'll answer mine."

Still nope. I couldn't for fear my stomach would reject everything I'd already stuffed into it this morning. I switched over to see who else needed an answer.

The simplicity of Mason's text made me feel a little better. *"Sorry about last night. When you get a chance today, can we talk?"*

We definitely had some things to discuss, but should I put it off until Dash and I finally have our say with each other first? Or should I give Mason the priority since he was the one who kissed me? And since I initiated the kiss the second time, didn't that mean he should be the first of the two men I responded to?

The name StupidPoutyPuppy popped up with another ding, interrupting my internal debate. Oops, I'd forgotten I'd changed Dash's name in my contacts. I swallowed a silent curse at my stomach flipping with too much anticipation when I checked what he sent me before answering Mason.

"I need to see you this morning."

"Of course you do," I muttered. My fingers poised over the screen to type my response, but another message came through.

"I can be at your house in minutes."

Panic killed the butterflies in my stomach. I glanced around the table at my friends who still and talked but kept watching me with amusement dancing in their eyes.

"*I'm not alone,*" I punched in. It didn't occur to me how it could be misinterpreted until the text was in the ether and out of my control.

I rushed to type out an explanation, but another text beat me to it. "*Neither am I.*"

Georgia's face flashed in my mind, and I frowned. I thought he said they were just friends. If that wasn't the case, then why would he want to bring her to my house?

Another ping, and I clicked on the text. "*Lucky needs to talk to you. It's urgent. Can we just come over?*"

"What did you just read that gave you that smile?" asked Lily.

I touched my mouth, not realizing what it was doing. Should the opportunity ever arise, I must remember to never ever gamble. Clearly, I lacked a poker face.

With my phone, I took a quick picture of my friends' eager faces and added it to my response. "*There are four nosy girls currently at my house. Does Lucky want to talk in front of them?*" I warned and waited.

The answer came as quick as I expected. "*No.*" Another followed, "*Meet at bar instead. Use side entrance.*"

If I didn't interpret his request to be urgent, I might spend a few extra seconds teasing him about day drinking. But given what happened to our leprechaun friend the night before, joking around wouldn't be helpful.

"*On my way,*" I typed.

I downed the last of my coffee. "I'm sorry girls, I've gotta go." Wiping my mouth and hands with the napkin, I got up from the table. "Ali Kat, is there any extra I might be able to take with me?" Maybe Lucky would feel better with some good food in his belly.

She got up as well. "Here's the deal. You go put on some clothes and I'll package you up some goodies to take with you."

My eyebrows shot up. "If?" I prompted.

Her smile beamed with mischief. "If you tell us who you're taking them to. Is it Mason? Or Dash?"

I clutched the back of my chair. "How do you know it's not my grandmother?"

Lily jerked her thumb at her cousin, and Lavender giggled. "Because I told you, love for your family members looks purple. Your aura is *not* purple."

"I hate you all," I declared, escaping their interrogation to run upstairs.

"No, you don't, and you didn't strike the bargain yet," Alison Kate reminded from the bottom step. "Who are you going to go see?"

At this point, I didn't feel comfortable breaking Nana's directive. If I told them Lucky wanted to talk to me, they'd change tactics and start interrogating me about why. They already knew more than I wanted them to, so a little half-truth white lie wouldn't hurt too much. "Fine. I'm going to meet up with Dash."

"Ha! Pay up," I heard Blythe exclaim.

"No way," protested Lily. "It's too early to tell who she's gonna choose."

I stomped on each wooden stair to try and drown out their betting on my love life. It took me three outfits until I found the right one that struck the right balance between *I'm-not-trying-too-hard* and *I-still-wanna-look-good*. I typed out a message letting Dash know I was about to leave my house before navigating the endless teasing of my friends on my way out the door.

On the road, I straddled my bicycle and sent magic through me and into my favorite mode of transportation since I'd lost Old Joe. It took off faster than normal, and I gripped the handlebars for dear life, holding on tight and trusting nothing ahead would knock me off course.

❧❧❧

AFTER PARKING my bike in the alley, I entered Lucky's bar through the side entrance and followed the murmuring voices into the bar.

"I brought some freshly baked goods with me," I chimed. No text could have prepared me for the look Lucky and Dash shot me. "What's going on?"

The two men glanced at each other, and my gut sank. I placed the container of goodies on the dark polished wooden bar and pulled up a stool. When neither of the boys responded to me, my stomach dropped again.

Lucky lifted a glass of dark lager to his lips and drained half the glass. A little foam rested on his red whiskers, but I refrained from teasing him about it.

"I need ye to do something for me, Charli girl," the leprechaun said in a voice that resonated to my bones.

Without hesitation, I responded, "Anything."

Dash placed his hand at the small of my back, and the shivers I didn't even know I had stopped. Why did the shifter feel the need to touch me at this particular moment?

Lucky finished what was left of the beer and slammed the glass on the bar. Taking a deep breath, he let it go and nodded at me. "Know this. I will pay ye whatever fee required."

The leprechaun's thicker Irish brogue sent chills over my arms and made the hairs stand on end. His accent only came out that sharp when he was overly excited, angry, or under duress.

"You don't have to pay me anything," I assured him.

"What I need ye to find is worth more to me than all the treasures in all the wide world." Lucky turned his head away and squeezed his eyes tight. "If only I could remember what happened."

"Stop blaming yourself," Dash demanded. "Someone did this to you deliberately."

I sucked in a sharp breath, wanting to ask more questions, but Lucky reached out his hand and grabbed mine. "The why is nae important. What ye need to search for is."

"And what's that?"

He stood on his tiptoes and leaned over the bar so he could face me head on. "Someone has taken me luck, and I need ye to bring it back to me."

Chapter Eight

"You want me to find your luck," I repeated, not believing what I'd just heard.

Lucky's head bobbed up and down. "And ye need to do it as soon as possible. Ye can do that by touchin' me, right?" He held out his hand.

Without thinking, I flinched away from him. "Wait a minute, I'm confused here. Are you talking about like a rabbit's foot or something?"

Dash huffed with impatience. "It's a bit bigger than that. Can't you just, you know, take his hand and figure out where it is?"

"I don't know yet," I insisted. "How big is the thing you want me to find?"

In my head, I tried to figure out what would represent a luck to a leprechaun. All I could come up with on the fly was a four-leaf clover or a pot of gold. I dismissed the clover for its size and marveled at my possible shot at being the one person in the world who got to find a real-life leprechaun's treasure at the end of a rainbow.

Lucky squinted at me. "I can tell by your smile that you'll be thinkin' of a pot o' gold. Ye of all people should be able to think beyond your typical misgivin's about the supernatural."

"Quit stalling, Charli," Dash demanded. "Will you help him or not?"

I swiveled to face the shifter, annoyed at his arrogance that he thought he could be the one to ask anything of me. "Sorry, but it's not that simple. I need to understand what it is I'm trying to find. If it's a tangible object, then yeah, I could probably do it, no problem. But that doesn't seem to be what we're talking about. I need to understand what I'm searching for before I can track it down."

The hopeful friendliness on the leprechaun's face faded. "I'm truly sorry, Charli, but I have to insist."

After not being able to help find Lucky last night, I more than owed it to him. Plus, what good was it to run a business finding things if I didn't do my job?

Shaking off my initial nerves, I slid off the stool. "Let's do this."

Lucky stepped down from his position and disappeared behind the bar, walking around the dark wooden barrier to join me in the middle of his place. "Do ye need to hold my hand?"

I nodded. "It helps." I accepted his hand and closed my eyes.

Over the past few months, my abilities had grown stronger and more consistent. Having my magic not work last night rattled my confidence. I needed to start fresh this morning.

"Try to focus on what it is you want to find. Bring it to the front of your mind. Make it what you want most," I instructed.

Testing where my powers were, at first I tried to find any type of connection without saying anything. When that didn't work, I doubled my efforts in concentration and threw in a whispered spell. *"Break the dam, let magic flow, and let me find what I still owe. From my friend's grasp, his power plucked, I need some help to find his luck."*

My body hummed with magic, but nothing as strong as I was used to feeling. The light buzz faded away without even the slightest thread intent on finding its target. I released Lucky with a squawk of disbelief.

"Did it work?" he asked with too much eagerness.

My panicked breaths increased in quick and uneven gasps. Even when I was little, I could at least make a minor connection. Now, only emptiness of nothing happening filled me. The room spun a little around me

"Whoa, I've got you." Dash bounded over to pick me up.

I warned him off. "I'm okay. Don't. Touch. Me." I ignored how mean my rejection might seem to him, but I didn't want to spread my failure around. "Just give me a minute."

I gripped the back of a chair to gain some balance and slow my breathing. Once rational thought returned, I silently reassured myself that failure was another way to learn. And if what my friend wanted me to find was something new, then I hadn't finished the lesson yet.

"Lucky, I think the problem is that finding something like a lost pair of glasses or keys is one thing. Connecting an object to a person is another that I struggle to master. But asking me to find something as abstract and intangible as luck? I wouldn't know where to begin." I pulled out the chair and slumped into it. "I need more to go on."

The leprechaun stroked his beard. "Aye. Tis a fair point." He went back behind the bar and busied himself pouring a tall glass of beer. When he returned, he set it on top of a coaster in front of me on the table. "Here, ye'll be needin' this."

"I don't typically drink in the morning," I protested.

Lucky sat down and invited Dash to join us.

"Where's mine?" the wolf shifter complained.

"Ye've already had some." Lucky pointed at me. "She may need it. Now, before ye start in with a lot of questions, I want your assurance that what I tell ye here does not get repeated. I cannae risk it findin' its way to the wrong ears." The leprechaun held out his hand in anticipation of the bargain.

It felt like such a little thing to agree. "Deal." As soon as our hands met to shake on the bargain, the great importance of it weighed on me.

Dash shook his hand after, and Lucky settled into his

chair. "I know it must seem a bit odd for a leprechaun with the name of Lucky to have lost his luck."

"It is," I agreed, wanting to follow up with a question.

He held up his hand to stop me. "Let me get through what I have to tell ye before you go needlin' for answers to things I may or may not be willin' to share."

"Plus, it'll go faster if you stay quiet," Dash murmured from his seat next to me. I kicked his shin and made him wince.

Lucky ignored us. "Although I may not look that old, I count myself as one of the oldest residents here in Honeysuckle Hollow. It is not me first home and it may not be me last. But I choose to live here because it is the first place that has felt like where I belong since I left my fair isle."

The leprechaun wasted no time in continuing his tale. "Once, in the place now called Ireland, the *aes sídhe* outnumbered the mortals that existed. Although we coexisted with man, we were more concerned with our own magic and power. In those days, we did not hide who we were and lived freely in our mounds o' the earth, roamin' the wide fields or livin' in the frothy sea."

I leaned forward, caught up in the visions Lucky's Irish brogue conjured. "I didn't know leprechauns lived in the ocean."

Lucky waved his hand in front of his face as if to brush away an annoying fly. "The term *aes sídhe* is an old one for all of the supernatural beings that existed then. I think in today's stories, they call us the *daoine sídhe*. Either term covers many races of fae. It makes no never mind what ye call them now."

Without asking, the leprechaun reached for the unclaimed glass of beer. He took one sip and wiped the froth away with the back of his hand. "By now, ye may have figured out that the word ye use for me is not the real one."

"You're not a leprechaun?" I asked.

"I am, although I am not as I used to be. But I mean me name, Lucky." He took another sip. "If I tell the two of you my real one, you must try and forget it as soon as you hear it, for it carries with it a terrible burden."

I nodded while Dash answered, "I promise."

"There is too much history to explain for ye to truly have a sense of who I was. I will need to skip to the most important parts." He fixed his eyes on a point we could not see, and they sparkled at some unknown memory. "It may surprise ye to know that I am the son of a king. Not the high king, mind ye, but the ruler of the southern half of Ulster, King Fergus mac Léti," explained the leprechaun.

I could barely contain my awe and excitement to find out we had royalty in Honeysuckle. Shutting my gaping mouth, I tried in vain to act cool and cover up my disbelief. "It sounds like you've always been a Southerner?"

Lucky cracked a smile. "I did not think of it in that way. Yes, I supposed the term fits. My real name was Fergus mac Róich. I served me da's kingdom well, trainin' to take over in his stead when the time arose. As his only son, me father's gifts passed onto me upon his death. He has his own tale that has been told and passed on over the ages, but the short of it is that he encountered three water sprites who dragged him into the sea for sport."

"They killed him?" I couldn't stop the question from bursting out of me.

"No, he had been sleepin' by the shore when they took him. He woke just in time and defeated the three sprites and earned favors for their misdeed. They granted him the power to swim and stay under water as well as the ability to produce and maintain good fortune. Me da counted himself more powerful than the northern half of Ulster, using his newfound powers to test what he could take." Lucky shook his head and paused.

Dash pressed his knee against mine. His face remained passive, but his fidgeting underneath the table signaled his own excitement. I guessed the leprechaun hadn't told him all of these details to justify needing my services.

"I'll admit," Lucky continued, "I supported me father, the king, in all of his endeavors. Some good, some bad, but he became a bigger hero to his own people the richer and stronger he grew. His head filled with desires to gain as much as he could in his lifetime, and he forgot the most important aspect to all of the *daoine sídhe*. All magic comes at a price, and no one ever struck a bargain without some sort of consequence."

It occurred to me that both Dash and I had done just that. Hanging my head, I hoped that our friend had no ill will in our own agreement.

He went on, his voice weaving the tale of his past. "The water sprites granted me father the ability to exist underwater with none of the weaknesses he formerly knew. However, he was warned nae to seek what lay beneath the waters of *Loch Rudraige*. With all of his success, it did not take long for the king to turn his eye to the lake in Ulster and what treasures lay beneath its murky depths. He gave no heed to the warnin' when he entered the lake. There he met a mighty creature of the water and faced its monstrosity with great fear. Although he survived, what he had laid eyes upon drained the life from him and affected him so deep, he ne'er spoke to me of what he saw. Before his passin', he willed all that was his to me, includin' his great sword Caladbolg, his title, and his powers."

A heavy silence stretched between the three of us when Lucky finished his tale, letting his words wash over Dash and me. He pushed back from the table and disappeared.

"Did he tell you any of this?" I whispered to Dash.

The wolf shifter shook his head. "He told me a very condensed version so I understood what he meant by losing his luck. All of this," Dash waved his hands in front of him. "It's incredible."

"And we've sworn not to tell anybody. Frosted fairy wings!" I exclaimed, grabbing onto Dash's arm. "Lucky's a king. Are we supposed to, you know, bow or genuflect or something?"

"None of that nonsense, now." Lucky set three glasses of beer on the table, one for each of us. He finished the rest of my drink and set it aside to grasp his full pint. "I figured ye could use a little help to keep up."

Without prompting, Dash and I both drank the thick, dark bitter ale from his homeland in large gulps. I left half the beer in the glass while the shifter finished all of his.

Lucky nodded in approval. "Remember that I was now king of the south of Ulster. The high king at the time, Fachtna Fáthach, took notice of me, and the two of us became allies and, in the end, friends. We ruled in tandem, and he supported me attempts to help those who lived underneath me, fae and human alike. While he knew of me father's powers and possibly suspected I possessed them after me da's passin', he never mentioned them in my presence nor asked me to use them for his own gain. Those were golden times for our people.

"But in all me time, I've found that darkness does not like the light. After days of glory and wonder, shadows come to block out the sun. King Fachtna's own son defeated him in a crushin' battle at a time when I was not there to fight at my friend's side. As the new high king, his son Conchobar mac Nessa, ruled over me. With nothin' more than his own greed drivin' his deeds, he demanded me fealty and forced me to use my inherited powers for his purposes. If not for one precious thing, me time spent under Conchobar's heel would have broken me. If ye cannae guess what it was that saved me, ye have never lived."

"A woman," growled Dash.

"Aye." Lucky rubbed his temple. "And not just any woman. Queen Medb, wife of Conchobar, who turned out to be as ruthless as her husband in the end. She would be the one to ruin me into diminishin' to what I am now, but not before we had lain together enough for her to become with child."

My eyes widened. "You have kids?"

"I did, but I ne'er laid eyes on them. When Conchobar learned of me treachery, it was all I could do to save me skin, a king's title of me own or not." Lucky wiped at his eyes.

Dash held up a finger. "Hold on, how did the high king find out you were the father?"

Lucky emitted a high-pitched word of exclamation in a language I didn't understand. "Medb told him herself. She used me ability to bring good fortune to become pregnant. But with her husband preoccupied with increasin' his own power, she was left with me to sire her offspring, givin' no thought to the consequences."

"How did you escape?" I asked.

The leprechaun flashed me a wry grin. "By testin' the power of luck on myself. I made it all the way to the coast and called upon the great Tuatha Dé Danann god of the sea, Manannán mac Lir. I asked him to help me leave the isle and bring me to safer shores. Already upset about the sea sprites grantin' my father powers to begin with, he readily set forth a bargain. If I were willin' to give back the gifted magic, he would bring me to a new land far away.

"I did not mind relenquishin' the gift of underwater magic as it never appealed to me. But I did not want to lose me power of good fortune in fear that me own destiny might crumble to dust without it. Manannán mac Lir demanded his price, so I countered with the gift of me fearsome sword,

Caladbolg. It was a great sacrifice as the weapon contained more power than to take life. The sea god accepted the offer but warned me that by holdin' on to the other gift from the sprites, it would be bound to me, body and soul. For magic always has a price."

Lucky's words hung in the air. The three of us finished our drinks. The sound of our glasses clinking on the table echoed in the empty bar.

"How is it you went from being a king to running The Rainbow's End?" I was sure the leprechaun had many more tales tucked away, but I had to know how he ended up in Honeysuckle.

"I am not what I once was. The longer I have been away from me home, the more I become less myself. And out of revenge, both Conchobar and Medb campaigned against me and my people. Some myths are created by reality and some are lies passed on through generations. All that the humans know of me kind exists because of greed and vindictiveness. They wanted to annihilate all leprechauns, and especially desired me to be hunted down. They spread rumors of us hoardin' away treasures from mortals and tales of how we bring luck. I suppose I chose my name as a reminder of my former life and to choose to live in the opposite manner."

"So, the luck you want me to find is a magic power?" I clarified, fear rising from the pits of my stomach.

Lucky's face dropped. "If ye cannae find it, then I don't know who else to turn to."

"I told you that you needed to help him." Dash bumped my knee again with his.

Panic rose in my chest, and I stood up fast. "I want to help, but I can't promise to succeed." The task loomed larger than our entire town in front of me. "Besides, you know I'm limited. I couldn't even find *you* last night." I pointed at the leprechaun.

Dash's eyebrows furrowed. "Lucky, are you sure your luck is actually gone?"

"If ye woke up in the mornin' and ye could nae turn into a wolf no matter what you tried, would ye think you lost something important?" the leprechaun challenged.

Dash growled at the thought. "Yes. But the ability might come back."

"Fine. What if ye woke up and all your arms and legs were gone. What would ye do then?" pressed Lucky.

I slumped into my chair again. "I'd do two things. One, I'd want to know how they were taken. And two, I'd want to find them. Especially if my life depended on me getting them back."

Lucky relaxed with a sigh. "Exactly."

"I didn't say I could do it. We need to consult someone way smarter than us." Taking out my phone, I pulled up the desired number and called it. "Hey, listen. Don't say anything until I'm done. I'm here at The End with Lucky and Dash. I need you to come here. Now."

MASON STOOD in front of the three of us with his arms crossed and a scowl on his face. "So Lucky wants something found, and you need my help. But you won't tell me what it is he's lost or why you need me here?"

The detective wasn't exactly the first person I called. Nana couldn't come due to needing to put on a good face in front of witch council members or some such political nonsense. If the situation wasn't as complicated as it was, I might have called in my gang. But since Lucky wanted to keep things quiet, there was only one person I thought I could trust in this situation.

"He has a point. If we want him to help us figure it out, he has to know something." I looked to Lucky to make the decision.

Dash muttered something under his breath and coughed to cover up his displeasure at my executed plan.

"What was that?" Mason asked.

Before those two could lock horns again, I cleared my throat. "Lucky, I think we can tell him what it is you lost without giving away anything else. He has to have some information to work with."

The leprechaun eyed each one of us. He dropped his guard and hung his head. "Fine. But I'll be needin' ye to guarantee that anything ye hear from me will stay between us." He stuck out his hand and struck a new bargain.

"Lucky's luck is gone," I declared, wanting to get things rolling fast.

Mason made a weird face. "That doesn't make sense."

"Get past that realization faster, please. It goes with his attack last night. Whoever it was did something to drain the power of luck from him. That's really all you need to know." I glanced over at my shorter friend. "Right?"

Lucky paused to think it over and gave me an approving grin. "That'll do."

Mason glanced at Dash, and I understood his unspoken question of why the wolf shifter was involved. To distract the detective, I volunteered the information I really didn't want to acknowledge. "I already tried once using my magic to find it. Nothing happened."

My confession knocked Mason off of whatever jealous path he was about to take. "Again? That's...something worth exploring. But, yeah, later." He cleared his throat. "Now that you've had some rest, can you remember any more details from last night?" he asked Lucky. Settling into his role of detective, he interrogated the leprechaun in rapid succession.

Dash approached me from the side and bumped me with his shoulder. "I've heard that you and the detective have gotten close over the last few months."

A burst of air escaped my lips. "Now? You want to start this conversation now? Our friend needs our help. I think any other talks can be put to the side until we figure things out."

"I didn't mean anything—" the shifter started.

"If you two can pay attention," interrupted Mason, glaring at Dash, "I could use your thoughts about how this is at all possible."

My brain had been working on that issue while Mason

caught up, but Dash had interrupted my thoughts. Back on track, I raised my hand. "I think it's important that you weren't born with good fortune. That magic was given to you."

"It was?" Mason asked.

Lucky narrowed his eyes at me, reminding me to be more careful with my words. "Tis true. I will nae tell you how it came to me."

"But Charli's right. If the power was given to you, then it stands to reason someone could take it away." The detective tapped his mouth with his finger.

"But how would whoever attacked Lucky know anything about the magic in the first place?" Dash asked. He gave a curt nod to the leprechaun to ensure he hadn't said too much.

"Aren't all of your kind expected to grant some level of luck to anyone who finds you, Lucky?" The detective's question reminded me of our friend's tale and how much Mason didn't know.

"I suspect whoever attacked me thought the same thing, to be sure," agreed Lucky.

"But," started the detective, "I've worked cases before where someone tried to steal another being's magic to use for themselves. It never lasted long and usually brought about some form of disaster for all involved. Which means, we need to figure this out before whoever did this is gone." He reached out his hand to grasp Lucky's shoulder and sucked in a harsh breath.

Mason closed his eyes and squeezed the leprechaun

tighter, his other hand grabbing onto the other shoulder. The detective bowed his head, his brow furrowed. Lucky endured the touch until he wrenched out of the detective's grip.

"What are you doing?" Dash took a step closer, preparing to step in.

Mason's chest rose and sank with deep breaths. "It's here. Whoever has your luck, they're still here. I'm sure of it."

Chapter Nine

꧁꧂

Neither Mason nor I spoke about our suspicions all the way to the event area. Dash and Lucky headed back to their teams in order to check in on things and to give the appearance of everything being normal. But the detective and I needed to consult with someone much more experienced and knowledgeable.

It took longer than I expected to locate Nana. Everyone we asked pointed us in the direction of where she had just been. We messaged people on our spell phones, and still couldn't locate her. Even though we spoke a few words to each other in the search, we avoided the important, big fat elephant-sized issue between us—how did *he* know something about Lucky's luck, and *I* didn't?

Mason's phone buzzed, and he checked it. "Big Willie says

I need to go to the administration tent. And that I should bring you."

"Does he say why?"

"I'm not asking my boss why. Let's go there and see if he or anyone in there knows where your grandmother is." He shoved his phone back in his pocket with haste.

A little bit of anger rose in my chest. Why the sudden wall of ice between us again? With quick steps, I hurried in front of him in order to beat him there.

"Charli, wait," he called from behind, eating my dust.

I zigged and zagged my way through the crowd, my stomach growling from the scent of grilling meat and other tempting foods floating in the breeze. Mason shouted at me a couple more times, but his calls only pushed me a little bit faster. I entered the tent at a hurried clip and almost knocked over a table with a taped poster board that read, "Information."

"So sorry," I gushed, but spotted Big Willie talking to Nana on the other side.

My grandmother held up her arms to greet me with a quick hug. "I was just tellin' Willie how you can help his son find his lost teddy bear."

The young sasquatch clutched his father's leg and hid behind it when I waved at him. I swallowed hard, not prepared to be called to duty.

"Tell Miss Charli here thank you for using her magic to help you," instructed the sheriff, shaking his leg.

I grasped my stomach, willing it not to burst from my nerves. "Uh, Nana, I don't think this is a good time."

"Nonsense." The smile my grandmother gave didn't reach her eyes. "Nothing's scheduled until after lunch, which means we have time a plenty. Stop kidding around and help, Charli Bird."

Mason approached from the side and addressed his boss first. "If you don't mind waiting, Sheriff, there's something we need to discuss with Ms. Goodwin first."

Nana huffed and bent over a little, wiggling her forefinger at the child. "Little Willie, can you come over here and let Miss Charli hold your hand? I promise, she won't hurt you."

Big Willie unhooked his son's grip from around his leg and encouraged the littlest sasquatch forward with a couple of pats on his back. The furry fella failed to meet my gaze, but he bravely held out his hand.

I begged Mason for help with a pleading look, but the detective only shrugged. Not sure I wanted a clear answer for my suspicions using a poor child as the test subject, I couldn't find a graceful way out of the situation and the tent.

"Try really hard to think about your teddy bear, Willie," I said, taking his tiny hand in mine.

"S'name's Willie," the child replied, finally glancing up at me.

The sheriff breathed out a dramatic huff. "We tried to get him to give the dang toy another name."

His son stuck his chin in the air. "My daddy's name is Willie. My name's Willie. And my bear's name is Willie, too."

I giggled and ruffled his hairy head. "You can't fight that logic." The little kid gave me the first reason to laugh today. For him, I would try. "Okay, Little Willie. Let's try this. Think really hard about your bear."

The boy did as I asked, shutting his eyes tight and sticking his tongue out in cute concentration. It didn't take long to figure out my magic, like Lucky's, wasn't there. My eyes flitted to the person who I would bet a good chunk of my late-uncle's inheritance possessed it instead.

Too many seconds ticked by with nothing happening. Confused, the young sasquatch whimpered with impatience.

"Hold on for one more minute, buddy." Mason leaned down and reached for his boss's son's shoulder with a gentle touch. It took him a few seconds to let the kid go, regret and confusion coming off of him in waves.

"Do you know where my bear is?" Little Willie asked, large tears pooling in his eyes.

"I think I do," admitted Mason. "If you can let us talk for one moment, I'll help you find him, okay?"

"What's going on?" pressed the Sheriff. "Whaddya mean, you know where the dang thing is?"

Nana glowered at Mason and me. "Willie, why don't you take your son there to get a funnel cake." She handed him some money. "It's on me. Get one for yourself, too. We'll meet you outside this tent in about fifteen."

"Vivi, what in tarnation—"

"You like funnel cakes, don't you?" my grandmother cooed

at the sheriff's son, getting the child all riled up and begging for food. "Fifteen minutes, Sheriff."

The larger sasquatch frowned but obeyed his distracted son, allowing his large body to be dragged outside by the child.

"Hey, y'all do me a favor and give me fifteen minutes to talk to my granddaughter," Nana requested, ushering out the few others sitting behind tables in the tent. She undid the ties at either end of the fabric flaps and closed the tent down. With a wave of her hands, she set up a magical seal around us.

"I don't know if that was necessary," started Mason.

Nana stopped him with one of her famous glares. "Child, I am worn slap out right now. Don't treat me like I've got one oar out of the water. Tell me quick what's goin' on."

I cringed, knowing she left no room for hemmin' or hawin'. "I think I no longer have my ability to find things."

"Because somehow I have them. We've switched magic, Ms. Goodwin," finished Mason.

"I...that...why..." Nana coughed. "Well, I'd call you both liars except I can see the truth as plain as day on your faces. Plus, I ain't so dumb that I didn't notice something was up last night. So, Charli, when you let Mason talk about finding Lucky, you were hiding that you couldn't do it?"

I pushed an invisible strand of hair out of my face, taking the beat to figure out how to answer. "Not hiding, exactly. I would say more unaware until this morning. I still don't know why it's happened, though."

"I do," volunteered Mason, flashing me an apologetic

glance. "I gave it a lot of thought last night because in my years as a warden, I've never once been able to pick up on a trail of a missing person or anything just by touching something. What I felt. How I just knew where Lucky was last night. It sounded so much like how Charli's described how things work for her."

"Why didn't you tell me before now?" I complained.

Mason lowered his voice. "I tried to get you to see me today when I texted you first thing this morning. It's not my fault other things took precedence."

"If you two are quite finished, we have to figure this out and quick. Detective, why do you think you've got Charli's magic?" Nana tapped her foot on the ground, waiting.

Before I could stop him, Mason told my grandmother about every single time he'd given me a flying lesson. Why would he want her to know all of our most intimate moments when we opened up and tethered our magic together? He explained the time I dropped all my barriers and let him see how different my powers were and how they sort of worked, and my cheeks heated to a blaze.

"Charlotte Vivian Goodwin, you should know better! I've taught you more than once not to play around with spells and such you don't understand. Only the most practiced and disciplined can share their magic, and even then it's not really encouraged." She swiveled to face Mason. "And you, Detective. No doubt you were taught at your wardens' academy that tandem magic could bring about harm if not handled correctly."

Mason didn't back down from my grandmother's scolding. "I am more than well-versed in its practice. I would never put Charli in danger."

Nana scoffed. "You've used it before with someone else?"

"With one of my partners. And it worked just fine." A slight tremor in his voice betrayed his doubt.

"And how did it affect your relationship with your partner? Did you feel more bonded with him or her?" pushed Nana.

Mason frowned and opened his mouth, but closed it while he considered my grandmother's question. "I think feeling bonded is normal for partners. *He* was a good friend."

"I'm not talkin' a basic friendship." Nana poked the detective's chest, her rage deepening her accent. "I'm askin' you to really examine what it did to your workplace partnership. Did you feel the need to partner together? Not like it if either one of you went out on the job with someone else? Have a more-than-normal increased sense of loyalty to him?"

"I—I never thought about it that way. But yeah, it tore me up when he wanted to transfer. Told me he needed a change. I couldn't understand his request since we had such a great track record." Mason bit his lip. "You're saying that what we did and why we felt that way is because we tethered our magic together?"

Nana stepped back and crossed her arms. "I can't say for sure because I wasn't there. You two might have been a good match for tandem magic, more than compatible. But it is possible to affect emotions and actions if used too much." She waved a finger between Mason and me. "And I suppose neither of you have felt things change between you lately? Maybe growing a little closer to each other. A little fonder?"

I clutched my stomach. No, that couldn't be the reason why Mason was becoming an important person in my life. Why I wanted to spend time with him the most these days. I liked him from when we first met, right?

No, I'd disliked him at first. My mind flashed over all our interactions. They weren't all tainted with the tandem magic. So, when did my attraction to the detective begin to really grow?

Mason put an arm around my shoulder. "I can tell you that my feelings for Charli were there before we ever connected in that way. And I think she feels the same."

I resisted the urge to peel out of his touch and run. Swallowing hard, I deflected as fast as possible. "It doesn't explain why you have my powers and I don't. It's never happened before when we tethered to fly." Mason withdrew his arm, and my heart sank.

He closed his eyes and let his head hang back. "Flying. That's what happened." He adjusted his shoulders to face my grandmother, but the move put me in a position where he couldn't see me. "I spellcast to give Charli my abilities to fly so she could experience it without being afraid."

"Charlotte Vivian Goodwin," Nana shouted, middle naming me again. "You allowed him to cast his magic into you? What have I always told you?"

I cast my eyes to the ground. "Not to do that," I mumbled in the voice of the girl I used to be.

"Did you two do a proper grounding before you spellcast? How about properly bringing the spell to an end? Based on the fact that you have her magic," my grandmother snatched Mason's hand and held it up, "I'm gonna say a big fat no. Both of you have your porch lights on, but nobody's home." She dropped the detective's hand and knocked on my forehead. With a not-so-genteel curse word, she paced away from us, mumbling hot words under her breath.

Mason refused to interact with me, and although he stood only inches away from me, it felt like a mile. "Did you know what we were doing was as dangerous as she says it was?" I asked, hoping to reach him.

"I already said I wouldn't do anything to harm you and I meant that. It was never my intent for you to lose your magic because I gave you a taste of mine. But you're grandmother's right. Both of us ignored the ancient rules of magic. Nothing comes for free. There's always a price to pay." He shook his head. "Can we switch our magic back, Ms. Goodwin?"

Nana stopped pacing. "That would be a lovely conclusion to fix an avoidable problem. How about we try that after you find the lost teddy bear for your boss's son?"

Right on cue, the little sasquatch squealed outside the tent. Big Willie yelled through the thin fabric. "Vivi, can you please drop your shield and help me? If I give the boy anymore sugar, he'll be up and runnin' around like a wild man until he's eighteen."

My grandmother waved her hand, and the air around us lightened when the spell dissipated. "Good luck. Come find me when you're done. There's definitely more we have to discuss."

"That's it?" I squeaked and covered my mouth when I heard my words out loud. Already in too deep, I dropped my hand. "How is this supposed to work?"

She lowered her glance at me. "You two have gotten yourselves into this. You're adults. Figure it out."

Mason and I walked out into the warm sun and joined Big Willie. The sheriff did his best to hold onto his rambunctious son trying to pull his massive body over for more food.

"I don't know what's going on, but I would appreciate any help either of you could give us," the sasquatch pleaded.

I elbowed Mason and spoke in a low tone so only he could hear me. "You know more than you think you do. Holding onto the boy's hand will help. You probably don't need to say the words out loud, but you should concentrate on helping him find the teddy bear."

"Hold his hand. Concentrate on the object. Got that." His finger wiped away the drop of sweat rolling down the side of his face. "What happens then?"

I shrugged. "You'll tell me what you feel, and I'll try to walk you through it. Don't worry, I've got you." Placing my hand in his, I squeezed it three times without thinking. With a gasp, I checked to see if he understood what I'd just done, but the detective was in the middle of psyching himself up for the task.

With a deep breath, he started the same process as before, having Little Willie concentrate on finding his bear. Mason took the boy's hand but squeezed mine a little tighter. The detective emitted a short grunt, and I knew he felt the connection.

"You can tell where the bear is," I stated, testing him out.

He nodded. "It's not far away. There's this glowing line outstretched in front of me. I want to grab it, but I've run out of hands."

I chuckled. "It's in your head. You don't have to physically grab it. Recognize it and will it to metaphorically tie it to you. You're the boss of it."

"I'm the boss," he repeated. Licking his lips, his entire face tensed with his efforts. He muttered the phrase over and over again under his breath.

"Is the thread attached to you?" I checked.

He nodded. "I think I know where the bear is. The thread thingy is kind of pulling me toward it."

Big Willie groaned. "Will you two get on with it already?"

I held up my free hand in front of the sheriff's face. "Hush, you." To the detective, I urged him on. "Okay, so now that you have the path waiting for you, open your eyes."

Mason obeyed and blinked a few times. "I can still see that glowing thing."

"Good. Now we're going to try something to test your limits. I want you to let go," I ordered. "Let's see if you can still see it without touch."

The detective paused a beat before letting go of the boy's

hand. He hung his head in exasperation. "Nope. It just disappeared."

I rubbed the back of his hand with my thumb. "That's okay. You're doing really well. Take Little Willie's hand again and see if it returns."

He sighed with relief. "Yes, it's there." Blowing out a long breath, Mason rolled his shoulders back. "You ready to go find your bear, little man?"

The sheriff's son whooped in his high-pitched voice, and his father assured him he would follow right behind.

"I think you can let me go now. You've got this from here." I squeezed Mason's hand and let my fingers relax.

He clasped me harder. "Oh no you don't. You're along for this ride," he insisted.

Taking longer than I would, Mason did his best to keep the boy distracted with questions while moving forward with slow steps. I walked beside him, impressed at his ability to multitask and not fall over. The magic might be mine, but he wielded it with more finesse than I sometimes did on his first intentional attempt.

Big Willie focused on his son's happiness rather than the bits he'd overheard while following right behind us. He pulled Mason over to talk to him, and I feared the detective might be forced to tell the sheriff what was going on. But they both shook hands, and Big Willie walked away with his boy bouncing alongside him.

"Did he interrogate you?" I asked.

The line between Mason's eyebrows deepened. "No, but I

think he might later. We're not going to be able to keep things quiet for long."

Somebody jostled me by accident followed by another person complaining about me being in their way. Reminded that the weekend's event would be huge and populated by a lot of people, I returned to the bigger problem that needed solving.

Pulling Mason by his shirt out of the middle of the crowd, I dragged him over to the side. "This whole field is gonna fill up if it's this crowded even before everything truly kicks off."

He straightened the wrinkle my fingers left in the fabric when I let go. "Figuring everything out is going to get much more complicated. And the clock is already ticking."

Mason grabbed my hand in his and took off with purpose. I stumbled a few steps to catch up to his quickened pace. "Where are we going?"

He pulled me out of the way of a loud group standing in the middle, holding me closer to him. "I think I need to test your magic out again."

His one success had gone straight to his ego. I hated to pop his balloon, but if he possessed my powers, he needed to know how fickle they could be. "You did good, but it's not as simple as that all the time."

Mason laughed off my warning. "It felt amazing afterwards," he exclaimed, weaving us around the side of two loud women.

"I bet I could make him say that about me if he'd let me take him home," one of the ladies said loud enough for me to catch. With the detective pulling me away too fast, I didn't have time to shoot her a dirty look or hex her hiney.

"Slow down, Mason," I implored. "Where are we going?"

He squeezed my hand and offered me a cocky grin. "We're going to find Lucky."

Chapter Ten

"I told you it wasn't that simple." Crossing my arms, I stood apart from Mason and Lucky at his team's campsite.

For about fifteen minutes after we arrived, the detective insisted he was the key to finding the leprechaun's lost luck. Hopes raised, he tried again and again, getting more frustrated at the challenge. No amount of hand holding with the leprechaun did the trick.

"Gah," Mason grunted again. "About the only thing I can get is that there's the presence of something connected to Lucky out there." He gestured at the entire event field. "What good is that?"

"If ye can't find me luck, then why are ye still grippin' me so hard?" Lucky pleaded for the detective to let him go. He flexed his hand when Mason let him go.

"There's a lot of good we can gather from what you have picked up," I reassured. "One, you still have the ability to sense something, which is more than I have right now. And two, what you detect is isn't fully gone. That means whoever took the luck is still here. The question is, why?"

"I'm still unclear as to why the detective's the one trying to track me luck." The leprechaun eyed both of us. "I'm sure there's a story to tell, but I appreciate ye both tacklin' me problem with such urgency."

The team's smoker lid shut with a metallic clang. Henry grabbed a drink out of the cooler and joined us. "I know y'all are trying to keep things quiet, and you don't have to tell me everything. But I've picked up enough to figure you might could use some insight." He popped the top on the can and took a sip, waiting.

"What can you add?" I prompted my assistant.

He swallowed and smacked his lips with dramatic emphasis. "We've got races and a food competition going on. There's plenty of reasons for someone to want to steal what our friend possessed to tip the scales in their favor."

"For a local barbecue competition and some exhibition races? That doesn't seem like enough of a reason for such a drastic act," Mason countered.

Henry finished the rest of his drink and crushed the can. "It is if there's serious money involved."

I scoffed. "We're not even offering that big of a cash prize for first place."

My assistant waved me off. "I'm not talking about the prize money. I'm talking about the betting pool."

Mason shifted his stance, crossing his arms. "A couple hundred bucks bet on a few locals isn't going to add up to much. Are you saying there's something bigger running?"

Lucky groaned and Henry wrinkled his nose. "Yeah, there may or may not be someone taking bets and collecting money on the side."

"Are you saying there's a professional bookie involved? Give me the person's name," Mason instructed, taking out his notebook and pencil.

Henry scratched the stubble on his chin. "There's a problem with that. See, nobody here knows who it is exactly. Only how to make a bet."

"How?" Mason pushed.

My assistant held up the crushed can and waved his fingers over it. "By setting up a system of proxies."

I waited, but nothing happened to the metal. "I don't get it," I said.

Henry shot me an impatient glare. "If you want to make a bet, word gets around about finding a certain object that someone has spelled as a proxy. You recite a secret code word or phrase, and a betting sheet with instructions on where to place your actual bet appears."

Mason wrote down the information with furious purpose. "It gives out a name?"

"Of course not," Lucky chimed in. "It gives ye another proxy to go to. You place your bet in the chosen receptacle. In return, ye get more information about where to collect your winnin's. So, whoever is runnin' the bets is never seen or known."

Henry held up a finger and quipped, "And the proxy changes whenever the bookie feels like it. By the time you hear about one object, the spell might be passed on to another."

My mind attempted to keep up with all of the steps. If someone went to that amount of trouble to keep themselves from being discovered, we might never find him or her. And while the information justified why someone here in Honeysuckle had a reason to attack Lucky, it didn't get us any closer to figuring out who that might be.

"Do you know what the object is right now?" Mason asked. When Henry paused, the detective promised he wasn't looking to arrest my assistant.

"When I placed my bet this morning, it was an abandoned shoe on the far edge of the field." Henry pointed to where Dash and I had been walking the previous night. "And then I was given instructions that led me to a charcoal grill sitting behind the campsite of a barbecue team from Kentucky to make my wager. I placed my bet and money in the center of the grill and closed the lid. I lifted it again to check, and all of it was indeed gone."

Mason wrote everything down. "I think I'm going to have to bring the wardens into this."

"I'd ask Nana first," I warned. The probability of keeping things quiet disintegrated the more we discovered.

The detective scowled. "This is getting too big for just a handful of us to handle. Even if we were so fortunate as to find the bookie, that doesn't mean we'd find the person who attacked Lucky."

"I think I might be able to help with that," a deep voice boomed. Dash approached the four of us with Georgia and her sister in tow.

He flashed a slight grin at me and tipped his head to Lucky and Henry. The detective earned a low grunt of recognition. After he introduced the two sisters, he pointed at them to explain.

Georgia cleared her throat. "Our friend has done his best to explain why you might need our services. He thinks that our psychic abilities might be useful, but without knowing what we're looking for, I'm not sure what we can really do for you."

I recalled what she'd revealed about my parents last night and wondered if they still remained close to me. She caught me looking to my left and right, and shook her head for a brief second. "No, I can't see them now, but that doesn't mean they're not there. Most of the time, I have to have some big shields up, otherwise, I can get a bit overwhelmed. It's why I usually don't drink alcohol, even from our family business."

Henry gazed at her with respect. "Wow, you can see spirits? It's been a long time since we've had a decent medium around these parts. You're right to throw up your shields here in Honeysuckle."

I made a mental note to question my assistant more about

his cryptic statement later. "What about you?" I asked the younger sister.

She held up her hands. "I'm only here to observe." After having heard her talk a mile a minute last night, her short response stunned me.

"Come on, Ginny. Dash says it's important." Georgia touched her sister's arm.

Ginny pulled away from her. "You know even if I try to help it always goes wrong. I can't risk doing that here. They don't even know us."

Dash addressed the younger sister, moving until he stood behind Lucky. "I can vouch for these people. I know what you've been through, and I keep telling you, nothing that happened was your fault. But you could at least try and use your magic here. It could make all the difference."

Ginny's face reddened with frustration and embarrassment. Georgia leaned in to her and whispered something in her ear. The two sisters quietly argued between themselves until the younger one pushed her older sister away.

"Fine," Ginny conceded. "I'll do what I can, but don't hold it against me in the end." She stepped forward and held out her hands with impatience.

Lucky approached her with caution. "And what is your particular talent, miss?"

"I can read people's fortunes. Well, sort of. Most of the time, I can see how things are supposed to be, but it's not always straightforward and it doesn't always come true,"

Ginny explained. "Knowing that what I tell you might not be easy to interpret, do you want to proceed?"

Lucky placed his hands in hers. "I don't have much of a choice. Do what ye can and I'll owe ye my gratitude. I'll not be holdin' you responsible no matter the outcome."

His kind words melted her reluctance, and she offered him a more confident grin. "Okay, then." She closed her eyes and concentrated. In a dreamy tone, she spoke, "You come from somewhere far away from here. The weight of your life is heavy. You are not who you once were."

Dash met my surprised gaze at the strength of her abilities. Pride filled his face, and he indicated I should keep watching.

Ginny shook her head. "You have hidden who you are for a long time. There are words and names that do not belong to you today."

"I thought she was a fortune teller?" I wondered out loud.

Georgia crossed her arms. "Just wait. In order to see beyond right now, she has to get a sense of a person's whole life. And don't worry, Dash already warned her about being careful about what she says out loud."

The relationship between the shifter and these two witch sisters baffled me. If we'd had enough time to talk last night, I might have understood how they all came to be friends. And I might believe his words that there was nothing between him and either one of the attractive girls.

Ginny threw her head back. "Someone has been tampering with your lifeline. I can see the thread of where it is supposed to be, but someone plucked it. Cut you wide open."

Lucky grimaced. "You're hurtin' me, girl." He tried to pull away, but the young witch held him tighter.

"Somebody has changed your fortune," she continued. "I can see...can see..." Ginny threw back her head and uttered strange words.

"What once was given was stripped away.
Your future bright has now turned gray.
Away it floats into the sky.
To bring it back, you have to fly.
Your future is unraveling thread.
Without the wind, you'll soon be—"

Drawing in a long rattled breath, Ginny slumped forward and dropped the leprechaun's hands. Georgia rushed to catch her sister, and Henry brought over a red plastic cup most likely filled with sweet tea.

Out of the corner of my eye, I caught my brother Matt staring at our scene with his mouth wide open. "What do y'all think you're doing? I don't think this qualifies as keeping things quiet and following Nana's edict to keep things under wraps."

"Where've you been?" I approached him and threw an arm around his side, needing a hug to ground myself and stop shaking.

"Between TJ being a little over a month away from having

our little girl and the ramped-up warden presence for the races, I haven't had time to participate in a seance," he admonished, kissing the top of my head. "There was enough power emanating from here to attract attention from the next town over."

Mason waved at Matt. "That's a bit of an exaggeration, but yeah, I wasn't expecting that."

"Can y'all shut up and give my sister a second?" Georgia commanded.

We all stopped talking and watched the poor girl try to recover. Deep, ragged breaths shook Ginny's body, and she bent over, grabbing her knees for balance.

When she composed herself enough to talk, she lifted her head, revealing her tear-stained cheeks. "I'm sorry," she uttered. Sniffing over and over, she did her best to stop crying.

Lucky lifted her chin with his fingers. "'Tis nothin' I didn't already know, girlie. Don't ye worry your pretty head with what's to come."

The weight of her sudden prediction dawned on me. The one word that had stopped Ginny cold hung in the air. If we didn't find the leprechaun's luck, the girl predicted Lucky's death. For a man who only heard the news a few seconds ago, he remained a little too calm.

"Did you know?" I asked Lucky, ignoring that not everybody in the circle understood.

His cold, wry grin chilled me. "Ye cannae expect me to reveal all o' me ol' blarney. What good would it have done for me to tell that me life might be forfeit?" He winked at me. "Always a price, Charli."

Only Dash and I understood Lucky's full meaning. Somehow, when the leprechaun met with the sea god to leave Ireland, part of the cost must have been fusing his luck together with his life. Without one, the other couldn't survive.

Ginny raised her hand and cleared her throat. "I don't understand whatever's being said right now, and I'm pretty sure nobody gets what spilled out of my mouth. Even me. But I do know one thing." She pointed a finger at Lucky. "Somebody's been messing around inside his head."

Georgia touched her sister's shoulder. "What do you mean?"

Her younger sister shivered and addressed Lucky. "When I was connecting with you, I could see your past and your present because I needed both to get to your future. I can't really explain it other than to say that for me, there's almost a flavor to a person's life. And there's a bitter taste to what should be your present."

"Everyone's talking in code and riddles," complained Matt.

Ginny ignored him and finished, "Someone has been inside his head and taken away his recent memories. Changed things and left a big gaping, spellbound hole." She tapped the side of her head to emphasize her point.

Henry spit on the ground. "That sounds like we've got someone with strong psychic abilities going rogue and messing with people's lives."

"And whoever it is, I think they're still here," suggested Mason. "We need to come up with a plan. And I think we have to involve more people whether your grandmother likes it or not. Sorry, Matt and Charli."

Matt nodded in agreement and waved his arms wide, ushering us all to step into a huddle. He spoke in a low, purposeful tone. "Actually, Nana already told me to select a few to bring in and help try and fix things before it got too big. Someone needs to bring me up to speed. Charli, you let our grandmother know what she—I'm sorry, I don't know your name."

The young witch pointed at herself. "Ginny."

"Right, Ginny," Matt continued. "Tell Nana what Ginny suspects so she can figure out what to do next on that end. Lucky, you're gonna have to decide how much information you want shared. There's clearly something that not all of us are privy, too. But we may need to know more if we're gonna maximize our strengths."

It was my turn to be proud. I rubbed Matt's back, encouraging him.

"Mason, you should take point on all this. With TJ experiencing false contractions, I can't be the one in charge. But I'll help in any way I can." My brother's ability to delegate increased my admiration.

"Right," breathed out the detective. "First things first, Dash, have Henry bring you up to speed about a potential betting ring. See if you can help him find out who's running it."

The wolf shifter nodded. "If it's all right with you, I'll get my brother in on this, too. He has a way of discovering the underbelly of things."

"Who'll watch our barbecue?" Georgia asked.

"We'll take turns, don't worry. Plus, the two of you shouldn't be seen trying to run around with the rest of us or it might draw attention from the locals. You two have helped more than enough." Waves of alpha authority poured out of Dash.

I bounded on my feet, ready to use my magic to help. Except, I had no powers to use. My heart sank, and I backed away from the group.

"I'm going to need Charli with me," instructed Mason.

Dash scoffed. "I'm sure you do." His response ruffled the detective's feathers.

I didn't need the two to challenge each other right now, here in front of everyone. "There are good reasons," I admitted, hoping to stop both of them before anything started.

Matt pointed at each person and repeated their task. When he finished, he clapped his hands in dismissal. "Everybody, keep your spell phones on you in case we need to communicate or change the game."

Georgia raised her hand. "Uh, we don't have one."

Henry tossed her his. "I'll get you both one. In the meantime, you can use mine."

The group scattered and left me standing with Mason and Lucky again. "I feel like we're almost exactly where we started. Except now I know how big the stakes are." I threw my arms around the leprechaun and hugged him tight.

Lucky patted me on the back. "There, there, child. No need to shed tears for me yet."

I chuckled into his shoulder. "I should be comforting you, not the other way around." With a sniff, I let him go. An idea occurred to me when I caught Mason watching us. "Lucky, do you have an object that we could use?"

"What kind of object?" the leprechaun asked.

"Something precious to you. A thing you wouldn't part with because your connection to it is so dear." An idea of what I could do to help blossomed.

"I'll have to go back to the bar. If I find something to use, where should I bring it?" Lucky asked.

Mason shot me a questioning gaze. My brother may have put him in charge, but I still remained the authority of the most important element we had to help the leprechaun.

"Bring whatever it is to my house," I exclaimed. "Mason and I have work to do."

Chapter Eleven

No amount of instruction or dragging him through a boot camp of learning my magic would bring Mason completely up to speed. I just needed to get him to a place where he could home in on whoever held the fate of Lucky's fortune and life. Luckily, my favorite test subject didn't have anything better to do.

"Could you hurry up," Beau whined from the front porch. "I've only eaten a fraction of the barbecue I intend to." He patted his generous stomach.

"Wait there," I instructed the vampire, waving Mason over to me. I handed the detective a small gold amulet that belonged to Beau, the glittering chain falling between my fingers. "Hold this and go touch him."

Mason's efforts had been hit or miss for the past hour. I'd put him through the paces of all my abilities, but his skills matched where mine were long before I left Honeysuckle to improve them. His desire to succeed pushed him harder than any of my expectations for him.

Mason trudged up the steps. "You ready?" he asked Beau.

My roommate flashed a fangy grin. "As a starvin' flea ridin' on the back of a hound dog, Detective," he drawled in exaggeration.

With a steady hand, Mason reached out and touched the vampire. He paused for a beat and asked me over his shoulder, "Now what?"

Calling on all my patience, I bounded up the old wooden stairs of the porch, ignoring the sharp creaks under my steps. "Concentrate on the object in your hand. Do you feel any sense of connection between it and Beau?"

The detective focused, furrowing his eyebrows. "Now that you mention it." He pursed his lips, focusing harder. "Yeah, I get that."

"Okay, let go of him and return to where we were just standing," I instructed. When he got to the right place, I called out, "Can you sense that the amulet is connected to Beau in some way?"

Mason held the piece of jewelry between his fingers and let it dangle. He scrunched up his nose. "It's faint, but if I'm looking for it, I can sense it. I don't think I'd be able to detect that on my own."

Uncontrolled laughter burst from my roommate. He sat down in one of the rocking chairs and slapped his knee.

"Beau, stop that," I scolded.

"But it's too funny, seeing the two of you with your magic swapped. It's like that movie where the mother and daughter switch places. Freaky something." The vampire chuckled behind his hand after I shot him my best imitation of Nana's searing glare.

"It's freaky all right," I admitted, rubbing the back of my head.

"If he got your special powers, what did you get?" Beau asked.

Huh. With everything going on and Lucky's life now hanging in the balance, I hadn't given it much thought. I recalled Nana's brief but important roasting of Mason and me about the last spell we cast together. "If I had to guess, then think I have his ability to fly on a broom."

Unable to stop himself, Beau broke into loud guffaws. "Doesn't sound like a fair trade to me."

Mason came back to the porch. "Trust me, I'd rather the skill remained with Charli. I don't think anybody else in the world could understand how powerful and yet frustrating it all is."

I sat on the porch railing. "Only others with similar abilities might. But I haven't crossed paths with anyone like me since I've been back."

I'd been told my magic was special, rare, desired by both good and horrible people. More than once, I'd wished it to be gone or to only have normal powers. Now that I no longer possessed them, I wanted them back. A little jealousy slithered through my veins.

"Do you think my magic will return?" I asked in a quieter voice.

Mason took my hand in his. "I don't know. Maybe your grandmother can help us, but understand that I will do everything I can to make sure you get it back."

Slipping out of his touch, I paced a few steps away, not wanting him to see the weakness of a few stray tears. The grind of a loud motor approaching in the near distance grabbed my attention. After the engine cut off, Dash and Lucky appeared at the edge of my field, bringing my pity party to a quick end. Concern for my friend replaced the worry for myself when I caught sight of the leprechaun.

"Is it me or does the color of Lucky's skin tone look more like mine?" Beau whispered into my ear.

"He doesn't look good," I replied out of the corner of my mouth.

Dash shook his head in warning, his shifter hearing catching my whisper. "I hope what Lucky has will work for your purposes."

The leprechaun glared at all of us. "Me fate might be up in the air but I ain't dead yet. Stop lookin' like you're already at me funeral. Here, Charli. I hope this'll do." He took out a lump wrapped in old cloth.

Jogging down my steps, I joined my friend and took the offered object. With great care, I unfolded the fabric until the sun shone on a medium-sized stone that sparkled a brilliant blue.

Mason and Beau joined me at my side, and my roommate

whistled long and low. "Is that what I think it is? It must be worth a fortune."

A desire to curl my fingers around the jewel and run for the hills ran through my body for a quick second. "It's not real a real sapphire, is it?"

"That it is. It was to be made into a pendant for a special lady." Lucky stopped himself from revealing more.

Dash and I shot each other knowing glances. "You've kept it for a long time," I said, my thumb stroking the glittering face of the gem.

"Aye, and please be gentle with it. If at all possible, I'd like it to come back to me." The leprechaun grinned with deep emotion. "'Tis a precious reminder."

It didn't matter if Lucky meant a reminder of Queen Medb or to not trust so easily. Either way, we needed to see if it would work.

"Since Lucky's here, we might as well test it out. Take and hold this in your dominant hand," I commanded to Mason. "Focus on it and repeat what you did with Beau."

The detective did as he was asked, touching the leprechaun, nodding once and letting go. He breathed out a relieved sigh. "The connection is definitely present and strong."

The others congratulated him, but I understood the bigger struggle. "You need to familiarize yourself with how it feels. Every thread of connection is different. It acts different. It smells different. It feels different. It can sometimes even taste different."

"Now you're sounding like Ginny," Dash accused.

Ignoring him, I stepped in front of them all and leaned into Mason. "You can't walk around holding Lucky's hand the whole time. You need to tether that connection between the jewel and him to you. Tie the bond strong."

"How? Do I have to recite a spell or something? Come up with a rhyme like you do?" he panicked.

Laying a hand on his shoulder, I gave him a reassuring squeeze. "Everyone's methods and needs are different. I rhyme because it keeps me focused and it's fun. Try visualizing the thread you sense tying around your middle like you're wrapping a present."

Mason shifted his stance. "I suck at wrapping presents. But I think I get what you mean." He closed his eyes and bent his head. After a few tense moments, he let go of the breath he held. "There. I think I did it."

"Good. Because you're going to have to use the sapphire as a substitute for having Lucky with you." I didn't want to take the time to explain all the ways it opened Mason up to searching for the lost luck. No need to remind everyone of how weak our situation was in our urgency or to give away all of my secrets.

Mason placed an arm around me. "You know, you're a pretty good teacher. You'll make a terrific mom someday."

The compliment should have caused me to blush. But my stomach flip had more to do with Dash's immediate displeasure than accepting the detective's flattery.

"We should get you back so you can rest," the shifter murmured to Lucky.

"So, me gem will work?" the leprechaun asked, hope gleaming in his eyes.

Forcing a smile on my face, I attempted a cheery response. "I think it will be the key and our best chance at finding where your luck went."

"Let's go." Dash escorted Lucky back to the road without looking at me again. His motorcycle roared to life, the sound slipping away into the distance.

I pushed Mason's arm off me. "I don't like that you do that."

"Do what?" His attempt at innocence annoyed me further.

"I think I'm gonna go back to join my team." Beau backed away from the two of us. "Good luck," he murmured before poofing into a bat and flying away. It was the first time I'd ever envied my roommate.

"You know exactly what you did right then. Every time you're around Dash, you both try to antagonize each other." Real fury ignited in my veins. Wanting to avoid saying anything I couldn't take back, I turned on my heel and headed toward my house.

"Can you really blame me? He's been gone for months, and the second he returns, the way you are with me completely changes," he called out from behind.

I stopped on the top step of the porch and whipped around. "Are you serious?"

Mason stopped following at my sudden confrontation. "I've gotten to know you pretty well, Charli. I can tell how you feel about him. And what about how you reacted when your grandmother told us about the effects of tandem magic? Right in front of her, I declared my true feelings. You said nothing."

I bit my lip, embarrassed that he did know me well. I reached inside and grabbed onto my anger, letting it burn away my discomfort. "That's two separate things. If you know how I feel about Dash, then I wish you'd tell me because the only thing I'm sure of is that he's stayed away, and I deserve to know why."

Not even the precious sapphire would be enough payment to make me admit the detective might be right. That more emotion than curiosity about the wolf shifter existed in my heart and mind.

Mason took the first step up the porch stairs, closing the distance between us. "What about the other thing? Do you really believe any feelings you have for me is because of the tandem magic? Are you really going to deny what was already there?" He took another cautious step. "What's still there?"

With his fingers, he brushed a strand of hair away from my face, stroking my cheek. I closed my eyes and gripped his hand. It should be easier than this, but the same doubt I'd ignored in the tent with my grandmother reared its ugly head again. Even if it hurt Mason, I couldn't give myself wholly to him until I trusted my feelings were real and not based on magic.

"Don't," I whispered.

Disappointment swam in the detective's eyes, and my heart ached that I put it there. "You're choosing him then?" He slipped his hand out of mine.

"No, that's not it."

"I think it is," Mason pushed.

I needed an exit strategy out of this conversation fast. "And I think there are more important issues at hand than a discussion about who I'm choosing. Like a friend's life."

I jumped over the side of the porch and ran to my backyard. The first spell to open the shed failed, and I did my best to calm down enough to cast the lock open.

"What are you doing?" Mason asked.

"Choosing myself." I rooted around until I found what I needed. When I laid my hands on the broom, I slammed the door shut, casting the simple locking spell over my shoulder.

"Hey, that's mine," he protested.

I rushed back to the front of the house and maneuvered the flying device onto the front basket of my bike. "Good observation skills, Detective."

Mason stood in front of the bike while I straddled it. "Where do you think you're taking *my* broom."

Refusing to meet his gaze, I pointed in the general direction of the weekend's event. "If you've got my magic, then I might as well make use of yours."

His jaw dropped. "You've got to be kidding. You don't even know if you still have the ability to fly. Do you really want to risk testing things out in a real race?"

His vocalizing the doubt swimming in the back of my

head did nothing to calm me down. Willing some power down into the bike, I felt it hum under my touch. "That's exactly what I'm going to do. Move," I commanded, the desire to get far away from him motivating my questionable decision to ride the bicycle over the bumpy grass and through tall weeds.

"You can't do this, Charli." Despite his words, Mason moved out of the way.

With an arrogant smirk, I lifted the kickstand off the ground with my foot. "Watch me."

Chapter Twelve

A bead of sweat trickled down the side of my face. Lots and lots of doubt swirled inside me, and I couldn't help but chastise myself. No good could come from making a snap decision while mad at a man. Standing in position behind the white-chalked starting line, I shuffled my feet and considered whether to stay or bolt.

A large figure cast a shadow over me. "My dear Charli, it is a wonder to find you here. I did not presume you to be a fan of broom racing."

Horatio wedged himself between the man standing to my left and me, towering over both of us. When the annoyed racer caught sight of the troll, he swallowed hard. No doubt the same surprise that popped up in my head ran through his.

"I think I could say the same to you, Horatio." I glanced

at the twig of a flying device he held. "Where'd you get your broom?"

He smiled wide and winked. "Lee magnanimously gifted me one of the first models he spellcast for non-witch use. He surmised that if I could fly, then anybody could. But my darling Juniper may have added a secret little extra boost."

"That sounds like cheating to me," quipped the smaller racer.

I leaned over far enough to notice his sour expression. "Not if the broom passed inspection like I'm sure yours did. If the officials deemed it fit to race, then I don't see what the problem is."

The guy took a step forward to see around Horatio's hulking mass, his toe coming close to crossing the starting line. "I think the problem is that racing is for those who should be flying on brooms. Witches only."

It wasn't the first pro-witch statement I'd heard while milling around the event since the night I registered the teams. Our town council prepared all of us in Honeysuckle about the negativity we might run into from those who didn't support a sanctuary town like ours. It was a different thing entirely to encounter such sentiment in real life.

"What's your name?" I asked the prejudiced racer.

He smirked. "You'll find out after they announce me as winner."

The need to beat this guy squelched all my jitters and second-guesses. Whether or not I still possessed Mason's racing abilities didn't matter anymore. I'd do my absolute best to win at all costs now.

One of the officials in a black and white striped shirt with goggles hanging around his arm and a clipboard in his hand walked down the line to check us in. When he got to me, his finger drifted down the page until it stopped. "Charli *'Birdy'* Goodwin?"

I smiled as wide as possible. "That's right."

"I hope you live up to your name." He chuckled, taking a pair of goggles off his arm. With a quick finger flourish over them, he matched the number to my name and handed them to me. "Good luck with your flying."

Holding the goggles, I couldn't figure out what made them special or necessary. But every contestant around me worked them over their heads. Fumbling, I did the same and felt the zing of magic as soon as I fixed them into the right place over my eyes. A flashing red line appeared in front of the starting chalk at the same time my name appeared on a board off to the side with the number thirteen.

"Great," I mumbled, wondering why I got stuck with that number. I ignored the rest of the names flashing across the board, determined to focus on the race itself.

"I wish you good fortune and flying." Horatio reached out his hand to give me fist bump.

"You, too." His massive mitt dwarfed mine, but the gesture increased my excitement.

With all of us at the ready, the official stood in the front. "This race is for amateurs aged eighteen and older. You've all been given goggles spelled with the course path. Do not deviate from it, but if you do get lost, don't panic. An additional spell will allow us to track your progress.

"There can be no use of magic other than within the parameters of flying the broom itself. However, physical contact will not be penalized. Should you get injured, stay where you are, and we will come to you. Are we clear?"

My stomach dropped at the mention of possible injury. "What does he mean by 'physical contact'?" I asked Horatio.

"The top two racers will automatically make it into the next round," the official continued, ignoring my panic. He held up his hand high in the air. "Mount your brooms."

Unable to get anyone to answer to my question, I kicked off the ground and floated in place, gripping the wooden handle even harder. It was too late to run away. The only path forward lay in front of me.

"On your mark," the official called out.

The blinking red line my goggles revealed changed to yellow.

"Get set. Go!"

The line turned solid and green, and everyone around me took off. "Pixie poop," I exclaimed and willed myself to go.

Adrenaline rushed through my veins, and I leaned forward, pushing the broom faster. Soon, I caught up to the racers in the back. Without any extra effort, my instincts kicked in and helped me find an opening to pass in between the first two.

I zipped around another few racers until I reached the

middle of the pack. Checking ahead, I saw that the path through the field would close off when we entered a forested area. With no time to lose, I visualized the clear openings the racers gave me to move ahead.

Wind rushed over and around me with each maneuver. The beginning to the path in the woods approached, and I took a chance to pass one more racer. My body grazed theirs at the last second, and whoever it was got knocked off the course, hitting a tree.

"Holy unicorn horn!" I exclaimed, not sure if I should stop to check on them or not. Another racer got knocked off ahead of me and was getting up off the ground on my left side when I passed. Remembering this was all part of the game, I blasted forward.

Once I made it around a big tree trunk and banked into and out of a tough turn, it wasn't hard to spot Horatio, even through the brush and trees. Whatever Juniper had done to enhance Lee's magic with the broom, it more than worked.

The troll seemed to be zooming ahead in front of all of us with only two others right behind him, using his mass and the narrow forest path to keep others from passing. An opening at the end of the wooded section shone bright through the shade of the woods up ahead. Once we all hit open air, the chances of the troll staying in first dwindled.

With sudden determination, I closed in on the three frontrunners. The person right in front of me swung back and forth to prevent me from passing. If I wanted to move around them, I would have to make contact.

"Here goes nothing." I stuck out my tongue and pulled up on their tail, waiting for my chance.

The racer looked over their left shoulder, which banked their broom in the same direction, and I shot forward. My body barely scraped them when I passed, and I couldn't help my grin of triumph. Only two left.

The sun almost blinded me when the three of us burst out of the woods. A cheering crowd lined both sides of the path through the field, and the black-and-white checkered finish line blinked in my view through the goggles.

Horatio couldn't see the racer approaching him from behind, preparing to ram him. "Look out," I yelled to my friend, knowing he wouldn't hear me.

Without any time to lose, I summoned all my strength and power to push into the broom. Wind whipped around me, and I leaned all the way over to make myself more aerodynamic. As I got close, I kept myself directly behind the other racer so they couldn't see me if they checked over their shoulder. At the last second, I zipped around from behind and rammed my body into the racer. The impact caused me to bounce off of them out of control. With great effort, I managed to stay on my broom across the finish line, but crashed on the other side, tumbling on the ground.

A voice boomed out of the nearby speakers, "Ladies and gentlemen, it looks like racer number fourteen takes first place. Let's hear a round of applause for Horatio."

Standing up and brushing myself off, I cheered for my

friend with a loud whoop. Too wound up and excited, I didn't notice the few people rushing to get to me.

"Charli, are you okay?" a concerned voice asked.

"That was a fool thing to do," complained another.

Nana and a few of my friends crowded around me, hands checking me over for injuries and asking me questions my brain couldn't comprehend with all the adrenaline and excitement buzzing through me.

Mason shook my arm, calling my name until my eyes lit on him. I didn't register what he asked me, but I threw my arms around him. "I can't believe I did it."

His body shook under my touch with laughter, and he tilted his head to speak in my ear. "Yeah, you did. Came in second place, too."

I pushed him away. "No way. Second?"

Whipping off the goggles, the world came into better focus. Horatio's name was at the top of the list and my name flashed second on the scoreboard by the finish line. All of my friends waited to pass me around for congratulatory hugs.

Nana placed her hand on my shoulder. "Birdy, sometimes you make me madder than a wet hen. I can't believe you'd do some fool thing like this without telling me." She pulled me into a tight hug and kissed the top of my head. "But I can't lie. It fills me to the brim with pride to see you win."

"I came in second," I murmured into her shoulder.

"It means you move on to the next qualifying round." Letting me go, she held my hands and sighed. "Guessin' we should figure out how long the switch of magic between you and the detective will last."

Horatio, Lee, and Juniper interrupted our private conversation, and my grandmother let go to give the troll her congratulations.

Lee high-fived me first before delivering a message to my grandmother. "Miss Vivi, the officials are looking for you."

"I'll be right back," Nana promised.

All of my friends surrounded the troll and me, asking us to pose for pictures with our fingers in *V*'s for victory. I told Horatio about how the last part of the race went since it all happened behind his back. Lee went on a little too long about how his spellcasting worked with Juniper's magic. Mason stood close by, but kept quiet, allowing the others to gush around us.

When Nana didn't return, concern replaced my elation. Excusing myself, I went to find her, glancing here and there until I spotted a tight group of people in black-and-white striped shirts discussing something in low voices with my grandmother and a few others. The prejudiced guy from the starting line gesticulated wildly, and his raised voice echoed through the air.

"You have to declare a disqualification," he yelled.

"For what?" I challenged, approaching the group.

The racer pointed his finger at me. "You." He spat a brown liquid on the ground in front of my feet. "You caused me to lose."

"Now, now, Earl, there ain't nothin' wrong with how this

little lady competed." A short and squat man patted the upset racer on the back, squinting his eyes at his friend. "What we want to address is the legitimacy of that monstrosity winning first. My friend here should be at least in second place."

My blood boiled. I didn't need the special goggles on to see red. "Horatio won fair and square."

Earl turned and closed the distance between us, poking my shoulder with his finger. "He shouldn't have been competing in the first place." His indignant spittle bounced off my face.

"If I were you, I would take a step back from my granddaughter," warned Nana. "I'm here to mediate in an official capacity. Make any more disparaging remarks, and I'll forget my Southern manners."

The racer did as he was asked, but anger still sparked in his eyes. "I want a judgment on whether or not the rankings stand."

"And I need you to refer to Horatio either by his name or call him by the position he earned...winner." I waited for Nana to busy herself in the discussion again and wiggled my fingers in a sarcastic wave at Earl.

With a few nods and grunts, the officials backed away. The one that started the race spoke out. "We are declaring that there are no restrictions as to who can enter the amateur races. With no violations occurring, the rankings still stand."

The officials dispersed, and Nana finished her conversation with the group I guessed were from the witches' councils. Earl stood his ground with his arms crossed, spitting more brown liquid onto the grass. "It ain't over yet."

A chuckle burst out of me. "You sound like a villain from a movie. A badly cast one."

He smirked. "You tell your big friend there, and any others who don't belong, to watch their backs."

When Nana approached, Earl held up his hands in temporary surrender, walking away. My grandmother shook her head and tsked her tongue. "Let's go get you some food before the adrenaline wears off and you pass out. Even though I don't approve that you took a huge risk, I'm actually really proud of you."

If my grandmother knew the reason I entered in the first place, she might not be so quick with her admiration. However, I hadn't been totally wrong when I declared I was choosing myself. Nobody else had earned second place for me. Although it might have been Mason's magic in me, how I wielded it earned my ranking.

"You know what, Nana? I'm proud of me, too."

Chapter Thirteen

The celebrations of our victories didn't last long. It took three whole pulled pork sandwiches piled high with coleslaw to clear my head. Competing in a broom race may have been awesome, but it didn't bring us any closer to figuring out how to help Lucky.

Excusing ourselves from our friend group, I pulled Mason aside. "Did you bring the sapphire with you?"

The detective pulled the cloth-wrapped lump out of his pocket far enough for me to see. "It makes me nervous carrying this around."

"Have you tried to use it to anchor the magic and see if you can pinpoint Lucky's lost luck yet?" I asked. The doubt in his face gave me my answer. "Look, I say you should just do it and not think about things too much."

The detective curled his fingers around the sapphire. "You

think I should take the jewel in my hand and find the luck. It'll be that simple."

Nothing would be simple, but we were running out of time. "Talking isn't gonna get you anywhere. Why not take a chance?" I encouraged him.

Mason watched the people milling around us. "Maybe we should find a more private spot."

I shook my head. "As long as you don't hold up the gem for all to see, I think you should try right here in the mix of things."

"I'm going to look weird with my eyes closed, walking around like a zombie trying to follow some invisible thread," he complained.

I hit him with the bristles of his broom. "Hey, I do not look like a zombie when I use my magic. Try to see if you can feel any kind of connection first. Then we'll go from there."

Mason turned his back to shield anyone from seeing him unwrap the sapphire. When he succeeded, he cradled it in his palm. "Here goes nothing." Taking a deep breath, he closed his eyes and whispered a spell. "*With this sapphire sparkling blue, I'll use the magic that belongs to you. Find the stolen luck that roams, and bring it back to its true home.*"

His rhyme wasn't bad, but I didn't detect any true power behind it. It was odd watching someone else use tracking magic like I did. When I'd traveled for that year away from Honeysuckle, I'd found a few people who possessed some level of the same powers. Each one mastered their skills in different ways and helped me figure out what worked for me.

I waited for something to happen, but Mason stood in the same spot, scrunching his face. With a grunt, he let out his breath and opened his eyes. "All I can feel is the same thing as before. That what we're looking for is still in this vicinity." He wiped his free hand down his disappointed face. "I think anything I do will be a failure."

A thought dawned on me and I switched his broom from my left to my right hand, holding it out in front of me. "We're not done trying yet. You want to know how I did so well today?"

The detective indulged me despite his gloomy expression. "How?"

I stepped closer. "Because I didn't overthink things. When it was time to race, I just went. Once I got into it, I didn't think about how it wasn't my magic to begin with or how you might use your skills to fly. I did what I had to do and let my instincts take over."

"I don't think flying around on a broom is the same as using tracking magic to search for something that, if we don't find it, might cost someone his life." Mason turned to walk away, but I grabbed his arm.

"Don't give up. Not yet," I insisted, letting my hand glide down his skin until I grasped his hand. "I think you need to forget everything I told you to do. Forget that the magic isn't even yours and definitely don't try to rhyme a spell. If it belonged to you from the beginning and you were training to use it while growing up, how would you conjure a spell to make it work?"

Doubt still lingered in his face, but Mason stopped to consider my question. Without letting me go, he closed his eyes again. "*I call on the magic to find that which has been lost. As I will it, so mote it be.*" He paused a beat before smiling.

"What? Did it work?" I pushed.

With his eyes wide open, he tugged on me. "Come on. I think I feel something in this direction."

We weaved in and out of the crowd. I didn't slow down to do more than call out a quick thanks to those who congratulated me on my race. A voice on a loud speaker boomed louder and louder as we reached the main stage of the event. Mason slowed down until he stood at the edge.

"Do you feel a connection?" I looked from him into the cheering crowd.

His telltale wrinkle of frustration appeared between his eyebrows. "This is as far as the thread tells me to go. There's so many of them."

My hope for success evaporated. "So, it could be anybody here."

"We're back to square one," Mason admitted.

I did my best to come up with a solution. Surely something that had worked for me in the past might help in our present. "Sometimes I can sense a direct connection if I'm touching the person. If we can find whoever it is that possesses Lucky's fortune, I'm betting you can figure it out."

"By touching every single person here? Not only is that weird, I don't think it's feasible." The detective let go of my hand. "But I won't be satisfied unless I've tried everything."

He pushed his way through the crowd, his hand lighting on as many people's shoulders as possible. To the average person, it looked like he wanted to get by each one. Mason paused as long as he could without things getting too awkward. We found ourselves at the front of the stage, no closer to finding a connection to the leprechaun's luck.

"Okay, ladies and gentlemen," announced Tucker, "let's get on with the first barbecue competition category. Please welcome to the stage your judges, Roddy 'Big Mouth' Bass, 'The Mud Dobber' himself, Billy Ray, and the First Lady of racing, Rita Ryder."

The three retired racers waved to the roaring crowd and took their seats at a table in the center of the stage.

Tucker waved the paper from which he read at the table of judges. "While some of these racers have joined their own barbecue teams, we've insured that none of them have a conflict of interest. The entries have been bottled and numbered so the judges won't be able to tell whose entry belongs to who. Appearance, taste, and texture are just three of the criteria they'll be using to judge. They'll try each sauce on its own and then try a bit of the grilled meat each team included."

"We should go," suggested Mason. "We're wasting time."

Out of the corner of my eye, I spotted Henry gesticulating wildly with his arms, trying to get my attention. He waved me and Mason over to the right side of the stage, pulling us behind it.

When we joined him, my assistant gathered us closer with

his arms. "Davis, Clint, and I are this close to finding who's running the betting." He held two fingers touching each other. "Dash's brother suggested we throw out some bait to try and catch someone's attention and maybe affect the betting itself. Nice win, by the way. Didn't know you had it in ya." He slapped my back hard enough to make me sputter.

Clint nodded, his beard waggling with his enthusiasm. "I think it's smart to watch the barbecue competition, too. Whoever may be counting on winning their bets may not be focusing solely on the racing."

"Did you guys enter a sauce? Or have you taken yourselves out of the competition all together considering..." I trailed off.

"Considering our friend might be dying? Yeah, Lucky told all of us what's going on," confirmed Henry.

It made sense that the leprechaun would inform his closest friends he was in trouble. But one person in the group hadn't known him for that long.

"Did he tell Billy Ray, too?" If the ex-racer had any involvement in Lucky's attack, nothing would save him from my grandmother's rage.

My assistant shook his head. "He's been too busy schmoozing the big wigs Vivi's dealing with as well as signing autographs and judging competitions. At my suggestion, he hasn't been told much. But that might all change tonight."

"What's going on tonight?" snapped Mason.

Clint excused himself to find Davis, and Henry stepped closer. "You hadn't heard? Your grandmother has called a few of us over to her house. She's gathering as many witches from Honeysuckle with psychic powers as possible to try and penetrate Lucky's lost memories."

When she wanted to get something done, Nana didn't do anything by halves. "And she's asked Billy Ray to be there?"

Henry shrugged. "I guess. Let's go find out who won the sauce competition is. Maybe it'll help narrow down things if anyone won money from betting on the winner."

"Or maybe the winner is the one with the luck," suggested Mason. He held his arm out for me to slip my hand through. "After you, ma'am."

Despite our little tiff from earlier and my still confused feelings, it warmed me all the way down to my toes when the detective did something so chivalrous. Did it matter if our dabbling in tandem magic affected my emotions about him or did it matter how I felt right now in this moment?

Walking around the corner, I reminded myself where my focus needed to be, watching Tucker hand the microphone to Rita.

"If the level of competition rises to the peak where we are, then this weekend is gonna be one heckuva ride." The retired racer waited for the crowd's pleased reaction to die down.

"You know, she's pretty easy on the eyes," remarked Henry, wiggling his eyebrows. "Once we square Lucky away, I might have to take my chances with her."

"But Lucky comes first." I bumped my assistant with my hip, acknowledging my own romantic hypocrisy in silence.

Rita continued. "All of the entries were more than

delicious, but let's celebrate the top three that got our attention. In third place, and we all loved the fruity peach flavor of the sauce, please put your hands together for the 'Q and Brew team from Georgia."

I clapped, remembering their friendly check in. It still surprised me that beyond the racers' teams, we had a lot of people here from all over. If we could save Lucky and keep things quiet and behind-the-scenes, Tucker would be the orchestrator of a very successful PR event.

Someone from the Georgia team jumped up on stage and accepted a small trophy from Rita. She clapped for them and checked her card. "In second place, I think this team might get a lot of applause because it's one of the hometown favorites, The Fiery Fangs."

I woohooed loud and long for Raif's team. The vampire insisted Sam Ayden join him on stage to accept the award. They all paused to take a picture holding the bigger award.

Henry sniffed. "I tasted their sauce. It's okay."

I tried not to grin at my assistant's displeasure. No doubt his team would have given the vampires a run for their money if they didn't have the troubles they did.

"And in first place—"

"That'll be my team for the win!" Fireball Irving jumped up onto the stage.

A murmuring chuckle passed through the audience, but Rita shot the diminutive racer a stern look. "I haven't even finished giving the introduction."

"But it's my team, right?" Fireball swayed on his feet,

lifting up his bottle of whiskey and taking a pre-celebratory swig from it.

Rita glared at the drunk racer, narrowing her eyes at him. The awkward silence spreading throughout the crowd pulled her out of her frustration. She cleared her throat. "And finally, the team from Kansas City wins with their signature barbecue sauce. Let's have a hand for Fireball's team, the Oink and Moo's."

The smaller racer spilled whiskey on the stage when he raised his hands in triumph. He snatched the trophy from Rita and poured the rest of the contents from the bottle into the shiny bowl, drinking straight from it. When he offered Rita a sip, she rushed past him, gathering her stuff from the table and leaving in a huff. Big Mouth got up from his seat and fetched Fireball, pulling him out of the spotlight and away from Tucker, who took the microphone back to give some closing remarks and go through some announcements.

Leaning into Mason, I pointed at the stage. "I think we should go talk to those two again."

Henry waved goodbye to us. "I'm gonna go check my sources and see how the betting has been affected. Hopefully, I'll be able to find who's running things soon enough. See you later tonight."

Mason and I rushed around to the back of the stage but slowed down when we heard the two men arguing with each other.

"Stop manhandling me. I'm fine," insisted Fireball.

"You almost gave everything away, you fool," answered the

expected voice of Big Mouth Bass. "Here. This belongs to you."

If we leaned our heads far enough out to see, the two might catch sight of us. I held my breath, hoping one of them would say something less cryptic and more incriminating.

"What are you two doing back here?" a woman's voice interrupted.

I jumped and clutched my chest, turning to find Rita Ryder's unhappy glare aimed at us. "Looking for my grandmother," I lied.

Her face relaxed. "Oh, right. You're related to Billy Ray's Vivian."

My whole body stiffened. "*His* Vivian?"

Mason put a steadying arm around me. "Not the point," he muttered to me.

Rita caught sight of the broom I still held, and her face lit up. "Are you the girl who won second place in the race?"

Not too happy she didn't clarify what she meant by her words, I offered her a weak smile. "I did."

"Congratulations. I'm glad they don't try to hold us girls back anymore. Good luck in the next round," she said with genuine fervor. "If you'll excuse me, I've got more autographs to sign."

Without waiting for a reply from either me or Mason, the retired racer walked past us in the direction of Big Mouth and Fireball. When I tried to follow her, I found the two men were already gone. We'd missed our chance.

With nobody else around, Mason pulled the sapphire out

of his pocket and held it in the palm of his hand. "Whatever I felt before is gone. We know someone involved was here, but I wish I could figure out how to make the magic be more specific."

"Let's hope Henry, with whatever he and the others have planned, has more luck than we just did," I cringed when I heard what I'd said. "Bad choice of words."

"I get it. And maybe tonight, your grandmother's efforts will help us figure out what happened to him. If we know how the luck was taken, maybe it will help."

I took Mason's hand in mine. "If you ever figure out how to make the powers be more specific, let me know." The detective was tasting only a fraction of the exasperating limits of being a tracker. "How about we get you some food and top off your fuel so you can try some more."

The detective pocketed the jewel again and took the broom away from me. "Let me carry this for now. It might be the last time I can call it mine if you keep winning."

We walked together in the direction of the food vendors, but my mind kept going over what we'd overheard. The two retired racers who'd seemed like jolly jokesters when we met, hid a much darker side. At some point, we needed to figure out what roll they played in the race to find the leprechaun's luck.

Chapter Fourteen

Mason spent most of the afternoon trying not to lose hope while milling around as many people as possible, touching their shoulders and hoping he could find a connection again. I did my best to cheer him up, holding onto enough hope for the both of us. Once in a while, he sensed a special presence in certain areas, but once we arrived, he couldn't pinpoint anything.

About the time the sun set and the sound of Jordy and the Jack-O'-Lanterns playing music on the stage echoed into the evening sky, we left the event field to go to Nana's house.

When we arrived, the sight of smoke billowing from the backyard plus the sound of voices beckoned us to join the small group out back. My grandmother's modest charcoal grill sizzled with cooking meat. The large smokers in high use for the competition might produce some good barbecue, but Nana could grill up some mighty fine chicken and steaks.

She greeted both of us with a glass of sweet tea. Kissing my cheek, she turned and gestured for someone to join us. Billy Ray stopped gabbing with Lee and Ben in the corner and sauntered over. When he stood next to my grandmother, he pecked her on the cheek.

Nana flushed bright pink. "Charli, you've already met this man here, but I guess I wanted you to officially know that we are an item."

Her confession rendered me speechless. Mason placed his hand on my lower back, but nothing he could do would calm my jangling nerves.

Billy Ray stuck out his hand to shake mine. "I know it may come as a bit of a shock, but I promise you, I intend to take good care of this here lady."

My eyes flicked down to his open palm, but I couldn't bring myself to take it.

"Charli Bird, don't make Billy Ray think me and your parents didn't teach you good manners." Nana's eyes bore into my soul.

Plastering on a smile that no one would believe was real, I accepted the handshake. "Make sure you do take good care of her. She only deserves the best."

Matt and TJ joined us. My brother slapped the ex-racer on the back. "It's kind of nice to have an inside track with a racer. Get what I said?" he asked, elbowing me in my side. "Inside track?"

TJ emitted a barfing sound, and my brother stopped laughing at his own joke to make sure she was okay. "You know," she chuckled, reaching out to stroke my brother's cheek. "You're going to be just fine when the baby comes. You've already got telling dad jokes perfected." She kissed him on the lips.

Entirely too much hankyin' and pankyin' was happening around me. I slipped away from Mason's touch and bolted for the drinks, hoping at least something my grandmother put out had some alcohol in it.

"Hey, Charli." Dash's deep greeting washed away my heebie jeebies.

"Hey, yourself. Did you bring Lucky with you?" Handing him a red plastic cup of sweet tea, I allowed myself a slight peek at his face.

The scars did nothing to take away from his looks. In fact, the injuries gave him even more a sense of mystery and intrigue.

The edges of the wolf shifter's eyes crinkled, and he flashed me a rare smile as he caught me looking. "I did. He's inside with a plate of food, eating what he can." The smile faded when he talked about the leprechaun. "He's not looking good. Any progress on your end? Has the detective been able to, you know, detect something?"

Dash's sarcasm turned on my sense of protection over Mason's attempts. "We've been working on things all day. There are a few theories, but we're hoping tonight we might be able to get some key information to help out."

He led me over to another table full of food and handed me a plate to load. "I don't know how much Lucky can endure. But the short guy is tougher than anyone I've ever encountered, and that's saying something."

I nudged his side with my hip. "You mean the short *king?*"

"Shh, don't say that too loud." Dash piled two scoops of creamy macaroni and cheese on my plate next to a smothering of collards. "There are times when I think the world can't surprise me anymore. And then Lucky tells us an unbelievable tale."

Neither of us gave voice to the worry devouring our insides. Instead, we prepared to stuff food in our mouths. To outsiders, they might think it strange that all of us gathered here at my grandmother's shouldn't be eating like it's a party. But we all understood the great magical undertaking about to happen and needed to be as fueled and ready as we could be.

The grilled chicken leg covered in barbecue sauce perched on top of the mound of food on my plate. If I wanted a slice of red velvet cake for dessert, I needed to gobble everything down. Lily called me over to sit with the group of girls staying at my place, so I shot a quick thanks to Dash and joined them, not giving him a chance to say the other things I thought I saw in his gaze. Color me a coward, but I'd rather face the firing squad of nosy questions from my friends than listen to Dash's explanations.

About the time my plate was empty enough for some cake, Nana stood on the back porch and addressed all of us in her yard. "Y'all know why it was important I asked you to be here tonight rather than at the festivities. A friend of ours is in trouble, and it will take all of our strength and will to help him out."

Lily grabbed her cousin's hand. "Are we doing it out here?"

"If I thought we could get away with going down to the Founders' tree and performing the ceremony round its magic, I'd drag y'all there. Since we're still trying to keep as low a profile as we can, we're gonna have to contain it all inside," my grandmother explained. "Finish eating and drinking, and then haul your behinds in here." The screened door slammed shut behind her.

Dash put down his plate of food and jogged over to greet his two friends who entered the scene with reluctant steps. I waved at the sisters in greeting while they surveyed with wide eyes how many of us were gathered. Hopefully Dash could explain to them how normal something like this could be in Honeysuckle and ease their worries.

TJ hugged me goodbye and headed home at Matt's insistence. Even though he was being overprotective, he had my full support. Magic, even when wielded carefully, could be wild and uncontrolled. No telling if it could cause her to go into premature labor, so no point risking an early appearance from Charli, Jr.

After I brought my plate into the kitchen, I made my way into the parlor. Someone had helped Nana clear out most of the furniture except some heavier antique pieces lining the walls. Several of the witches found a place to stand on the edges to start a makeshift circle. Lily and Lavender joined their grandmother Mimsy on the interior where Lucky lay on his back on some cushions in the middle of the room.

My stomach rolled when I spied the color of his face. Dash hadn't been exaggerating when he said our friend wasn't doing well. More gray than pale, he looked like he would fade away into the shadows before long.

"Should I give him back his jewel?" Mason asked, popping up beside me.

"I honestly don't know, although I think it can't hurt. Why don't you ask Nana?" I suggested, too unsure and shaken to give him a definite answer.

Dash escorted the two witches from the mountains inside the room, but they lingered outside the circle. I did my best to clear away my concern for Lucky and welcome them.

"I think my grandmother wants you to join the other witches who have some psychic abilities." Taking both by their hands, I dragged them over and introduced them to Lily and Lavender, letting the cousins take over the rest of the introductions and instructions.

The wolf shifter stood away from us and refused when I jerked my head in invitation to join us. With most of us in place, what came next weighed heavy on us. Soft voices lowered until the creaks of us shifting on our feet or the occasional cough or sigh sounded like loud intrusions.

Nana stood at the far end of the parlor. She looked around the room, taking stock of each and every one of us, nodding her approval and thanks to each individual for coming.

"Dashiel Thaddeus Channing, you take your place inside

the circle." she ordered. "We need all the help we can get, and your friendship to Lucky is worth just as much, if not more, than a witch's magic."

With a grunt, the shifter obeyed, sidling up to my right-hand side. Mason stood a little taller on my immediate left. At least both men were smart enough not to say anything.

Nana held out her arms wide. "Y'all hold the hand of the person beside you. We form a barrier of magic, friendship, and hope around you witches in the middle. May it protect you and feed your good works." Nana waited for the five in the center surrounding Lucky to also come together.

The air around us crackled with anticipation, matching my nervous energy. Mason squeezed my left hand and Dash stroked the back of my right with his thumb, both of them distracting me. With a deep breath, I did my best to center myself and push my personal conflict away.

Nana uttered the words to build the spell. "What we have, we give. What we give, we offer freely amongst all gathered here tonight." A spark of magic rushed through me, and I opened my shields to let it weave its way through those of us in the outer circle.

It didn't escape my notice when the power flowed stronger between Mason and me than with Dash. Perhaps the magic recognized two witches who'd shared before, or maybe the wolf shifter's power couldn't be a good match, no matter how hard the magic tried to work.

The five witches in the middle bent their heads, Mimsy Blackwood murmuring low and rocking back and forth where she sat behind the top of Lucky's body. With intent, she placed flowers all around the leprechaun with the help of her granddaughters. I recognized the daisies and sprigs of lavender but would have to ask my friends about the significance of the other flowers.

Mimsy rubbed a cutting of what looked like rosemary between her hands and drew a line across Lucky's head and down both his cheeks. The scent of the herb permeated the room, and my head lightened a little. I squeezed the hands of Mason and Dash to keep myself upright.

My friends' grandmother leaned back and closed her eyes. Both granddaughters flanked her and laid one hand on each of her shoulders. All five completed a circle around the leprechaun by touching the witch next to them. With her hands free, Mimsy placed her fingers on either side of Lucky's temples and drew in a hard breath.

The older woman labored to continue breathing and her eyes rolled into the back of her head. "The shield around his mind is strong. Whoever cast it is very skilled."

Magic pulsed through my body as she bent her head again in greater concentration.

Georgia's eyes whipped open and she glanced around the room with great awe and fear. Swallowing hard, she tried not to freak out. "There are a lot of spirits here."

"Focus, girl," Mimsy called out. "Any that might be of use to us?"

The sister from the mountains shook her head and searched around the circle for Dash to get her out of there.

Her gaze found me, and I did my best to mouth her some encouragement and send some good will directly to her.

"I don't like this," muttered Dash.

"Don't you dare break the circle. Not now. Not if you care about Lucky," I demanded.

Georgia licked her lips, still not appearing any bolder, but she gave a slight nod to let me know she wouldn't run away. Blowing out a calming breath, she opened herself up.

Her head turned and tilted to the side, seeing something there the rest of us couldn't. "There are three faded figures hovering about. They are too much in the shadow to communicate with me, but I feel like they belong here with him."

Lucky held up a shaky hand. "It cannae be! Ask them if they are me offspring."

The air around the leprechaun shivered, and I swore I saw three shadows hovering above him. Each figure wavered when Georgia addressed them, as if taking turns.

"They're a little stronger now, speaking some language I don't understand. But each one repeats a different word over and over again." She closed her eyes to concentrate. "It sounds like what they're conveying starts with a *C*," explained the witch.

Lucky smiled. "It is me kin. Conmac, Ciar, and Corc." He proceeded to whisper something so low, none of us could hear anything for sure. I knew the ancient tongue he used wouldn't be understood by us anyway.

"Lucky had kids?" Mason asked under his breath.

"I was thinking the same thing," added Dash.

I nodded. "Me, too."

Nana widened her eyes to get us to hush.

The three shimmering shadows gathered together until they formed one stronger and darker mass. We watched it rise in the air above the leprechaun, pause, and then dive right into Lucky's chest.

"Keep the circle intact," ordered my grandmother.

All five of the psychics drew in hard breaths, their voices coming out fast.

"He never saw it coming," Lavender cried out.

Lily followed. "It hurt when his mind was invaded."

"The one who did it forced Lucky to do their bidding, emptying him of his will and compelling him to fulfill theirs, like a marionette and its master." Georgia's voice sounded distant.

Ginny coughed and sputtered, her body convulsing. Breaking her hold on the two witches beside her, she dropped forward, her hands touching Lucky's leg.

The overwhelmed girl uttered a long, low moan until her voice rasped out her prediction.

"A rabbit's foot, a golden coin,
All good things for luck to join.
To drain from one into a vessel,
You search for something in which to nestle.
Fly fast and far or all is lost,
To fail is much too high a cost."

A sharp scream ripped through the younger witch and reverberated in all our chests. The tingle of magic reached a peak, signaling its limits.

"Wait," cried out Dash, pulling his hand out of mine and rushing forward to catch a fainting Ginny. "Do you see who did this to him? Does he remember anything about the one who attacked him?"

The shared power in the room blasted through all of us and dissipated. I collapsed forward and grabbed my thighs, putting my head between my knees to keep from retching. Alison Kate didn't make it, and Lee held her hair out of the way. Ben approached Lily and knelt down beside her, catching her as she broke down into sobs.

Henry slumped down and sat against the parlor wall as the rest of the people in the room attempted to recover. I joined my assistant, too tired to make it any further and having missed where Mason had disappeared to.

"So, what do you think?" I asked him.

Henry blew out a breath. "I think whoever did this, it wasn't their first time. We're dealing with a nasty piece of work who is more than capable of covering their tracks. I also think it's possible that we might lose..." He waved me off and turned his head away so I couldn't see the tears forming in his eyes.

When I looked for Lucky, I found him talking to Nana with Mason helping him to sit up. Dash hovered over the two sisters, crouching down to talk with them and rub both of their backs. When he caught me staring, he quirked his eyebrow, checking to make sure I was okay.

"I'm fine," I mouthed. Pointing at each sister, I gave him a thumbs up in definite approval. They had more than earned our respect tonight.

A few of the guys helped bring Nana's furniture back into the room, so Henry pushed himself up from the floor with a whole lot of grunts and groans. He offered me a hand to help me stand, and we busied ourselves in straightening up the place and ignoring the somber mood that blanketed the parlor.

Nana thanked as many as she could before they left until only the few of us who'd been clued in since the beginning were left. Matt and Ben helped Lucky to his feet and escorted him out to the warden's patrol car parked outside. Dash promised he would return after taking care of Georgia and Ginny. My grandmother forced them to take some food back with them to their campsite. I guessed she gave them an open invitation to return to Honeysuckle anytime they wanted and to call on her if they were ever in need of her services.

Blythe and I returned to the backyard and poured sweet tea into plastic cups, bringing them inside and distributing them around. Once everyone had at least a sugary drink to shore them up, Nana collapsed onto the stiff couch.

"What do y'all think?" she asked, the exhaustion on her face causing her to look a little older and less sure.

"I think I need to shower those two new girls with a whole lot of baked goods," exclaimed Alison Kate.

Lavender still clung to her cousin's hand. "They were pretty amazing and possess a whole lot more power than I think they know. I feel like it supercharged me. I can see all of your auras with more clarity than ever before."

"Not that it's a super power," remarked Lily, "but if any of you are thinking of purchasing any flowers, I know exactly what you need."

Mimsy hugged her granddaughter. "That's a fine use of magic, my dear. And perhaps it's high time we teach you how to expand your gifts."

Nana raised her hand in the air. "Stop this dithering. We don't have time for pleasantries or general observations. I need concrete thoughts and interpretations. If someone has an idea of how what just happened could help Lucky, speak out now."

I obeyed my grandmother because she'd train me well not to ignore her special tone. "Henry thinks whoever did it is very skilled and can probably cover his or her tracks well."

"I can talk for myself," my assistant complained.

I ignored him and continued. "But did anybody else catch it when Ginny talked about a rabbit's foot or golden coin?"

"I did." Henry raised his hand, giving me a side-eyed glance. "I think she said the word 'vessel'. So maybe whoever forced Lucky to give them his luck used something to put it in."

I couldn't help the smile that spread across my face. "That's the first piece of good news we've had so far."

"Why, Charli Bird?" Nana asked.

My eyes went to Mason. "Because we've, I mean, *I've* been searching for something that wasn't tangible." I didn't know how many in the room knew about Mason and the magical switcheroo Mason and I had accidentally set in motion. "How can you find the concept of luck if it has no form to find? Knowing we're tracking an actual object narrows things down." At least I hoped it did.

"Charli, you won second in a race today when before, you would fall off a broom if you tried to mount it. I think we know that somehow or another, you and Mason have swapped powers." Lee shook his head at the two of us.

"Fine," I admitted. "I think I might be able to help Mason hone the tracking magic to search for a tangible object. As a last resort, we can close down our borders and have him check every single possession on each person before they leave."

Nana cringed. "I'd prefer if we could do something else long before the event ends. The contingency of naysayers from Charleston are really pushing the regional council to take umbrage with how we do things here in Honeysuckle. A disastrous ending like that could tip the scales in their favor."

Billy Ray leaned in to say something personal to my grandmother, and I pursed my lips. Matt flopped down next to me, taking too much pleasure in my discomfort.

"Let me clarify, I don't mean that I would put the town's well-being over Lucky's. I think y'all know me better than that," Nana conceded. "If it comes to shutting everything down to save our friend, I'll do it."

Mason took out his notebook. "Let's make a list of anybody we think might be a candidate."

A few names or descriptions of people got shouted out. I added my dislike of Earl and his friend that tried to disqualify Horatio. I still wanted to talk to Big Mouth Bass and Fireball, but other than hearing a minor argument, I didn't have a solid reason to say their names.

Henry added, "Steve and I are still trying to track down whoever's running the bets."

An idea dawned on me. "Maybe we could use me as bait."

A collective groan rose in the room. Matt ruffled my hair. "Explain what you mean, Birdy."

I batted his arm away. "Don't call me that." Running my fingers through my hair to fix it, I followed my train of thought. "Henry, do you think it's possible to get anyone who places a bet to believe I'm a dark horse to win? In other words, can we affect the betting?"

My assistant considered the idea. "I see where you're going with this. If everyone here tells whoever they can that your flying today was a fluke, maybe we could affect the odds. And then if you place either first or second and they win even more money because they bet on you—"

"Then the likelihood that he or she is the one who possesses Lucky's fortune increases," finished my brother. "Not bad, Birdy. And before you tell me to stop calling you that, remember you registered under it for racing. I think a whole lot of people are going to be cheering for you with that name after tomorrow."

Nana sighed. "It's the best plan we've got so far, and your next race is first thing in the morning. Huh," she exclaimed. "I never thought I'd be saying this, but I can't wait to hear Charli 'Birdy' Goodwin being called out a broom racing champion."

Instead of a cheer, a yawn escaped my open mouth. Nana dismissed everyone, reminding them to keep their spell phones charged and on the ready in case things changed. I promised the girls I'd be home soon and stayed to help my grandmother clean up. Averting my eyes, I concentrated on collecting the stray plastic cups instead of watching Nana kiss Billy Ray goodnight.

Mason helped me collect plates and start bringing in food to be packaged up. "You really think it'll be easier knowing we're looking for something that could hold the luck?"

I shrugged, too tired to give a further interpretation of my powers. "It's worth a shot at least." Taking the empty plate from him and dumping it into the sink full of dish soap, I leaned up and pecked him on the cheek. "Thanks for helping. You should go get some rest."

"What about you?" he asked.

"I'd like to talk to Nana in private for a few minutes. Don't worry, I'll get home safe on my own."

Mason pulled me into a warm hug. "I know that," he murmured into my head. Throwing the damp dish towel at me, he backed away. "I'll have enough time to pull off one more task tonight."

"What's that?"

The left corner of his mouth lifted in a sly grin. "I'm going to enlist Lee's help in making T-shirts emblazoned with 'Team Birdy' and the number thirteen on them."

I splashed a large amount of soapy bubbles in his direction, but he hurried off, laughing.

Left alone, the gravity of my plan settled into my gut, and I ignored my creeping doubt and forced hope to replace it. For tomorrow, I intended to place my highest bet on myself.

Chapter Fifteen

After making one last pass through the parlor, I found Nana slumped in her seat at the small wooden table in her kitchen. I rubbed her back in slow circles.

"Can I get you anything?" I offered.

She shook her head but remained eerily silent. Even the song the cicadas chirped didn't seem to cheer her up. I pulled out the seat next to her and waited.

"I don't know if I can keep doing this," Nana muttered.

It freaked me out to hear my grandmother admit any form of weakness. "Doing what?"

She placed both hands on the table to steady herself. "Be the leader Honeysuckle needs. Maybe I'm too old for this stuff."

All my life, Nana had loomed larger than anything else in

the world to me. Even when Pop Pop was still alive, she took up most of the air in any room she entered, and he adored her for her strength. It was his choice to legally change his last name to hers to keep the Goodwin name front and center. To hear her doubt herself crushed me.

"You'll never be too old for anything," I reassured her.

Nana scoffed. "Child, you out of most people should understand that life is fleeting."

"And you always tell me to live it to its fullest, right?" I reminded her.

She furrowed her brow but the sparkle in her eyes relieved me. "Don't be usin' my own words against me, Birdy."

I covered her hand with mine. "I'll use whatever I need to keep you from giving up too soon. Besides, I think Matt has enough on his plate with the birth of his first child coming up quick to take over on the council."

"That's right." Nana snapped her fingers. "I'm about to have a great-grandbaby to spoil. Although you could take over on the town council. Tucker's success so far proves that maybe we need more young blood to shake us up."

With a gasp, I pulled my hand away. "I can't take the council seat. I'm not a full Goodwin."

Nana scooted closer and cradled my chin with her fingers. "I dare anyone to deny that you are my family and deserve a seat on the council as much as your brother does."

I met her gaze with doubt. "I'm not saying I'm not a part of the family. But I'm not blood-related, which means I shouldn't take on the family legacy."

"Well, I think the magic that holds our town together has already recognized your authority before. But I guess I'm not ready to find out for sure anyway." She released me and got up from the table. "And now that I'm done feeling sorry for myself, let's discuss what's going on with you and those two boys."

"*Men*, Nana," I corrected.

She filled up an old kettle from the tap and clicked on the gas burner to boil some water. "I think both of them have been a bit childish in their mistakes with you. Until they correct their courses, they're both boys to me."

I rolled my eyes and then checked to see if my grandmother saw. "I've been putting off discussing anything big with them until we solve this thing with Lucky."

Nana grabbed two mugs out of the cupboard and set them on the counter. "Don't you mean King Fergus?"

"You know?" Of course, Nana knew.

"He told me back when he came to Honeysuckle. Wanted me to know his background and if I was comfortable that he chose to live here. I told him anybody who was the source of the mythology surrounding the sword Excalibur could take care of themselves when the time arose." Nana turned off the burner when the kettle whistled. "He didn't understand at the time that when he became a part of our town, it meant we would fight for him, too."

I scooted back in my chair. "Wait, how is he part of the myth of King Arthur's sword?"

Nana scooped a mix of herbs and leaves into small

strainers to steep. "How do you think he exchanged his sword with the sea god?"

I thought hard and came up with the answer. "He threw it into the water."

My grandmother winked. "All myths start somewhere." She quieted down while she finished preparing our drinks. Despite the warm temperatures where we lived, she believed in the healing properties of a good cup of hot tea.

Taking a sip, I pondered where I stood with Mason and Dash. Both had made their interest in me known at some time or another, but what happened between me and them on an individual basis clouded my emotions.

"You gonna tell me what's going on with those two *men?*" Nana emphasized the last word.

"You gonna tell me what's really going on between you and Billy Ray?" I deflected.

My grandmother grinned. "Sure. He pursued me about a month after he moved here, and I accepted his advances. We've been dating steadily for a couple of months." She blew on her tea. "He's even stayed over—"

I put my mug down on the table and placed my hands over my ears. "La, la, la, I don't want to hear any more about this."

Nana giggled. "You're the one who said I wasn't too old. Guess my body already knew that since it still remembers how to—"

I threw a hand over her mouth. "Don't finish that sentence, I beg of you."

She licked me, and I pulled my hand away, wiping it on my

shirt. The grossness of it all worked as a nice distraction from my serious man problems.

When her amusement faded, my grandmother pushed me again. "Are you going to tell me what's happened so I can help you figure things out?"

I opened my mouth but closed it again with a sudden realization. Nana had always been my safe spot, and when I had a problem to work out, she was the one I came running to. But this time, I figured both guys deserved better.

"You know, Nana, I think I'm going to figure things out on my own first. If I hit a brick wall, maybe I'll ask for your help. But don't worry, I'll keep in mind all the advice you've ever given me about boys." I brought my mug to my mouth. "I'll see if it's worth anything."

"I'll always be here when you need me, Birdy," she said with a wink. "And you're getting awfully good at doing that for me, too."

AN OWL HOOTED in the distance when I opened the front door of Nana's house to walk home. The light of the moon shone bright through the trees, casting moving shadows on the ground and reminding me of those we'd seen tonight hovering over Lucky. A slight shiver ran down my spine.

"Can I walk you home?" Dash stepped out of a dark corner of my grandmother's front porch.

I jumped a mile high, clasping my chest. "Don't scare me like that."

He chuckled low. "Sorry. I've been a little too used to hiding lately." His footsteps creaked on the wooden porch. "Didn't mean to startle you. But I'd like to walk you home if you don't mind."

I'd told Mason I could make it on my own, and it didn't take magic to conjure up the reason why Dash wanted to be my escort. The walk would give him the opportunity to finally tell me what had happened to him and anything else he wanted to say to me.

Curiosity forced my brain to go blank when trying to find a reason to tell him no thanks. With a sigh, I gave in. "Okay."

Cool moonlight let me see the corner of the wolf shifter's mouth curve up. "That was easier than I thought."

I walked down the porch stairs and headed in the right direction. Dash caught up to me with his long strides until he reached my side. I focused on the crunch of our feet on the ground, giving him space to start the conversation.

After more than thirty crunching steps, he finally spoke. "I almost died."

His words sucked the oxygen out of my lungs, and I stopped. "What does that mean?"

He shuffled forward, encouraging me to start walking again. "It means that without help from several friends, including Georgia and her two sisters, I'd be a ghost who haunted you."

I didn't want to admit to him that even alive, he'd been

haunting me a little bit ever since I'd met him. "It sounds like you have a lot more to tell me than I expected."

Dash reached out and took my hand in his grasp without asking. "Leaving Honeysuckle when I did, that was the hardest thing I've ever done. Until I went to war with my own brother."

He slowed his steps so I didn't have to rush to keep up with his pace. My hand squeezed his to encourage him to keep talking.

"If you remember what I told you, I created the vacuum of power that allowed my middle brother Kash to take control of the Red Ridge pack. That was after I'd killed my own father." Dash snorted at whatever memory he relived. "If I was strong enough to take down one bad leader, I should have been strong enough to take over and run things."

Regret soaked every one of his words, earning my sympathy. "So, you came here to Honeysuckle to hide. I remember," I admitted.

He snorted. "I'd like to think I came here to recover, but you're right. I was hiding. And then you came barreling into my life, forcing me to remember that there were things worth living for. Shining the light of hope into the darkest crevices of my pain."

I shivered again, his words shaking me to my very core. Dash stopped walking and pulled me into a warm embrace, asking me if I was cold. The only response I could give was a nod of my head. I couldn't let him know how much I needed to hear him confirm my importance in his life out loud.

"I mean it, Charli," he mumbled into my hair. "You saved me. I only wish I could have been a better match for you."

I closed my eyes, swallowing the response that he could be if he tried. "I know," I muttered into his shoulder. Needing to protect myself, I pushed him away with more reluctance than I expected.

He didn't take my hand again but matched my strides while he talked. "A shifter battle over territory and pack leadership can get ugly in the best of times. With Kash, I had to wage an all-out war to beat him. Do you remember Trey?"

I would never forget one of the rogue wolf shifters who helped Damien almost kidnap me. Who tried to choke me. "Yes," I grunted.

Dash bumped into me to break me out of my memories. "He was lost and going down a dark road when you met him."

"No kidding."

He clarified, "Trey wasn't such a bad guy really. And his connections were crucial to recruiting allies to fight my brother."

"How could he help from jail?" I asked. After he'd been caught, he was supposed to be serving time.

"It took a little convincing and some promises made, but I had some legal help to get Trey's sentence shortened to time served and released on probation."

"Ben," I muttered. "Did he help you?"

Dash waved off my accusation. "You're focusing on the wrong thing. Trey helped me gather enough support from those under Kash's thumb to help me attack my brother from the outside in. First, we took down his drug trafficking business, which was trickier than we expected because he'd involved humans. With his main source of money cut off, we went after his biggest supporters. That's where we got into some trouble."

A low rumble of a growl underlined his words. I guessed he might be holding back specific details if telling me the basics caused his animal to reveal itself.

"Kash had a couple of nasty witches working for him," Dash continued. "He had them strung out on some kind of drug that lowered their inhibitions, allowing them to use every ounce of their magic to help him. For a hot minute, I thought I should save these two pathetic, skinny strung out kids."

In my year of traveling around, I'd come across cases of witches addicted to human drugs and magical ones. Goblin fruit gave wardens the biggest headaches. Once a supernatural got hooked on the stuff, it became the only thing that mattered. A witch could drain their bodies by not protecting themselves when they used magic. Even if Dash wanted to save his brother's witches, they'd probably die anyway doing everything they could to get their hands on more of the foul stuff.

"Do you think he was dealing magical drugs, too?" I asked.

Dash shrugged. "I told the local wardens about it afterwards. It's up to them and any other organization to figure that shit out. My problem came with my brother's clever way of using the witches' powers to help defend himself." A growl ripped out of his throat and his golden eyes glowed in the dark. He held out a hand to stop us. "Give me a minute."

My heart thumped in my chest when we stopped. Dash struggled to gain more control over his animal. If he was so volatile while recounting his story, maybe he was too dangerous to be around.

Panting, he blinked his eyes open and shut until the glow disappeared. He started again with heavier steps. "Sorry. It's all still too fresh."

I wanted to touch him, to reassure him. But the closeness of his animal scared me enough to force my hand into my pocket. "It's okay."

"No, it's not," Dash said. "But I'm doing the best I can, and I need to get through this so you can understand."

I waited for him to choose what else he thought I needed to know or why he didn't think I understood his good intentions for all the violence.

The shifter chuckled a couple of times. "You know, I credit you for how things turned around in our favor."

His words surprised me. "I didn't even know you were going through any of this. How could I have helped you?"

He reached for my hand once again. "Because I kept thinking of you the whole time. Remembering that there was something, someone out there in the world worth all the fighting so I could see them again. See you."

Dash stopped and lifted my hand up to his mouth, planting a light kiss on my skin. Confused emotions or not, his touch caused excitement to spark to life, buzzing through my veins.

He pulled me a little closer until the heat from his body warmed me. The last time we were this close, he'd broken my heart when he left. But I couldn't find it in me to tell him to stop.

Tipping his forehead against mine, he breathed in deep. "Your scent was always with me, calling me back when I gave up on hope. Helping me push harder to win." He clasped my face with both his hands. "I shouldn't do this."

"Do what?" I squeaked, my heart beating a wild rhythm in my chest.

With one finger, he tilted my chin up. "This."

Dash covered my mouth with his. Fireworks exploded behind my fluttering eyelids. My hands moved of their own accord. One cradled his scarred cheek while the other cupped the back of his neck, pulling him in a little closer.

A low growl returned to his throat, but it sounded more pleased than threatening, rumbling like a satisfied purr. He deepened the kiss, smashing his lips against mine with raw need.

All sense flew out of my head, and I let my body do the talking. I stood on my tiptoes to get as close as possible, hoping he'd take the lead. Instead, he loosened his tight grip on my face and fluttered my lips with light kisses until he stopped with a sigh.

"I shouldn't have done that," he murmured.

It was my turn to place my forehead against his. "It's not like I stopped you. Or hated it."

Dash's thumb stroked my cheek. "Oh, Charli, if only..." He squeezed his eyes shut. With a grunt of effort, he took a step away from me.

The short distance cooled my body and awakened my senses. What had I just done? Half of me wanted to throw myself at the shifter and attack him again. The other half pictured Mason and how he'd react if he found out. My fingers touched my swollen lips, and I tried my hardest not to start comparing. This wasn't about apples and oranges. This was about the difference between a pixie and a unicorn. Or a shifter and a witch.

Dash blew out a breath and stuffed his hands in his pockets. "I don't mean to complicate your life. But I couldn't help myself. So many nights, I stayed up dreaming about what that would be like."

"Awful? Terrible? Completely yucky?" My sarcasm acted as the last resort to shield my heart.

He grunted one short sad chuckle and smirked. "Far from. But it won't be happening again. It can't." He held up a finger over my lips. "And don't ask me why."

I almost bit off the offending digit stopping that exact question. Crossing my arms, I tried on my best challenging glare.

My attempts at being more kick butt than mushy puddle earned me sad amusement. He removed his index finger from my mouth. "I haven't finished yet. When I do, you'll understand what I mean."

Flustered and a little hurt, I raised my hands in the air. "Sweet honeysuckle iced tea, get on with it then."

My frustration didn't stop the shifter, who kept us on the track to my house. "Fine. We lost the first couple rounds of attacks on Kash because one of the witches had psychic abilities of his own. He was kept sober enough to foresee when we were coming. That's how I got these." He pointed at his scars.

I reached up to touch the gashes again, but he pulled back. A flash of pain ripped through me at his rejection, and I held in a wince.

"After that, I figured I needed a little witchy help on our side," Dash continued. "Like I said, I credit you for our ultimate winning of the war. I sought out a similar private community like Honeysuckle where I'd heard a few witches lived. That's when I found the Whitaker sisters."

My goodwill for Georgia and Ginny vanished with a shot of old-fashioned jealousy. "I'm glad they helped," I croaked with a little too much whine in my voice.

"You're messin' with my ego, being all jealous," Dash crowed. "But it wasn't like that. Caro, the oldest of the three, has a way with creatures. She works as a large animal vet, which helps pay the bills. But she's like the creature whisperer. I've never seen someone be able to work with animals and magical beasts like she can. Because of her, we got a hippogriff to use in attacking Kash."

"No, that's not right," I countered. "Hippogriffs only exist in really popular wizard books and movie series."

Dash lifted his eyebrows. "I'm being serious. She enlisted a Yeti, too. I'm not lying, although even I had some problems believing she knew one until I met George."

Spit blew out of my mouth when I scoffed. "You had a Yeti named George who joined your side?"

"His name isn't really George, but he said we didn't need to take the time to learn how to pronounce his real one. Caro helped in recruiting creatures while Georgia risked her sanity talking to spirits."

"And what did Ginny do? Did she use her fortunetelling abilities to help?" I asked.

Dash pursed his lips. "I don't think she'd want me to tell you exactly what happened. She blames herself for my brother's current state. You can't tell anyone I told you this, but I trust you. Because of our interpretation of one of her predictions, Davis got injured in the fight more permanently than we expected.

That got my attention and stoked my interest. "What happened?"

"He can't shift into his wolf now." Regret and anger mixed in Dash's tone. "He's moved out of our family home in Red Ridge territory and is living near the sisters. I don't know how long it will take for him to get better. And Kash is gone now."

Dash didn't have to say who killed his middle brother. With such a high body count, I didn't know if I could excuse the amount of blood the shifter had on his hands despite the reasons.

I thought about what I'd overheard Trey and Dash talking about in the alley next to the bar and why he left to fight in the first place. "Who's left running the Red Ridge pack?"

Dash halted one more time but didn't answer.

His silence reeked of the truth. "It's you. You're the new pack leader. You're coming back here this weekend isn't a permanent return, is it?" My last question came out in a thin whisper.

The lights of my house loomed in the near distance and the moon shone bright in the sky, casting its cold light over the field.

Dash took my hand in his one more time. "I told you things were complicated. It seems you were right when you said we take two steps forward and then fall way behind in the long run. No matter how much we try to dance with each other, we can never get the steps right."

The tiny rips in my heart that cracked when he refused to kiss me again tore open a little further. I swallowed hard, wanting to find a solution but failing.

He brought my hand up to his lips and brushed a light kiss against my skin again. "Also, I'm still hurt from everything. Not my scars. Those I can live with. But you've witnessed how close my animal is to the surface. I don't trust him or myself enough yet. And there's one more thing."

What else could I take? Tears pooled at the corners of my eyes, and I did nothing to stop them from falling.

Dash squeezed my hand and let go. "You seem to have found someone who's good for you."

"Mason," I screeched. "You're using Mason as an excuse?"

He crossed his arms. "No, not as an excuse for anything. Just an observation. Sure, it bugs me to no end when he's so smug about whatever's going on between the two of you. I can't stand the fact that he can pursue you when I can't."

I wanted to tell him he still had a chance, but nothing came out when I opened my mouth.

Dash kicked a rock. "Even I can tell that you'd be good together. And I shouldn't hold you back from anything that could ultimately make you happy."

My vision blurred from the tears. "You could try."

Dash wiped away the wetness from my cheeks with a gentle touch. "I wish I could."

His tenderness tore the rest of the cracks wide open. I smacked my hands against his muscled chest. "No," I roared and poked him in the pec. "You don't get to make the decision for me. Don't go telling me that Mason is who I should end up with or that things can't work out with you. Nobody gets to decide who I'm with. Except. Me." My finger hurt from each jab.

"Charli," Dash protested.

The reality of my world crashed down over my head. We had a friend's life in terrible jeopardy. A culprit to catch. Luck to find and return. Races to win. Who I kissed or even chose had to wait.

I took a few steps toward my house and away from the

wolf shifter. "I'm tired. I've got to get some rest before the race tomorrow." Pointing a finger at him, I gave him a final order. "Do not leave town again before we discuss this one more time."

Remorse filled Dash's face. Pursing his lips, he nodded.

I stomped through the field, allowing the light of my house to guide me, never looking back. Despite everything tumbling down around me, I made it to the top of my front porch before I completely lost it and collapsed in sobs and tears.

Chapter Sixteen

ound sleep eluded me most of the night. All the girls
did their best to cheer me up, but I knew they heard
me crying on and off at all hours. Peaches curled up
on my pillow to show her support even though she left me
with no place to lay my head. When dawn lit up the sky, I still
didn't know if I was mourning the lost opportunity with Dash
or destroying what was only beginning with Mason.

Exhausted, my nerves affected me even more while
waiting for the race to start. I'd given Mason a quick lesson on
how to sharpen the magic to search for objects, but left him
when the qualifying round approached.

Horatio and Juniper waited with me while Lee checked
Mason's broom and tightened up a few mechanical spells. I
spotted Earl patting the back of a fellow racer. When he
caught me staring, he stuck his middle finger in the air.

Using all the creativity of a snail, he tapped his wrist and mouthed, "Watch."

Earl pointed at me and said, "Your."

Turning around, he used both hands to gesture at his body. He glanced over his shoulder and finished, "Back."

Power sizzled across my fingers and I counted the people standing in between us who might get hit by my stinging hex.

"Charli, don't get yourself disqualified." Mason came up from behind, looking between me and the ignoramus still trying to taunt me from afar.

"He started it," I pouted. My lack of rest apparently turned me into a five-year-old.

The detective raised a disapproving eyebrow. "You can't ruin the only plans we have in place. Henry says he and a few others have taken care of their side of things. Now it's up to you."

I closed my eyes and reminded myself to stay focused on what we really needed to win here. A warm pair of lips on mine caught me off guard, and I blinked my eyes open again.

Mason smiled and wrapped an arm around my waist and pulled me closer. "That was for luck. This one's because I want to."

The detective's body brushed against mine. Still in shock, I didn't fight him off. My traitorous body took a step closer, giving Mason a signal to deepen our connection. His hand swept through my hair and held onto the back of my head, and a little warmth bloomed in my chest.

He knocked the broom out of my grasp and intertwined

our fingers, holding onto me while his lips explored mine. Heat flared to life and burned away all my protests. This kiss was no less pleasurable than the other one I'd received last night. Both melted my brain like butter on hot biscuits.

The comparison startled me out of my romantic haze. Ending our contact, I placed a hand on the detective's shoulder. "Mason, we need to talk."

He answered with a cocky grin. "I know we do, but after you win. Good luck, Birdy." Stepping away, he pointed at the T-shirt he wore in support of me.

I picked up the broom with one hand and hit my forehead with the other. "I am in so much trouble."

The official for this race checked us all in like before, and our names appeared on the scoreboard. When mine showed up, a small group of recognizable voices cheered from somewhere nearby. The same thing happened for Horatio.

"May you fly true," wished the troll, giving me another massive fist bump. We both adjusted our goggles and waited for the instructions from the official.

In her black and white striped shirt, she raised her hand in the air. "Lady and gentlemen, this is the qualifying round for amateurs aged eighteen and up. Whoever wins the top two spots will move on to race with the professionals in today's final event. No pressure, right?"

Her joke earned a few nervous chuckles. When she called for us to mount, I did so and kicked off the ground. A stray memory about the two kisses invaded my head, causing my stomach to stir and the broom to dip.

"Get a grip," I admonished myself, obeying and holding onto the broom handle a little tighter.

When the blinking light through my goggles turned green, I shot forward. The path through the field toward the forest was the same. I aimed my broom in that direction, leaning forward to soar faster. At the front of the pack, I tried to focus on what came next rather than what happened behind me. The path narrowed as I flew into the woods.

The blinking light directed me through a different direction than before. I took one curve a little too wide, and the broom wavered under my touch. The gut instinct I counted on lessened. A body zoomed past my left side, and I recognized the taller frame of Eric Mosely, the clever boy from the first permit class I'd taught.

Instead of following his lead and catching up to him, the broom wobbled underneath me for a brief second, allowing the racer who Earl favored to pass me.

"Oh, no you don't," I called out. With renewed determination, I zipped forward.

He looked over his shoulder and found me riding his tail. Brown liquid came hurtling over his back and splattered across the left side of my face. I seriously considered hexing his behind, but with my focus on winning to help Lucky, I couldn't risk it.

Instead, I had to rely on my swapped magic to help me fly. I pulled up to the right side of the spitting man, who smiled a toothless grin of a challenge. Aiming his body at mine, he bumped me almost hard enough to run me into a fast-approaching tree. With a quick recovery, I caught back up to him as the light of the last section of the race approached at the edge of the woods.

Eric was long gone by the time we broke into the sunlit field. The other racer and I traded body hits back and forth. Sweat poured down my face as the effort to fly and attempt to come in second exhausted me. I didn't remember it being this hard in the last race. A little fear coursed through my veins, and my broom wobbled again.

Sensing a weakness, the spitting racer aimed his broom to bump me off course one last time. Sending more magic than I wanted through me and into the broom, I zipped ahead by a fraction, and he missed my body. However, he did catch the bristles of my broom, knocking me into a horizontal spin.

The world spun faster and faster around me, and I couldn't find a direction to choose to pull out. The watching crowd gasped with horror, and everything happened in slow motion. Something collided with the broom, throwing me off balance. The earth stopped spinning only because it approached my face with great speed.

Dirt filled my mouth and nose when I impacted with the ground, and pain seared across my shoulder. I must have tumbled a couple of times because when I opened my eyes, the world appeared upside down.

Voices shouted and I lay on the ground, waiting for Doc or any other healer to help. Nana reached me first, her professional demeanor destroyed by her concern for me.

"How many fingers am I holding up, Birdy?" She waited with worried eyes for my response.

"Who's Birdy?" I joked, wincing as I rolled to my side. "I'm fine, Nana."

The zap of pain fired from my right shoulder and into my upper arm, throbbing with more intensity. Would it be a good time now or later to tell my grandmother I couldn't move it?

Doc Andrews and Mason rushed over to me. The doctor tried to examine me while pushing the detective's concerned hands out of the way.

"I'm sorry I didn't do what I promised I would," I exclaimed.

Mason relaxed his expression. "After all that, you're worried about the results of the race? You've got grass and dirt in your hair, scratches on your face, and you want to apologize. You know, you're pretty amazing."

Still focused on the task I failed to complete, I reached out with my good arm and grabbed his. "Seriously. What are we going to do? I think I lost your broom and someone else won the race."

Nana requested Doc to have my head checked. He assured everyone I was in a little shock. "I'm going to have to reset your shoulder, Charli. You dislocated it when you landed."

"When she crashed, you mean," corrected the detective. He leaned a little closer so I could hear him. "You didn't lose my broom. It's still clutched in your hand. That's why you won second place. Even though you crashed over the finish line, you kept ahold of the broom."

Doc insisted I lay back down. "I don't think that's what's important right now."

Under his careful touch, the pain subsided a bit and my head lightened. "I don't think I'm actually hurt," I declared, fighting to sit again.

Mason assisted the doctor in holding me down. Doc pursed his lips. "That's because I've spellcast a little help to numb the pain. This next part you're gonna feel. Take a couple of deep breaths for me." He pulled the injured arm out to the side.

Before I could ask him what came next, he gripped my wrist firmly and pulled my arm at an angle. His foot braced against my chest, and he moved slow and steady until I heard and felt an internal *clunk* in my shoulder. I cried out despite the immediate reduction of pain.

"There. One more thing." Doc knelt beside me and laid his hands over my skin. It felt like someone poured warm liquid over the injured spot. The magic trickled down my arm until the throbbing stopped. The warmth changed to stinging cold as his spell finished.

"What did you do to me?" I asked, rubbing my arm.

"That should reduce any swelling. I'd give you a sling and tell you to go home and rest, but I don't think you'll listen. So, I cast a spell to help your body heal a little faster," Doc explained. "And I would advise you not to enter the final race."

I sat up, my head a little clearer. "I'll make that decision after I clean myself up."

With a little help, I got on my feet and the crowd cheered for me. I waved back using my good arm. When I walked, I did my best not to limp off the end of the course and over to the side where my friends waited for me.

"Y'all give her some breathing room," insisted Nana.

I looked around for my troll friend, wanting to know how he did. "Where's Horatio?"

"Filing a formal complaint," my grandmother pursed her lips while she and Blythe attempted to clean the dirt from my face and hair. "The racer that hit you in the end had an accomplice who antagonized Horatio during the race."

"That makes three jerks, including Earl. Why would they do what they did?" I asked.

Nana stopped fussing over me. "Hate rots things from the inside out. Big Willie's decided that whole group of boys will wait out the rest of the event in a warden's cell."

"Won't that affect how Honeysuckle is viewed by the outside witches' council?" I whispered to my grandmother.

She scoffed and licked the rag she was cleaning me with. "I'd rather them see that we're not scared and do the right thing when something wrong happens than roll over and take it. Now stay still so I can get this last smudge."

Henry rushed over to our group. He approached Mason and whispered something in his ear. "You sure?" clarified the detective.

"As a fox in a henhouse," replied my assistant. He whispered something to Nana, who nodded her approval.

"What's going on?" I insisted.

Mason promised Henry he'd be right behind him. "We've caught who's been orchestrating all the betting. I've got to go."

With my bad arm, I held him in place, asking through clenched teeth, "Where do you think you're going?"

The detective laid his hand over mine. "I'm going to the station to perform an interrogation." He patted me twice. "You stay here and take care of yourself."

I brushed Blythe's hand away from my hair. "It would take all the hippogriffs in the world to keep me from coming with you."

Mason and Nana tag-teamed and listed several reasons why I shouldn't go. The detective crossed his arms and mustered up a little authority. "Plus, hippogriffs aren't real."

I kissed my grandmother's cheek and pushed past Mason. "That's what you think," I muttered.

"What did you say?" he challenged.

I turned and walked backwards. "Hurry up, Detective. I wouldn't want you to lose *this* race and let me get there first."

Chapter Seventeen

I stared out the window from the patrol car Mason borrowed from Zeke to take me with him to the warden station. He asked me questions about the race, but I only offered short responses to avoid the bigger issue I should be telling him about.

"Are you sure you're feeling up to this?" Mason placed a hand on my knee. "I can easily drop you off at your place first."

Guilt throbbed more than the pain in my shoulder and arm. The nicer the detective became, the more it gnawed at my insides.

"No, thanks." I patted his hand, hoping he'd remove it.

Instead, he turned his palm up and laced his fingers through mine. "That's fine. We're almost there anyway. I trust you."

His words sliced through me like sharp knives. I wondered how much more hurt I'd become if I opened the door and rolled out onto the ground to get away from the cloud of shame threatening to choke me in the car.

Mason pulled up to the station and waved at my brother through the window. I rushed to open the door, panicking when the handle didn't work. "What. Is. Wrong. With. This. Thing," I grunted.

He gave me an odd look and hit a button on his side. The lock on the door clicked up. "There you go."

"Thanks." With forced patience, I slid out of the car determined not to run away.

The detective escorted me inside. The few staff in the lobby cheered for me like I was a big deal. Matt walked over with a wide grin and pulled me into a big bear hug.

"Ouch," I complained, pain shooting down my arm.

My brother placed me back on the floor with greater care. "Oops. I forgot Nana's first order in her text not to hurt you. I'm just so danged proud of you, sis."

"Not gonna call me, Birdy?" I teased.

He clicked his tongue. "What good is a nickname that bothers you if everyone uses it to praise you?"

Dash's brother Davis appeared, walking out of the bathroom and wiping his hands on his pants. "Took you long enough."

"What's he doing here?" Mason asked Matt.

"Hey, a little respect, please." Davis held his head up with pride. "I'm the one who figured it out and came up with the plan to catch them in the end. Y'all ready to stop interrogating me and start talking to the masterminds of the betting?"

Mason stopped checking over the younger wolf shifter, his head snapping up. "Mastermind-s-s-s? There's more than one? All you said was that we caught whoever was in charge."

Something crashed at the back of the station and a loud voice yelled out, "Hey! Can we get somethin' to drink back here? I know my rights." A banging of metal followed the complaint.

Matt groaned and rubbed his hand down his face. "I know Nana wanted those fools detained to keep them away from the event for the rest of the day, but we could have kicked them out and sent them on their merry."

"Is that Earl and his gang?" I asked.

"You mean the barrel full of jerks? Yep," Matt confirmed. "They were mostly shnockered to begin with, so they deserve what they're getting. Then the one who attempted to assault Horatio on the race course also threw a punch at Zeke. We nabbed a couple of their other buddies who were drunk and disorderly for good measure."

"Great," exhaled Mason. "You got enough people here to handle them if they get out of control?"

My brother sniffed. "Where are they gonna go? We've got things handled. I'll call back a couple of the others if TJ texts me she needs something."

My eyebrows raised in alarm. "Is she okay?" Maybe some of the magic we conjured last night had affected her anyway.

"Oh, she's fine. I think she's upset that she's so close to giving birth yet too far away, in her words. Doc Andrews suggested she should stay home and avoid too much excitement, which I completely agreed with," Matt added.

"Pfft, you'd practically handcuff her to the bed to keep anything from happening to her," I accused.

My brother wiggled his eyebrows. "How do you think we made the baby?"

Davis snickered. I punched Matt with my weaker arm, and he fake flinched. Why did all my family members think I needed to hear about their sexy times?

Mason laughed, and I swung to hit him, too. He caught my hand mid-air. "Don't even try it. I'm going to take Charli to my office and then I'll go check out these masterminds, plural, in the interrogation room. Davis, we'll see you later." Placing a hand on the small of my back, he escorted me down the hall.

"You weren't very nice to the guy who helped break down the betting bookie. And don't think you're going to stash me out of the way in your office, Detective." I halted in front of the door and attempted to cross my arms, except the injured one wouldn't cooperate without shooting pain.

Mason smirked. "First, I treated Dash's brother just fine. Second, you think I don't know I couldn't keep you in there if I wanted to? I wasn't about to tell your brother I was allowing you to accompany me to interview the big bad bookies. But you've got to let me do the talking in there."

"Deal." I stuck out the hand from my bad arm to shake on it.

The detective gripped it with care and rubbed his thumb against my skin. I couldn't meet his adoring gaze without guilt forcing the truth to burst out of my mouth. I promised myself I'd tell him as soon as we were finished with the interview.

The detective ordered me to wait for his signal before I followed him inside. He opened the door and took a step in. I waited, but nothing happened.

His body blocked the entrance, and I tapped his shoulder. "What's going on?"

"You've gotta get in here to see." Mason stepped to the side, giving me a full view.

A kid and a gnome sat in metal chairs behind the table. Two pixies flanked them, floating in the air with their wings flapping as fast as a hummingbird's.

The boy, who couldn't be older than ten or eleven, uncrossed his arms and cocked an eyebrow at me. "You think bringing a hottie in here will get us to talk? If you cleaned her up a little more, she might be worth it."

"I feel like I've walked into the middle of a joke," I exclaimed. "You are the betting masterminds? What are you, kid, ten years old?"

The boy slapped the table. "My name is Owen and I'm thirteen. I told the idiot who threw us in here that I'm small for my age but much smarter than any of you wardens."

"I'm twenty-six," quipped the gnome. "You can call me Jasper, and I don't mind the dirt on you."

"Congratulations," replied Mason. "You're old enough to know better." He turned his attention back to the kid. "Why do you think you're smarter?"

Owen leaned forward. "Because everyone ignores you when you're small. Most witches don't even acknowledge other supernatural races as being equal, and they definitely think those of us who are smaller are weaker. Witches have no clue that the smallest of all the magical beings in the world could outstrip any of their collective magic."

The realization of who we were dealing with stunned me, and I tried to cover up my surprise with a cough, sitting down in the seat in front of the kid. "You sound older than you are."

He jutted his chin out with pride. "My grandpa raised me. He taught me a lot of valuable things."

The more information he gave up, the better my chances increased to get what we wanted out of him. "My grandmother had a hand in raising me, too. What would your grandpa think about you being at the warden station for illegal gambling?" I pushed.

"He'd be proud to bail me out. Who do you think taught me the business?" replied Owen. "And that's all I've got to say to you."

"Then you can talk to me." Mason sat down on my right.

The boy crossed his arms. "Aren't you gonna ask Pip and Nip how old they are?" Owen snarked, sitting back in his seat. "That's why we're smarter than both of you."

I greeted the two pixies by their names, and they squealed with glee in their high-pitched tone. One of them fluttered its wings and flew over to me. It rubbed its head against my hurt shoulder a couple of times, reminding me of my cat Peaches and her displays of affection.

Mason waved the pixie away from me, and the little creature shook a minuscule finger at him and then pointed at my shoulder.

"Don't," I suggested. "I think Pip is trying to help." My shoulder had stopped throbbing after the pixie touched it.

"That's Nip," corrected Owen. "He must like you to waste his power like that."

"My sincerest apologies, Nip," I addressed the pixie. "Did you just do something to help my injury?"

The creature flapped its wings and nodded its head up and down. He spoke too fast for me to understand, but I guessed he was explaining how his powers would heal me. Bowing out of respect, Nip flew forward and placed his hands on my scraped cheek. The sting of the impending bruises and open cuts disappeared.

"Wow." Mason didn't say anything else while he watched the pixie share its power with me.

The brush of Nip's fragile wings against my skin tickled. He uttered something I couldn't understand, so I nodded without comprehension. He flew at me and kissed my cheek, giving me a tiny peck that tingled with the hint of bigger magic.

Owen snickered. "You're in for it now. You just agreed he could woo you."

"Get in line," Mason grunted, his eyes narrowing on the

poor pixie. If he felt that strongly about the tiny creature expressing his interest, how would he react when I told him about Dash's romantic moment with me?

"Oh, now I get it. She's your girlfriend, and you brought her in here to impress her. Well, I'm sorry if we can't help you out, sir," Owen stated. "We ain't tellin' you nothin'."

"Nothin'," echoed the gnome.

"But if you're as smart as you claim to be, then don't you think it would be wiser to work with the wardens? You don't know why you were pulled in other than assuming you were in trouble." I dangled the bait. "What if there's something else they want?"

Jasper blinked, looking too confused to give a helpful response. Nip and Pip got into a heated discussion with each other above the gnome and kid's heads.

Owen shouted at the two pixies to stop. He whispered something to Jasper, who nodded. When the boy sat straighter in his seat, he asked, "What do you want to know?"

Mason took out his notebook and pencil. "Tell me how you were running things."

For the most part, Henry got it right when he told us how things worked yesterday. The pixies spelled proxy objects to give out betting info and collect the actual money. Their diminutive size did make them practically invisible to everyone else, allowing Owen and Jasper to run things smoothly.

"If it weren't for another gnome and a fairy with her army

of pixies, we would have gotten away with everything," complained Owen. "I didn't know towns like yours existed."

Pride for our special town filled me to the brim. "Maybe that makes us a whole lot smarter than you thought," I jabbed back.

Clint wouldn't need to pay for a drink for a long time. Juniper earned herself a whole lot of home cooked meals as did her boyfriend Horatio, who had the intelligence to ask for her help. I'd make sure Alison Kate baked whatever any of them wanted for an entire month.

"You know, we've been making a decent living across most of the South," piped up Jasper.

"Shut up, idiot," Owen hissed.

Mason interrupted before all four of them erupted into an all-out brawl. "We want to know who has been the biggest winner all weekend."

"What's in it for us?" The kid leaned forward in his chair. "If we give you what you want, how will that help our current situation?"

As much as I'd like to see someone in authority interfere and try to give the kid a better life as well as rehabilitate the other three to live within the limits of the law, we didn't have time for things to go the way a warden might demand.

"Give us the name and we'll let you go," I proposed.

Mason turned to face me. "You don't have the authority to offer that."

I gritted my teeth in a fake smile. "And we can't delay any

longer." I pointed at the clock on the wall. "See the minutes ticking by?"

The detective frowned, caught in the web of his internal struggle to follow the letter of the law or bend the rules a little to help a dying friend. Without looking up, he grunted, "What she said. But I want the top three winners for your freedom."

Owen smirked again. "And if we give those names to you, we get to leave with all our earnings and nobody arresting us?"

"As long as those names check out to be real." I stood up and placed both hands on the table, leaning forward to intimidate them. "You give us bogus information, and we'll make sure you never see the light of day again." I might have seen one too many police procedurals.

Owen consulted with his associates. The one pixie squeaked a lot of words to the others. Nip took the time to wave at me and blow kisses.

Mason glanced at the clock again. "The offer expires in three, two, one."

"Okay! There's only two names of people who placed bets that always won despite the odds." Owen pointed at me. "Funny enough, if I'm right and you're Birdy Goodwin, then someone won big bucks when they bet on you in the last race."

It took a lot of restraint not to bounce in my seat. My efforts were worth it if we had the key to who might have stolen Lucky's fortune.

Mason held the pencil poised over the paper in his notebook. "I'm ready."

⚜

WE LEFT the odd little gang inside the interrogation room. They'd have to be contained at the station until we checked the validity of their claims.

Once outside the room, I lost all my cool points at once. "Holy unicorn horn, I can't believe it," I sputtered, tugging on Mason's shirt that read "Team Birdy" on the back of it.

"Shh, try to stay calm," the detective said. "At least wait until we're in a more private space before jumping up and down. Still, it is pretty unbelievable."

"Roddy 'Big Mouth' Bass and Franklin 'Fireball' Irving." I whistled long and low. "I knew they were up to something when we overheard them talking after the sauce competition."

"They've been working together all this time to hustle a little money on the side. They're taking a huge risk though, especially attacking Lucky." Mason took out his spell phone.

"Are you calling Nana?" I asked, stretching to look over his shoulder.

"No, I'm texting Ben. We need to dig into their financial backgrounds quickly, and he's the only one with the skills and connections to do so." His fingers flew over the buttons of his phone.

The same loud voice from before barked out from the

back, interrupting us. "Hey! Whoever's standing out there, bring us something to drink."

With a brilliant idea, I covered the detective's mouth to stop him from replying. "Where's your break room?"

Mason pointed in the direction behind me, removing my hand. "Over there. Why? What are you going to do?"

I winked at him. "I've got this."

When I returned, I held one plastic cup of sweet iced tea. "Could you open the door for me?" I asked the detective.

"I don't like you going in there alone," he complained.

"They're locked up. Besides, you're coming with me." I grinned, a little too pleased with my idea of revenge.

Mason unlocked the door and gave me room to walk in first. The rowdy men uttered disgusting comments about me, and I waited until there was a break in their insults and cheesy come-ons.

"You kiss your mamas with those mouths?" I provoked. "Besides, I don't know why you're antagonizing the person bringing you what you asked for."

"Hey." The racer who'd gone after me pushed the others out of the way. "Ain't you that girl? I thought you was hurt."

I looked up and down my body. "No injuries here. Guess you failed to take me out *and* completely trashed your opportunity to win a place in the final exhibition race with the professionals."

"Move over, Cleetus." Earl pushed to the front of the bars, gripping them and shoving his face in between two. "Give us whatever you brought to drink."

I held up the plastic cup. "Here it is."

"That's one cup. Where's the rest of them?" Earl complained.

I waved my forefinger at them. "You asked for a drink. I brought you *a* drink. It's a cold glass of sweet tea, too. Who wants it?"

The men pushed and shoved each other, trying to claim the tea for themselves. I watched their chaos with glee and set the cup on the floor just out of reach. They glared at it from behind the bars.

"What are you doin'?" Cleetus croaked, turning sideways and straining to reach the cup.

"I'm giving you what you asked for. Consider this a free lesson. Don't mess with any of us from Honeysuckle Hollow." I turned around to sashay away and thought of one more thing. "Oh, and boys. If one of you does manage to reach the tea, you might wanna consider this. Am I too much of a lady to have spit in it? Or am I a wicked witch who cast a diuretic hex on it?"

"You can't do this to us." Earl spat on the floor, the glob missing my shoes by a good foot.

"Or," I continued, ignoring his thinly-veiled threat. "Maybe it's just tea. Have fun, fellas." I waved my fingers in a final farewell, leaving the hateful group silently pondering if I'd messed with their desired drink.

Cleetus whispered loud enough for me to hear, "What does *dye-your-attic* mean?" The door closed shut with a metallic thunk, and I burst into uncontrolled giggles.

Mason grabbed my hand and dragged me into his office. He kicked his door shut and hugged me tight. The pressure didn't bother my shoulder at all, and I filed away the idea to research just how strong the magic of pixies really was for another day.

"You are too much, Charli," he declared. "If we didn't have to go find those two ex-racers now, I'd kiss you silly right here on my desk."

His proposal reignited the guilt I'd temporarily been able to avoid. I opened his door and stepped through it before he could complain. "But we do need to talk to Big Mouth and Fireball. Let's go."

If I waited to tell him after we talked to the retired racers, I wasn't technically breaking the promise I'd made to myself. Delaying the inevitable truth gave me a quick reprieve.

I hoped we were on our way to figuring everything out so that the thrill of triumph and saving Lucky's life might overshadow the sting of betrayal.

The finish line loomed ahead, and it was time to lean into the wind to finish strong.

Chapter Eighteen

We arrived back at the event and found almost everyone crowding around the stage. Tucker addressed the audience with a microphone, his bright smile showing off his gleaming white teeth. If I had time, I'd stay to enjoy his success.

My stomach churned with the urgency of our mission. "Where should we start first?" I asked Mason.

The detective escorted me through the throng with a protective arm around me. "I've already contacted Henry, who was supposed to let the others know to look out for Big Mouth and Fireball."

I narrowly avoided a lady holding her toddler, although a bit of the melted ice cream the little girl was enjoying smeared across my shirt sleeve.

"Have you used Lucky's gem to try and locate them?"

When Mason didn't answer me, I stopped in my tracks. "Tell me that's the first thing you did."

"You've been with me since we got out of the car, so no," the detective answered, "I haven't tried."

"Why not?" My voice got a little too loud, and a few heads turned in our direction.

Mason pulled me into his body and whispered in my ear, "Because whatever I was able to do before isn't working anymore. When I hold the sapphire, I feel absolutely nothing. And I didn't want to tell you because you had enough you were dealing with."

There was a time and place for chivalry, and now wasn't it. "We don't have a choice. You need to try right now," I hissed back.

We chose a spot at the back of the crowd and checked to see if anybody else watched us. Mason dug in his pocket and pulled out the fabric-covered jewel. When the blue stone glittered in the palm of his hand, he did everything I taught him.

After only a minute passed, he opened his eyes, grunting in frustration. "See, it's not working."

"You must be doing something wrong or different. Here, let me hold the sapphire and show you how again." I plucked the stone with my fingertips and cradled it in my hand.

Something buzzed in the back of my head, and the jewel vibrated in my hand. "This used to be embedded in the hilt of Lucky's sword," I exhaled.

"Lucky owns a sword?" Mason stared at me, perplexed.

Drawing in a quick breath, I closed my eyes and visualized clear images that matched the story the leprechaun had told Dash and me. Power and success pulsed through the heart of the gem that had once adorned the weapon called Caladbolg. Fights and battles gave way to the image of a beautiful woman with flowing red hair wearing a crown.

"Queen Medb," I whispered.

"What are you talking about, Charli? You're making no sense." Mason shook me by my shoulders, and the images faded away.

I stumbled forward, sweat soaking my shirt. "Get me something to eat or drink," I rasped out, clutching my chest and willing my heart to slow down.

The detective first took the sapphire away from me, wrapping it up in the fabric again and placing it in his pocket. I stayed put until he brought me back a full cup of iced tea. It disappeared down my throat in only a few gulps.

"Did you just connect the jewel to Lucky?" Mason asked.

I nodded, wiping the last dribble of tea off my chin. "Yes. It showed me things I wish I could tell you about, but I made a promise."

My brief vision of Lucky's former life deepened my desperation to find his luck and help him live until my grandchildren's children could listen to his stories. But the stone had only shown me his past, not right now when we needed help the most.

"If this means your magic is returning to you, then you

should use it again to find Big Mouth and Fireball." His hand went to his pocket, but I stopped him.

I pulled my sweat-soaked shirt away from my body and let it fall back with a sticky *thwop* on my chest. "Based on how I'm feeling a little shaky, I don't think me trying again is a good idea. It was one connection and to the wrong time period. If we're going to find the retired racers, we need to figure out the most likely place they'd be."

The audience clapped, and I stood on my tiptoes to see someone walking across the stage and accepting a small trophy from Nana. Tucker had arranged for the winners of the barbecue competition to be announced before the finale of the entire weekend with the retired broom racers flying in an exhibition competition. The one I had qualified to participate in.

I grasped Mason's hand and dragged him forward. "We need to get closer to the stage."

If either Big Mouth's or Fireball's barbecue teams won something, they'd show up on the stage. If that didn't happen, there was one more opportunity to know exactly where they'd be, and I had a reason to be right up close to both of them.

The detective and I pushed our way through the crowd until we got to the very front. Clementine spotted me and came over. "Isn't he doing great?" she gushed, beaming up at her husband.

"He really is, Clem." I gave her a quick side hug. "Can you do me a favor and tell Tucker to stall things for a moment? I need to get my grandmother's attention."

"Sure," my cousin agreed. "Is everything okay?"

"It will be." I waited for Tucker to spot his wife and let her give the message. He flashed me a disapproving glance but did as she asked.

The new council member put on a good show. "Ladies and gentlemen, I'd like to take a minute to give a brief history of our fair town and how we put together this entire event."

I ran up to the front of the stage. "Psst, Nana." Calling her over, I talked as fast as possible, explaining the new plan.

"You want me to completely ignore the list of actual winners and call out Big Mouth Bass's team as one of them?" she checked. "And why do you look like something the cat dragged in?"

"It doesn't matter," I brushed her questions off. "And try to get Fireball and his team up there, too. It's important to get both racers on stage and keep them there. If you don't want to lie, then make up a new category for Big Mouth's team to win, like best brisket." Based on his bragging on the first night, it might not be a complete falsehood.

"Brisket, right." My grandmother concentrated to remember my point. "And what about Fireball?"

My mind raced to find anything to lure him to where we wanted him, too. "His team already won in the barbecue sauce category. Call him up to receive more attention. He'll love that."

Nana agreed with a nod. "What happens after they both get to the stage?"

"Keep them there," I insisted. "Don't let them leave until Mason and I talk to them."

Tucker waved furiously and called out my grandmother's name. He couldn't stall for much longer.

Nana nodded. "Consider it done. I hope you and your detective know what you're doing." She backed away and took her place beside the table full of shiny trophies, indicating for Tucker to proceed.

Mason got caught up quickly with my plan, and he texted Zeke to help surround the stage on all sides. I clenched my hands into fists, impatiently waiting for Nana to find her moment. By the time the trophy table was down to the last few awards, I knew she couldn't wait any longer.

"Come on, Nana," I urged, bouncing on my feet..

Keeping her composure and air of authority about her, my grandmother interrupted the proceedings. "Before we go any further, I think we all need to give a warm round of applause to Tucker Hawthorne, our newest town council member. Because of him, this weekend has been a huge success."

Cheers and applause spread through the crowd, and I watched my cousin jumping up and down next to her stern mother. Aunt Nora's mouth rested in a disapproving bow. She ignored her excited daughter, choosing to talk instead to a few snooty people standing beside her, who weren't clapping either.

"And if Tucker wouldn't mind, I'd like a chance to call out a couple of the winners myself." She ignored the younger council member's disappointment and acted like she read off the piece of paper she held in her hand. "First up, I'd like to congratulate the Texas Hexes team captained by good ol' Roddy 'Big Mouth' Bass, one of our star racers. His team won the best brisket category. Come on up here, Big Mouth, and bring the rest of your team with you."

A lot of whooping and hollering rose from the back of the crowd, and a group of guys belted out, "Deep in the Heart of Texas," as they weaved their way to the stage. Big Mouth stuck his head out from behind a backstage curtain. With reluctant steps, he joined his team to accept their reward.

Nana shot a worried glance at me and fiddled around with all the trophies left on the table. "Oh my, it looks like we've misplaced your trophy. But that doesn't matter, we can get that to you afterwards. Let's hear it for the team with the best brisket."

Big Mouth's look of confusion disappeared, and his laugh boomed across the stage. "You're darn tootin' we've got the best brisket." He fashioned his hands into guns and shot them in the air like an overgrown cowboy, whooping louder than anybody else.

"That's one down," whispered Mason. "I gotta say, Owen was definitely wrong about him being the smartest in the room." He placed a hand on my lower back to steady me as we waited for Nana to set the trap for our other suspect.

She waved Tucker off when he tried to take the microphone back. "And we really should recognize one of the earliest winners in the competition. Please welcome to the stage Franklin 'Fireball' Irving and his team from Kansas City who won for best barbecue sauce. Let's get them up here on the—"

A sharp scream ripped through the air and interrupted the awards ceremony. A hesitant hush fell over the crowd, but the temporary silence shattered with a second horrified shriek.

Mason and I ignored Tucker's instructions for everybody to say where they were, and we rushed to find the source of the person wailing for help. We pushed ahead of other nosy onlookers and made it to the area backstage.

A small group clustered around on the ground, and I spotted a pair of cowboy boots peeking out from the mass. The detective instructed everyone to back up, and I pressed forward enough to identify who it was. Fireball Irving lay sprawled out on the grass. His eyes and mouth were wide open, frozen in a scream. We didn't have to wait for Doc Andrews to arrive. I knew in an instant the retired racer was dead.

Another body lay crumpled next to him. Rita Ryder stirred and attempted to sit up. Mason took over the scene and insisted she take it easy until the doctor arrived.

Nana rushed off the back of the stage and joined us. "What happened?"

I pointed at Fireball, refusing to look at his contorted face. "He's dead and Rita's hurt."

My grandmother cursed under her breath. "Do you think it might be the work of the same person who hurt Lucky?"

Mason interrupted, calling me over. "You need to hear this, too." He prompted the lady racer to start over.

Rita insisted on sitting up, refusing any help from Zeke. "I'm fine, young man. I didn't get to be as successful of a racer as I was without getting a few bruises." She rubbed the back of her head and winced. "Granted, this feels a little more like someone pierced my head with a needle. How's Fireball?"

When we didn't answer her, she narrowed her eyes, watching Mason and I exchange knowing glances. Rita tried to get to her feet, but her knees buckled, and she crashed on the ground. Crawling, she made it inch by inch until she fell across the dead racer's body.

"No, no, no, no," she wailed, tears brimming in her eyes. "Why'd it have to happen to him?"

"What's going on?" Billy Ray approached us, confusion spreading on his face. "Is that Fireball? What happened?"

A wild thought took root in my head. I spun on my heels and confronted the new arrival. "Where have you been?"

"Charli, leave him alone," Nana insisted.

"Not until he tells us where he's been. If those two racers were attacked, why wasn't he?" I looked to Mason for back up.

Billy Ray couldn't take his eyes off the lifeless body. "I left to go use the facilities. I wasn't here when whatever happened occurred."

"Which means you could have done it," I accused, holding my finger in the air.

Nana grabbed me and pulled me away. "What do you think you're doing, attacking him like that?"

Although it pained me to stand up to my grandmother,

she needed to accept the truth. "He wasn't the one attacked, they were. Don't you want to know who did it? And if Billy Ray's still okay, then he must be considered as the one who did it."

Nana's face dropped as she pondered my point. "It's just, I know him. He wouldn't hurt anybody."

Placing a hand on her shoulder, I tried to offer her a little support. "I know, Nana. I'm sorry."

"Wait." Her eyes sparkled in defiance. "He wasn't the only racer not attacked. Big Mouth Bass was on stage just like you asked when it happened. Maybe he's the culprit."

I groaned. Mason and I had completely forgotten about the larger-than-life racer and my little trap. Rushing back to the scene that now had more observers gathered around, I found the detective writing down the details that Rita gave him.

"Mason, we forgot about Big Mouth," I interrupted.

The detective excused himself and took out his spell phone. "I should call Flint and tell him to close the border and lock everything down."

"So-o-o," Aunt Nora crooned from the side. "Everything isn't as hunky dory as you'd like us to believe, is it Vivian? I'm sure my new friends would love to hear all about whatever it is you've been trying to keep secret."

One of the people she escorted jumped back. "Is that a dead body?"

A guy wearing a suit despite the heat from the hot sun stepped forward. "I think we deserve an explanation."

There was a mighty scramble to figure out who should start the explanations between Mason, my grandmother, Tucker, and the newly arrived doctor. Aunt Nora stood back with a smug smile on her face, enjoying the chaos.

The stranger in the suit challenged a little harder. "I've heard that there's also a group of men being detained in a cell at the warden station for no reason."

"Oh, there's a reason," I piped up.

"Have they been formally charged with something?" Suit ignored me and addressed Mason in a lilting hoity-toity Southern accent. "If not, then I have to wonder how efficient your law enforcement can really be to handle a murder of this magnitude."

Offended, I blurted out, "We've solved a whole bunch of murders here."

Nana shot me an alarmed glare, and I realized my mistake too late.

The antagonizer grinned at me and turned to address the others in the group. "I believe those of you from the regional council should go ahead and vote now for Charleston to take over Honeysuckle Hollow so that we can get rid of the chaos and fix everything that's wrong here."

Nana dropped her professional demeanor and poked an angry finger in the suited man's chest while blasting him with words. Mason did his best to defend the wardens and the work they did to the outside council members. Too stunned to jump in, I watched the future of our town and my friend's life go up in flames.

Rita interrupted everyone. "Listen up. Here's the skinny. Someone attacked me from behind. I don't know who it was, so I'm not going to be any help figuring that part out. Whoever it was seems to have taken my friend's life in the process."

"Who put her in charge?" asked Mason.

The female racer impressed the heck out of me. "Shh, she's doing a good job taking the lead." Every single person who Aunt Nora had brought with her clung to every word Rita said.

"Right now, only a few of us know that somebody's been killed, but we're not going to be able to keep it a secret for long," the lady racer continued. "Everybody who's here is expecting the weekend to end with a fun race between retired racers and a couple of amateurs who qualified to compete. Why don't we admit that Fireball is gone and dedicate the race in his honor in front of the audience? It will cover up what actually happened and give the local wardens a chance to figure things out."

I almost applauded her when she finished. She commanded attention and respect in everything she did. And what she proposed made a whole lot of sense. It solved the PR problem Nana faced and provided the space for us to keep searching for the attacker. I spotted Fireball's cowboy boots again. Now we were searching for a killer.

Mason's spell phone rang, and he frowned while he took the call. "You got him? You sure? We'll be right there." The detective pulled my grandmother and me aside. "That was

Flint. He stopped Big Mouth Bass at the border and has him detained at the gate."

Nana's shoulders slumped in relief. "That's a good piece of news. You two, go do what you were going to do in the first place with that man. I think Rita's plan is the best we've got and may be our only chance to salvage Honeysuckle. I'll make sure Zeke takes charge of the scene here while Rita comes with me to make her announcement on stage."

Mason and I started to leave, but Rita called out my name. She moved with pained steps to catch up to me.

"Should you be racing today?" I asked.

"I'll be fine. We girls are tough. Here, I intended to give this to you." She held out a pair of goggles.

I fell in love with her a little harder at her kind gesture. "Wow, that's a big gift. Would you sign them for me?"

She chuckled and winced, touching the side of her head. "They're not my goggles. I mean, they were, but now they're yours. They're an extra pair I brought with me, but I think you should use them in the final race."

"Thank you so much." I reached out to take the goggles. As soon as my hand touched them, tingles of power crawled up my fingers.

Rita saw my surprised reaction and winked. "Oh, I may have spellcast them with a little extra juice to help you out. Like I said, we girls have to stick together."

"I'm honored," I uttered.

Mason plastered a smile on his lips. "Flint's waiting for us. We need to go."

I shouted over my shoulder one more thanks and followed after the detective. Even with a dead body added to the mix, I couldn't help but give in to hope, letting it clear the doubt and fear from my heart.

If all went well, we were about to cross the finish line.

Chapter Nineteen

✿❦✿

Big Mouth struggled to get loose from the ropes tying his pudgy hands behind his back while sitting on a tree stump. He grunted, unable to speak because of a piece of duct tape slapped across his mouth. The ex-racer spotted us and shouted unintelligible words that, by the sound of them, weren't very friendly.

Flint greeted Mason and me while his brother Clint threatened to throw tape on other hairier parts of the racer. The spectacle distracted us for an extra minute.

"Why is he all tied up like that?" asked the detective.

Flint crossed his arms. "Because he's too big to fit in our makeshift guardhouse. Although he isn't too big to get caught. Clint and me found him trying to cross at the edge of the southwest woods."

The gnome's brother joined us. "The fool flew his broom

right into the border line. The wood of it splintered since it took the brunt of the shield magic. If he had been leaning a little further forward..." Clint mimed Big Mouth's head exploding.

Having heard what might have happened to him, the racer's struggle renewed, and he wiggled his way right off the stump. His corpulent body flopped around like a blubbery whale out of water.

"Is he the one who hurt Lucky?" Flint clenched his small fists.

"That's what we're here to find out." Mason approached the red-faced racer. "If I help you back onto the seat and take off the tape, will you behave?"

Big Mouth did his best to hurl insults at the detective through the tape. Clint pushed Mason out of the way and kicked the racer in his flabby stomach.

"Clint," I cried out.

"He'll get a lot more if he doesn't tell us what he did to our friend," threatened the small gnome in a high-pitched voice. "You going to arrest me, Detective?"

Mason shook his head. "No, but don't do it again. Charli, help me out."

It took us a good five minutes to hoist the racer back to his seated position. Leaves hung off the wispy hairs in the middle of Big Mouth's bald head. His cowboy hat lay nearby, and I refused to put it back into place.

The detective ripped off the tape, and Big Mouth howled.

"Get over it, Mr. Bass." Even Mason's professionalism had its limits.

"You're making a huge mistake," Big Mouth countered. "I swear, it's not me you want."

I picked up the hat and dusted the dirt and leaves off it. "Why do you think we're chasing after you?"

"If you aren't, then for the love of all that's magical, you've got to let me leave," he begged.

"Why? So you can get away with attacking a friend of ours. Or killing the one who seemed to be your bestie?" My eyes stayed glued to the racer's face, wanting to see the guilt overwhelm him.

His fear gave way to sorrow and his voice wavered with deep emotion. "Are you tellin' me that Fireball's dead?"

"Did you kill him?" Mason knew we didn't have time to draw out a formal investigation. We needed answers and had to get them as quickly as possible.

Big Mouth lurched forward, attempting to stand on his own. The momentum threw him off balance, and he fell to the ground face first.

"I would never. He was my closest friend." To my surprise, the big guy wailed a guttural cry so pitiful, it melted a little of my anger.

The two gnome brothers stood back and watched in disgust while Mason scratched the back of his head. "I'll admit, I'm not sure how to proceed."

We were so close to figuring things out, and we had no time for sentimentality. Using my shoulder and pushing hard,

I heaved the racer over onto his back. Rivulets of tears washed down his dirty face.

"I didn't mean to get him into things so deep," Big Mouth moaned. "I had a good thing going for years. But Fireball could never stay on the straight and narrow for very long. Instead of accepting the odd dollar here and there from me, he wanted in."

"On what?" I pressed.

Big Mouth closed his eyes and blew out a long breath. "Ever since I turned professional, not many of the actual races were straight."

Mason took a step closer. "You cheated?"

The big guy nodded. "It was little things at first. Totally harmless. Nothing that would do permanent damage. I would help with the set up and then profit off of the winnings I placed knowing the final outcome. We did a good job covering our tracks. Sometimes, we lost just to make sure we weren't caught. But for the most part, we made big bucks together. Being here with the barbecue and racing competition, well, I guess we fell back into our old ways."

Mason wrote down all the details, so I asked the important question. "You keep saying 'we.' Do you mean you and Fireball?"

Big Mouth frowned. "We brought Fireball in this weekend because he could help win more money. And if something happened—"

"Then he could be a decent scapegoat. Some best friend

you are," finished Clint. He charged to kick the racer again, and I held him back.

"But if it's not Fireball that you partnered with, then it has to be another racer." I hated to call out the name I knew would break Nana's heart. "Is it Billy Ray?"

Big Mouth scoffed, and a bit of dirt and spit dribbled from the corner of his lips. "That stiff? I mean, he's an all right kind of guy, but he wouldn't drag a toe out of line. He's the biggest rule follower of them all. If Mud Dobber ever found out, he would have reported us for sure, even if it meant that some of the races he won would be disqualified."

Relieved I didn't have to tell my grandmother that her boyfriend was involved, I looked to Mason to give the last push.

"Then who is your partner?" he asked.

"Rita Ryder." The large racer's words hung in the still air.

My ears heard the words, but my brain refused to accept them. "It can't be her. She was attacked at the same time Fireball was."

"It'd be a cold day in Hades if that woman was tellin' the truth," exclaimed Big Mouth. "Did she cry big tears and make you feel sorry for her and everything? Rita is the biggest fake of them all. And if she can't make you believe with her actions, she sure as shinola can force your brain to accept it. I've never met a witch with bigger psychic abilities than her. It's why you've got to let me go."

Flint leaned over the beached racer so he could be seen. "You're not going anywhere. If I have to, I'll beef up the border shield until you'll explode into oblivion if you try to leave."

Mason shepherded the angry gnome away from Big Mouth. "I'll see if I can move you to more comfortable quarters, but first I want you to start from the beginning. Explain everything Rita does and how she involved you."

Big Mouth burst like a thin balloon filled with too much air. Every single detail tumbled out from his lips. Rita had grown up in a foster system that somehow lost her, so she'd never registered her magic. Cleverer than most, she'd used her powers to survive, and when she fell in love with broom racing, she'd wielded them to rise within the ranks of the sport.

With another racer involved, Rita could trap other competitors and push her psychic powers into their minds to either make them forget things or to mess with their sense of direction. Big Mouth revealed all kinds of ways she'd manipulated races, and he acted as the friendly trusted friend who lured others for her to use or would place bets based on how she affected the races.

"The only reason either of us stopped was because our bodies let us down." He poked his finger into his rotund middle. "I can still fly, but I'm not going to be winning anything ever again."

Off in the distance, a horn blared, and the cheers of the crowd floated in the air.

"They must be preparing for the final race." I'd left the

goggles Rita had given me in the patrol car. "I'm going to miss it."

"Not if we finish up here fast." Mason crouched down to get as close as possible to Big Mouth. "Were you involved in Lucky getting attacked?"

"That was Fireball's job. He was the one who set off the big explosion to pull everyone's attention. Rita used her powers to steal the luck off the leprechaun." The racer grinned for a second. "Man, we couldn't get one bet wrong after that."

Clint lunged forward and slapped the racer's face. "She took something that didn't belong to her. If the law don't punish you, you can be sure I'll make it my mission in life you get what you deserve."

For a gnome who worked with plants and greenery, he possessed a fiery disposition. I made a quick mental note never to get on his bad side.

"What's her plan now?" I asked, adrenaline pumping my heart rate faster.

Big Mouth flinched, expecting another slap. "I don't know. But I can tell you she thinks the gold coin she's keeping in her pocket will keep her out of any trouble."

Bingo! Now we had something to work with. Mason must have thought the same thing because he closed his notebook and blurted out instructions to the two gnomes to keep the racer secured until he came back for him.

"Hey, you said you would take me somewhere comfortable," Big Mouth complained.

I wanted to tell him that murderers didn't always get what they wanted. He had a hand in Lucky's predicament, but he didn't know that the leprechaun might die if I didn't find Rita Ryder and retrieve the lucky coin before her stolen good fortune helped her escape.

"Hang out here and see if a genie comes along to grant your wish," I called out, rushing to get into Mason's car.

I slammed the door and turned to the detective. "We never spent enough time interpreting what Ginny predicted. All we could focus on was the possibility of Lucky dying. But she's been telling us all along how things are supposed to end."

Mason cut the engine on and threw it into drive. We hurdled down the canopied road and turned off to drive through the edge of the field. "How are things going to end?" he asked.

I grabbed his broom from the backseat where I'd left it after I crashed during my race. "First, I'm gonna get on that starting line. Then, I'm gonna lean into the wind and soar as fast as possible until I beat Rita Ryder. In other words, I intend to fly for the win."

Chapter Twenty

J umping out of the car, I sprinted for the race. Mason carried the broom for me so I could hustle a little faster. We broke through a line of fans and made it to the starting line right when the official raised his hand in the air.

My name and number flashed on the scoreboard at the same time he announced, "Get set. Go!"

Rita, Billy Ray, and Eric took off. Without the other racers, the competition wouldn't be as difficult, except for the fact I was already behind before I even started. It would take everything I had in me to catch up to two professionals.

With shaking fingers, I fixed the goggles Rita had given me over my eyes and yanked the broom out of Mason's grasp. I threw a leg over and kicked off the ground.

Mason startled me when he patted my hip, ignoring the

official's warning about my impending disqualification if he didn't leave. "You don't need luck to do this, Charli. Focus on catching up to her and trust that you won't be alone." Mason gave me a quick peck on the cheek and smacked my behind. "Get going."

I pitched forward with less grace than I'd had in the first two races. Already way behind, I didn't have time to doubt myself. Leaning over the wooden handle, I pushed the broom and my body to their limits.

I closed in on the first racer, Eric Mosely, a hometown favorite. The kid had good skills and could probably make a career as a professional in a few years with some help. But he couldn't keep up with Rita or Billy Ray. My mission spurred me on, and I forced as much magic as I could down into the wood of the broom handle. I zoomed around my former student with unapologetic dexterity.

"Come on. This is the last time, I promise," I begged the flying object underneath me.

When I followed the course and passed through the opening into the woods, spots of dappled sunlight flickered through the canopy of leaves. It took me a second to notice the green line that showed me the way was blinking on and off. At full speed, if my guided path disappeared, I would be flying blind.

"Thanks a lot, Rita," I cried out, not caring that she couldn't hear me from so far ahead.

A strong tingle of magic pulsed in my pocket. Instinct allowed my hand to release the broom handle and touch the strange lump. Power rippled through my fingers and across my entire body. Instead of freaking out, I grinned, recognizing my own magic flaring back to life.

The wonky green line vanished from my sight, but I no longer needed it. Energized to feel my magic rekindle inside me, I cast the quickest spell I could come up with. *"Get Lucky's fortune that she stole. Help me catch her blackened soul."*

Relief and happiness caused tears to pool in my eyes when a golden thread glimmered and stretched in front of me. Binding the connection to me, I willed it to pull me forward. With a loud whoop, I whipped off Rita's damaged gift and threw it into the forest bed passing below me. I'd bet on my magic beating out enchanted goggles any day.

Up ahead, I detected one racer's outline zipping through the brush and tree trunks. I tried to force myself to move faster, but the broom faltered in the air, dipping up and down. In all the haste of the day and consumed by the need to find Rita, I didn't question whether or not I should fly. The fact that my power was back thrilled me, but its return must mean I no longer possessed Mason's flying skills.

The thread between me and Rita stretched thinner, and I panicked. If I couldn't master flying in the next few seconds, I might lose her. Trusting that Big Mouth told the truth and Rita intended to use Lucky's stolen fortune in her favor to get away, I had no choice but to pull up my big girl panties and fly the heck out of the broom on my own.

Leaning forward again, I opened myself to the indescribable pull of the object Rita controlled and let the magical connection guide me. In the spur of the moment, I tied the same glowing thread to the wooden handle itself. The broom stopped wavering underneath me and zipped a little faster and with more purpose.

Unfortunately, the magical connection didn't understand that I needed to stay on the cleared path of the race course. It demanded I follow the shortest trail possible, and the broom obeyed it, unaware it took us deeper into the woods. I ducked out of the way of the first low-hanging branch just in time.

"That was close." Glancing over my shoulder, I marveled at my luck.

When I turned back around, I squealed and held a hand up to protect my face. The broom carried me right through a group of bushes and pine saplings. I squeezed my thighs a little tighter to stay on board, and my left hand pounded from gripping so hard.

No longer on the right path for the race, I had no reason to hesitate. If I concentrated hard enough, I could weave in and out of the woods to reach the bright opening of the field straight ahead. Refusing to give into the fear bubbling inside of me, I bobbed back and forth, combining my magic with my experience from the last two races to help me wing through the forest.

My confidence faltered when the thread of connection changed course. Instead of stretching out in front of me, it banked right, arcing and moving like the second hand of a watch. Unsure of what to do, I slowed my pace, and twisted my head around until the thread of connection tugged on me in the opposite direction. Instead of me pursuing Rita, she gained the upper hand, flying right behind me.

"Pixie poop," I exclaimed, losing my momentum to turn around and find her.

The glowing thread shortened, and a blur closed in fast on my right. A woman's evil laugh echoed through the woods, and I knew Rita was playing with me. I lurched forward to match her speed when she caught me.

The lady racer pulled up close, avoiding brush and branches with ease as if it was child's play. "I see you figured out the goggles I gave you weren't meant to help."

I dodged a particularly tall sapling, swinging wide to the left. Rita stayed parallel to me, refusing to make her next move.

"Once a cheater, always a cheater," I taunted, banking in her direction to knock her off balance.

Although I wanted to catch Rita, since I was off course, I didn't know how anybody would find us. And if she managed to get me off the broom out here alone, there was no telling how she would use her psychic magic on me. I needed every single one of my memories to stay intact.

The professional racer snorted in derision. "Do you really think an amateur like you, who hasn't finished a race in the upright position, can take me on? Please. Give up, Charli." She saluted and dashed away, dodging the trees with a smooth deftness I envied.

I couldn't let her win, even if she was no longer in the

official race. The one we still competed in counted for far more.

Something the gnome brothers had said rung in my ears. If I could push her to the new extended boundary, maybe even into it, I might be able to stop her. If Flint's descriptions were true, I could force her into the border, either obliterating her mode of transportation or hurting her enough to slow her down. If her head blew up like Clint implied, I wouldn't shed any tears.

The woods we were in had to be the ones that sat outside our normal borders as a natural barrier to unwanted guests. If I could flank her on her left and keep her from maneuvering around me, I would be able to either force her into the shield at the western side of the woods or bring her out into the more immediate land beyond the southwestern line of trees. If my mental calculations weren't off, I might have a secret weapon I could use waiting in the clearing.

The Founders' tree grew in the field close to where this woodland ended. Having used its magic before to protect our town, I hoped it would allow me to tap into its power one more time. A lot of *if*'s hung in the balance for me to succeed, but I didn't have a choice but to cling to hope and fly my behind off.

I took a deliberate sharp angled detour to the left to swing outside of her peripheral vision. It almost did me in trying to watch Rita and look out for tree-like obstacles at the same time. When I saw my best opening, I zoomed on the diagonal until I pulled up beside the racer.

"Oh, Charli, you're still trying? I respect your moxie, girl, but you're not going to win any prizes." Rita tapped a spot right in the middle of her chest. "I've got luck on my side."

We both rose up and over a downed tree, and Rita swerved in an attempt to slam into my body. If I flinched for even a second, she might succeed in knocking me off. Instead of moving out of the way, I leaned in and aimed to hit her. Our bodies collided again and again, each time a little harder. I had no explanation as to how I remained on my broom other than the sheer will to make it to the Founders' tree.

"You stupid idiot." Rita rammed me so hard, both of our brooms tilted and wobbled.

"You'll knock us both off," I yelled, trying to swat her away.

Occupied with the task of staying upright, we both missed the oncoming holly bush. It wedged in between us, its branches and pointy leaves scraping our skin. I managed to stay on my broom, but felt the air blowing over open cuts and scratches.

The bright light of the sun filtered through the space between the trees ahead of us, and my heart leapt. In only a few more seconds, we'd burst out into the field on a direct line to the Founders' tree. Rita flew straight only a few clicks in front of me. She tried to shake me off, but I remained glued to her tail.

Without the goggles, the sun blinded me when we made it out of the woods. Now that I'd gotten Rita to where I wanted her to be, I had to figure out how to get as close to the special tree as possible and then stop her. A good old-fashioned hex might do the trick, but with all my energy being spent on wielding my renewed magic and flying the broom, I didn't know how much oomph it would have.

A gray shadow appeared on my right flank, and I glanced over to see a massive wolf with golden eyes running at full speed next to me. It tilted its head for me to know exactly who it was and took off after Rita.

The wolf's paws lifted off the ground as it vaulted into the air. The animal had its prey in its sight, but he attacked too soon.

I screamed out with all my might, "Dash, no!"

In one gigantic leap, he knocked the witch off her broom and sent her tumbling across the ground. Dash's wolf crashed too, having chosen the explosion of a chaotic attack over a controlled take down of his prey.

With my magic draining me and not an ounce of Mason's flying powers remained, my sudden landing went predictably wrong, but I'd gotten used to pain when I touched down. There was no time to moan or check how hurt I might be. I had to get up to make sure Rita hadn't recovered yet. My rattled brain struggled to come up with a brilliant next step to save the day while I worked my way off the ground.

I rolled on my side, and the lump in my pocket pressed into my hip. Making it to a shaky standing position, I reached inside my pants and touched the familiar cloth. Another prickle of power danced over my fingers, and the thread of connection pulsed strong and unwavering.

"I could kiss you!" I shouted into the air, silently thanking Mason for sneaking the sapphire into my pocket.

Standing up, I unwrapped the jewel with my fingers and held it in my palm. The blue glittered with so much brilliance, I almost had to shade my eyes. Somehow, it recognized the nearness of Lucky's fortune. Not sure of how the gem would come into play, I placed it back in my pocket for safe keeping.

With Rita still crumpled on the ground, I had limited time to try to strip her of the gold coin she used to contain the leprechaun's luck. I stomped over to her, pausing about a foot away to first do a visual check on her condition. Her chest rose and fell at a rapid pace, so she hadn't died. Holding my own breath, I gathered my courage and scooted closer. I kicked her foot once to see if she would react. The racer's body lay still and unmoving.

Working my way around to where her head lay, I crouched down and leaned over her face. She'd touched her chest when she talked about luck being on her side, so I gambled on finding the coin hanging around her neck by a chain. My breath quickened, and I rubbed my fingers together in anticipation of grabbing the necklace and ripping it off her.

Just as I got close enough to move her shirt out of the way, Rita's hand shot up and grabbed me by my hair. She yanked hard, pulling my head closer to hers, enjoying my yowls of pain.

"You lose," she hissed through her bloody split lip.

"No, you do. Let go of Charli." Mason hovered close to us

on another broom. He got off and held out his hand in front of him, summoning power at his command. "Now."

Rita's body shook, and I checked to see what caused her convulsions. Her amused chuckles morphed into uncontrolled cackles, proving how far she'd lost her mind.

She released my hair. "Well, this will be interesting."

I clambered away, fear of what she might do next making me forget about taking the coin away from her. "Why?"

Mason warned her to stay still, but Rita rolled over anyway and smiled, showing off her bloody mouth and teeth.

"Because I finally get to find out just how lucky I am."

Chapter Twenty-One

✦✦✦

"Aw, the detective has come to save his maiden fair," teased Rita. "I didn't take you for a damsel-in-distress type, Charli."

The racer stood up slowly, placing her hands in the air with a wry grin. Only a fool would believe she intended to surrender. Neither Mason nor I were fools.

I scurried backwards to put some distance between me and the crazy witch until something warm and furry blocked my escape. A growl rumbled and vibrated against my back, and now I was the one smiling.

Mason willed magic to crackle across his fingertips. "This is your last warning. Get down on the ground with your hands behind your head."

Rita didn't budge. She lowered her arms and placed one hand on her hip. "Looks like I get to play a little before I leave. Who should I mess. With. First?" She pointed at each one of us while toying with her choices.

Dash's wolf pushed against my body, preparing me to expect another attack. His lip curled up in a snarl, and I rolled out of the way.

"Uh, uh, uh, wolf boy." Rita snapped her fingers and searing pain pierced my head, blinding me.

Mason cried out and grabbed his temples. Dash's wolf whimpered and lay low to the ground, his paws covering his snout.

The ex-racer laughed, pulling on the chain around her neck and revealing the gold coin. "I've never tried a psychic attack on three people at once, but something told me I'd get my way. Oh, excuse me, two people and a wolf. I think it's about time you shifted back, don't you?" She snapped again.

Dash's animal yowled and cowered as low as its body would go. The air around him shimmered and flickered with power. Gray fur receded and the muzzle shortened. His wolf howl morphed into a human groan of pain from the forced shift. Dash's body curled in the fetal position and his face contorted in agony.

Rita stared with no shame at the shifter's nakedness. "If I had more time at my disposal, I might try to turn you into my own personal pooch." She blew a kiss at Dash.

Hot fury boiled in my veins, dulling the pain she caused. "Big Mouth told us everything," I gritted. "We know you killed Fireball."

If I could distract her by talking, then maybe she wouldn't

be able to affect all three of us. I was willing to take the brunt
of her powers if it meant Mason or Dash could take her down.

Rita shrugged. "It only took him a few decades to finally
earn his nickname. If the big oaf hadn't been called to the
stage, I would have wiped his memory of his entire
association with me. And don't think because I'm talking with
you that you've distracted me."

A hundred elephants stomped my brain into a pulp. I
clasped my head, trying to keep it from exploding from the
torment. Maybe it was a bad idea to call attention to myself. I
lurched forward and braced myself against the ground.

My fingers dug into grass and dirt. We were farther away
from the Founders' tree than I'd intended. I could try and use
what was left of my magic to call to its power even from this
distance. But I needed my head to stop pounding for one
second.

Rita rolled her shoulders back and stretched her neck
from side to side. "You know, it's been *murder* having to hide
my true strength all these years. Sure, a little mind
manipulation here and there did the trick, but it wasn't very...
what's the word?" She flourished her fingers, curling them to
make a fist, and Mason dropped to his knees. "Satisfying."

Nana had hammered the lesson into me that if a witch
used magic to harm others, it took a toll on them. Frosted
fairy wings, I'd taught that to a couple of spell classes. And
after seeing what Hollis's actions did to him, I knew the truth
of the consequences. So why was Rita not a withering husk?

"That's a good question, and yes, I can read your mind

because you're so weak that you can't keep me out." Her shoes appeared in my sight when she stood right above my prostrate body. "And since I won't be here long, I'll give you a real gift and tell you the truth."

The pain in my head eased up, and I panted hard to recover. She lifted my chin with her fingers, and I had no choice but to watch her smug explanation.

"My early life was less than pleasant. No fairy tale for me and my magic. As soon as I could, I skipped out of the foster system and survived on my own. Little by little, I experimented to find the limits of my power. When none came, I did what I wanted to sustain the life I created." She stared off into the distance, caught in her memories.

Mason grunted. "A hard childhood doesn't justify what you've done."

Rita made a motion with her hand, closing her fingers to her thumb. "No more talking for you, Detective. It's rude to interrupt." She rolled her eyes with dramatic effect. "Men. Always trying to interfere in our lives, am I right? Now, where was I?"

Dash's eyes blinked open, glowing gold and irate. He remained still but he kept the insane racer locked in his line of sight.

"You were explaining to me why you're still so healthy despite hurting others with your talents," I said, participating in her game but hopefully preparing the chance for the three of us to take her by surprise.

"Oh, right. The fact is, I'm not." She pointed at her chest. "Cancer. Stage four. I'm dying, Charli."

"Then why in the hell are you still hurting people? Killing them?" I screamed. None of it made any sense.

Rita crouched down to my eye-level. "Because I can. And if I don't have long to live, then I'm going to go out my way. I'll take what I can and leave a path of destruction in my wake. I didn't expect some backwards podunk town like yours to be the starting point, but it'll do just fine."

As she leaned forward, a cocky smile spreading on her lips, the gold coin swung away from her body. With one quick swoop, I could take it from her. I drew in a breath and prepared to snatch it.

Dash chose that moment to attack her again in his human form. Rita scrambled away from me, and I hit the ground in frustration at the missed opportunity. He failed to tackle her with his full body, but his shoulder caught her in the chest, knocking her onto her butt. The throbbing in my head stopped, and I breathed a sigh of relief.

Mason recovered at the same time and pushed himself off the ground. He raised his hand in the air and took aim. "With the authority of the wardens, I order you to—"

Rita chuckled ruefully. "Oh, please." With a snap, Mason froze in place. She reached out with her other hand and crooked her finger at Dash. "And I think I'd like to have you right by my side, dog."

I watched in horror as Dash crawled on his hands and

knees and sat down, leaning against her leg like an obedient hound.

Rita placed her hand on his head, stroking his hair and spreading her fingers wide. Her eyes closed, and she breathed in deep. "My, this one has some serious power, but he uses all of that yummy strength to hide his true nature from you. You've fought some battles, haven't you, poochy?"

"Take your hand off of him," I demanded.

She placed a finger to her lip. "Shh, I'm not done listening to his mind. It's too delicious, all the secrets he's keeping. Oh Dash, I think you should tell Charli how you really feel. Every woman deserves to hear the words from the man she desires."

Dash struggled to keep his mouth from moving. When Rita tightened her grip on his scalp, he winced. "I...won't. You can't..." He panted with the effort of fighting her.

She leaned over and spoke in his ear. "Open your eyes and tell her."

With Rita's will pushing him to obey, Dash did as he was told. His glowing gold eyes snapped to mine. "I love you," he rasped.

"There. Doesn't that make you feel good?" Rita asked me. "But that's not all." She focused on Dash again. "Tell her the thing you definitely didn't want her to know. And if you fight me again, I'll take one good memory you have with her and erase it forever."

Dash snarled low. "Please don't," he begged.

"Tell her," Rita repeated, singing the words.

The wolf shifter gazed at me with absolute regret pooling

in his eyes. "I won the war for my pack at a cost. I owe a debt that must be paid."

The witch narrowed her eyes. "Don't try to get around it. Tell it all now, or I'm going to strip the one memory you treasure the most clean out of your skull."

"I'm engaged to be married," Dash grunted.

My heart shattered into a million pieces. I had no right to care as much as I did, but I couldn't help the tears that fell in mourning of something that never had a chance to begin with.

"I made a blood pact with Trey that if something happened to him, I would marry and always take care of his younger sister, Dina. He died fighting for me, and I'm left to honor my word. I came here this weekend to say goodbye." Dash bent his head, unable to watch me cry.

I sniffed and turned my head to find Mason watching me with a scowl. My reaction to what Dash was forced to tell me broke something between the detective and me. In a few quick seconds, everything I had with either man disintegrated.

A seed of hate rooted deep in my gut. I let it fester and slither inside me until it thrived and bloomed, fueling my anger and rage. The more fury that pumped through my veins, the less I felt the effects of Rita's psychic assault.

She patted Dash's head and waved her hand in front of her face. "Whoa, the emotions coming off of you, Detective, are so strong. I don't even have to touch you at all to feel the tangible love you have for Charli. And I can tell you haven't been brave enough to tell her either. What is it with you two cowards?"

"You're the coward," I snapped.

Rita raised her eyebrows. "Really? So, you've told the detective about your delicious kiss with the shifter?" She closed her eyes and licked her lips. "Tasting Dash's memory, it was a toe-curling moment. So much heat and lust and anticipation finally finding a little release."

Mason's face fell, and my anger faltered with guilt. "I was going to tell you, but I wanted to wait until—"

I couldn't tell him there was never a good time to share the truth with him and face the consequences. Rita was right. I was a coward, and now my lack of bravery fractured any chance I might have left with Mason.

In anger, I planted my hands on the ground and squeezed my eyes shut. If I could tap into the tree's power, I could blast this witch with a gigantic *B* into oblivion.

"Come on, tree. Let me have it one more time," I ordered under my breath. No tingle of power answered me.

"Charli, get up off the dirt." Rita snapped her fingers, and my body obeyed. "You'll learn that men aren't worth your time. They only want to take and take from you. Don't waste a second allowing your heart to hurt over either of them. Love is overrated."

"Love is everything," I barked back. "Even if it gets broken or ends too soon." With my eyes, I tried to convey my apologies to both men.

Rita scoffed. "Sure, and it hasn't tied you in knots trying

to decide which one of them you should choose? I have a brilliant idea. Let's have them fight each other to see which one of you loves you more."

"Don't," I yelled in alarm, but with a few of her hand gestures, Mason and Dash approached each other, pacing and sizing up their rival.

"This ought to be good." Rita took her place next to me and threw an arm over my shoulder. "Get on with it. I want to see who's willing to shed more blood for you."

With a growl, Dash made the first move, crouching lower and driving his shoulder into Mason's gut. The detective grunted and pounded his fists on Dash's back. The sickening sound of flesh and bone colliding turned my stomach. I wanted to look away, but I couldn't take my eyes off the spectacle. I couldn't bear to see either of the men I cared about hurt, especially in this twisted way.

The fight distracted me, and it took me too long to notice Rita's fingers had inched away from my shoulder and dug into the back of my scalp. White-cold icy tendrils froze my brain from the inside out, and I shut my eyes in utter anguish. Rita trespassed on my most intimate life with her violent invasion.

"If you don't fight me, it won't hurt so much," she whispered in my ear, holding me close. "I can see everything. I know what you want most even more than you do yourself. Do you want me to tell you what it is, or should I just do a little rearranging and change your desires to my liking?"

Panic flooded my system and I squirmed to get away. My parents' faces and the feel of their hugs poured out of my head. The happiness from eating at Nana's table and teasing my brother added to the mix. The confusion and frustration of who I was and who I wanted to be blended with the rest. My heart beat faster at the memory of riding behind Dash on his motorcycle compared to flying on a broom with Mason's arms wrapped around me.

My eyes hurt from squeezing them so tight. "It's too much," I whimpered. "Stop it."

Rita's fingers dug in harder. "I can make it go away. Surgically remove all memories involving either of them." She pointed at Mason and Dash, still slashing, beating, and brawling with each other.

I made one last-ditch effort to stop her. Shoving my hand in my pocket, I took out the fabric-wrapped gem. "If you'll let me go, you can have this."

The memories she battered me with stopped. "What is it?"

I unwrapped the fabric and let it fall away, revealing the shining sapphire in my palm. "It's yours if you'll leave me alone."

The jewel wasn't mine to bargain with, but desperation will make a liar out of anyone. If I could get her to consider the bribe, maybe I could free myself enough to save the guys, too.

Rita's grip on my head loosened. "It's a tempting offer, and that's one big sapphire. It could sustain me for a long while. Then again," she tightened her hold on me, "I can feel your magic swimming around in there. It would be handier for me to change your mind and convince you to come with me. Then you could use your magic to find all the treasures in the world."

I remembered how I'd broken her psychic hold on me before with extreme emotions. Closing my eyes, I tried to stoke the fires of anger. Rita had assaulted more than just Dash, Mason, and me. With her terrible will, she forced our hearts to be broken. And if she got away free without any consequences, I wouldn't be able to live with myself.

Some of her icy tendrils melted and the pressure inside my head eased up, but not enough. I needed something strong enough to kick her out, and I knew exactly what would do it. I reached for the one emotion that drove me to be better every day. That made me want to be a good sister, daughter, granddaughter, friend, and potential partner.

Love didn't make me weaker. It was the solid foundation I built my life on. Recalling all of the people I would die for and kindling my feelings for Dash and Mason, I pushed the warm, blazing emotion of love through my veins until it burned away all of the psychic's presence.

Rita let go of me with a yelp, and I threw my head back, connecting with her face. The crunch of bone was unmistakable, and I swept my leg around to trip her. In all of my sudden movements, the sapphire dropped out of my grip, but I didn't have time to recover it.

Crawling on top of her, I pulled the gold chain and held the coin in my hand. "This doesn't belong to you." With a snap, I ripped it off of her.

Rita cradled her face, drops of blood seeping through the cracks of her fingers. "You broke my nose!"

"And you'll be getting a black eye, too!" I shouted. Clenching my fist, I punched her as hard as I could.

My hand throbbed after I made contact, but I would gladly break all my bones if it meant I could beat the smugness right out of the ex-racer.

Someone pulled me off Rita, and I kicked and thrashed to break free. "Charli, let us handle it," Dash hissed in my ear.

Mason wiped blood running down from his nose away with the back of his hand and held it up in front of him. "By the authority of the wardens, I arrest you, Rita Ryder." A magic shield formed around her and tightened until it wavered mere millimeters over her skin.

Voices called out our names from across the field. Finally, others from Honeysuckle had found us. I bent over and placed my hands above my knees, relieved the fight was over.

Mason forced Rita to stand and waited for his colleagues to come help him. Dash touched my shoulder, and I jumped at the contact. I wanted to let him hug me, but his lack of clothes stopped me from accepting an embrace.

"I should probably change back into my wolf so I don't scandalize the population," he joked, but no smile reached his lips.

A shrill shriek echoed behind us, and a shockwave of power emanated from Rita's body. She broke free of Mason's hold and placed her hand on either side of the detective's face.

"I'd love nothing but to punch you back, Charli." She spit blood at me. "But I think I'll hit you where it'll do the most damage. I'm stripping all of his memories of you out, and I'll make it hurt." She smirked at me, and her hands pulsed with power.

Mason roared in agony, and my vision turned red. "You said you manipulated and killed because you were dying. Because you had nothing to lose. Well, I guess we girls have to stick together."

Not caring what happened to me anymore, I ran at full speed toward her. If she wanted to stop me, she'd have to take her focus off Mason to defend herself.

Imitating Dash, I lowered my body stance and barreled into Rita's chest, knocking her over. Adrenaline fueled my actions, and I flattened her on her back. My legs straddled her upper torso and my knees pinned her arms down so she couldn't reach my head.

"I don't have to touch you to mess with your mind." She struggled to say each word because my hands closed in around her throat, choking the life out of her.

I was done playing the part of a pawn. Her magic had caused too much devastation. Only one solution came to mind, and I let go of her neck and placed both hands over her heart. Without hesitation, I cast my spell.

"With all the harm that has been done, it's time the awful game is won. Now is the time and now is the hour that I'll strip you of your power. With my magic you will find. I'll take your power of the mind. With all my heart, I will this switch, and now I win, you evil witch."

I called on every ounce of my strength, willing my magic to flow through my body and out of my hands. Rita cried out at my forced invasion, but I ignored each and every one of her pleas.

With my eyes closed, I visualized my powers pouring into her body, our two magics mixing like oil and water. I pushed and fought to fill her full of mine and compelled hers to spill out of her.

"No, you can't do this!" Rita thrashed underneath me, but the spell bound me to her.

The longer I stayed connected, the more I lost myself. My magic emptied out of me, leaving a vacant void needing to be filled. The darkness that ate away at her insides attempted to cross over to me. Weakened and drained, I couldn't fight much longer. If this would be my last act, at least I did it to save those who meant the most to me.

With my last breath, I uttered the one thing I hoped both Dash and Mason heard.

"I love you."

Chapter Twenty-Two

"Charlotte Vivian Goodwin, you are in so much trouble." Nana cuddled me into her shoulder, rocking me back and forth and kissing the top of my head.

I snotted on her shirt. "Quit middle naming me."

The fact that I didn't die surprised me. I hadn't even passed out like I had too often in the past. It took my grandmother's powerful magic to stop the progress of my spell. Big Willie and the other wardens took Rita into custody. All of Lucky's barbecue team scoured the ground until Henry found the sapphire and Clint picked up the golden coin.

"Do you want me to take you home?" Nana asked, letting go of me just enough so she could see my face.

I shook my head. "I want to make sure Lucky gets back what's his."

A gray wolf sauntered over beside us and nudged its head underneath my hand. I ran my fingers through Dash's fur and scratched between his ears. His tongue lolled out in a wolfy grin, the only smile I imagined he could muster.

Nana rubbed one of his ears. "You did good, Dash. We'll meet you at The Rainbow's End."

With a satisfied growl, he bounded off, no doubt to find some clothes to put on. I sighed and looked around me, searching all the faces in the scattering of people left.

"If you're looking for Mason, he's not here. I sent him to Doc Andrew's and called Mimsy to meet them there." She watched me with concern.

"Is he...did Rita erase...?" My lip quivered as I closed my eyes and replayed her cruelty that I couldn't stop in time.

Nana hugged me tighter and rubbed my back. "Hush, child. We won't know how badly he's affected for a little while. Until then, let me carry your troubles."

I lost all control and sobbed until my body ached from my sorrow. My knees buckled underneath me, and I almost went down. My grandmother called for help, and my assistant rushed over to hold me up. I'd been strong enough to beat Rita at her game, and now I could let go and allow others to help.

At Lucky's bar, all the members of his team plus Nana, Dash, and I surrounded the leprechaun. We leaned over him, still aghast at his appearance.

"Either somebody start singin' a sorrowful dirge for me

and bury me body in the ground or give me back what's mine and get on with it," Lucky managed with labored breath.

Clint held out the coin dangling from the golden chain for me to take. "You found it. You give it back to him."

I opened my mouth to protest but closed it. The price required to win the prize might have come at too high a cost if Mason's mind was lost. Laying the chain and coin on top of Lucky, I backed away. Henry placed the sapphire he'd recovered next to the coin.

For a brief moment when nothing happened, I feared that Rita had drained all of the luck until there was nothing left. But the coin and the sapphire shimmered to life, and a bright glow poured out of both items and flowed over the leprechaun's body. It hovered over him like sparkling particles of dust until the magic seeped into his body.

Lucky drew in a long, hard breath and sat up. The color of his skin changed from gray to pale peach, and the leprechaun stretched as if getting up from a long nap. "Somebody bring me a pint of lager and a barbecue sandwich. Not necessarily in that order." He pocketed the sapphire, and when he caught me watching, he winked.

All of us cheered and whooped as loud as possible. His team did the best they could to pick Lucky up and carry him around the bar like a champion. Horatio hoisted him on his shoulders and Henry and Steve grabbed onto the leprechaun's arms while Leland Chalmers Jr. and Sr. took the legs. Not wanting to be left out, Clint grabbed hold of the troll's pant leg while they trotted around. Little did all of them know, they were toting around royalty.

I wiped the happy tears from my eyes and leaned against Nana. "All hail the King," I quipped.

She poked me in my ribs with her elbow. "In a small town like ours, secrets are hard to keep. No doubt he'll have to tell some tales sooner or later."

I counted the men having fun with their healed friend. "They're one short. Where's Billy Ray?"

Nana's smile broke and she cleared her throat. "Even though I told the silly man none of this was his fault, he feels responsible. I think he might be leaving Honeysuckle."

"Oh, Nana, I'm so sorry." I took my turn to offer comfort and hugged her for all I was worth.

She sniffed and wiped her tears and nose on my shirt. "It's okay. I understand why he feels that way, and I'm not going to stop him from going."

"He's not worth fighting for?" I asked.

Nana regained her composure and held up her head. "Charli, you'll learn that some loves are worth the battles and some you have to let go and let live. Either way, you'll be far richer for having loved at all in the end." She brushed a gentle finger down my cheek.

A pounding on the door interrupted our private celebration. My grandmother stepped away and went to answer the insistent knocks.

The sun's light outlined the tall figure of Raif. "Is it possible for myself and the rest of the Fiery Fangs to enter?

We would like an opportunity to talk with Lucky and his team."

Horatio placed the leprechaun down on the floor, and Lucky cleared his throat. "Go on. Come in, all of ye."

Nana and I moved out of the way to allow Raif and the other vampires to walk into the bar. Every single one of them carried food with them, and my stomach rumbled embarrassingly loud in hunger. I hoped whatever they had to discuss wouldn't take long so we could dig in and eat.

Raif motioned for Sam to stand next to him. The famous barbecue pit master held a large trophy in his hand. "We would count it an honor if you would display this award for best barbecue right here in your bar."

Lucky narrowed his eyes. "And why would that be?"

"We mean no disrespect," insisted Raif. "But we could not help but notice your team's withdrawal from the competition. I am sure there is some good reason behind it, but it was a shame we could not compete together."

"Ye mean ye think we might have given ye a run for your money if we were at full steam?" Tension silenced all of us until Lucky chuckled. "Aye and I'm sure t'would have been a grand struggle for first place. Ms. Vivi, as you sit as the high seat on the town council, perhaps ye could put in a good word. We'll be needin' another barbecue event to fight for the top spot soon enough. Drinks are on me, lads and lasses. Let's feast!"

Forgetting my manners, I grabbed a barbecue sandwich and stuffed it in my mouth. The vinegar base of the sauce hit the back of my tongue while the cayenne and red pepper flakes added just the right level of spice.

"Don't you want some coleslaw on it?" Sam asked.

"No thanks," I muffled through my full mouth. "Maybe on the next one."

It took me three more sandwiches, two scoopfuls of potato salad, and almost an entire pitcher of sweet tea before I started feeling close to normal again.

Dash slammed the door open, his face stuck in a frown. He jabbed his thumb behind him. "You might want to prepare yourself for what's coming."

Aunt Nora strutted in with her snooty friends following behind her. The dislikable suit guy surveyed the mess of food and our makeshift celebration with disdain. Next to his group, another less intimidating group filed into Lucky's bar.

Nana placed her plate on a nearby table and wiped her hands on a napkin. "Ladies and gentlemen, I was hoping we could resume our discussion at a later date. Right now, as you can see, we're sharing in the honors of the top team."

Nora sniffed and crossed her arms. "I would think there were more important issues at hand than eating barbecue. This is Calhoun Ravenel, and he runs the council in Charleston. Cal, why don't you start."

So, the suit had a name. He stepped forward, sticking his nose in the air. "After everything we've observed this weekend, we've come to the conclusion that Honeysuckle Hollow is a danger unto itself."

Lucky, feeling much better and back to his old self,

approached the outsider. "And what danger might ye be referrin' to?"

"Well, the murder for one. And by all accounts, it isn't the only one that has occurred in your supposedly safe small town," Calhoun Ravenel countered.

Nana stood her ground. "If you'd like to check with our sheriff, we've captured the witch responsible for Fireball's death. In less than a day. And she ain't from Honeysuckle either." She tapped her foot on the ground, daring them to say something else.

Aunt Nora snapped her fingers, and I cringed at the sound. "I heard that somebody got attacked on Friday night and, Vivi, you went out of your way to make sure nobody found out about it."

Although Lucky only came up to the guy in the suit's midriff, his presence felt grander than all the authority figures in the room put together. Except Nana.

The leprechaun crossed his arms. "Oh, ye may have heard about the scuffle I was in. Tis no surprise when you mix whiskey and grillin' together that a little shenanigans might occur." He slapped his chest. "As ye can see for yourselves, I'm fit as a fiddle."

Calhoun Ravenel looked around the room. "Who did you get into a scuffle with?" His eyes landed on Horatio and his mouth drooped into a frown. "Perhaps whatever...person you fought with should be dealt with in the strictest manner. Of course, there would be a dramatic decrease in potential problems and bad influences if there were a purer citizenry here."

Dash growled. "I'd think twice about saying words like that in here. Look around you. Do you think any of us are less pure than exactly what we are? And if you're pure anything, then I'd say you're a genuine ass—"

"I've got this, Dash, thank you," Nana interrupted. "Cal, I won't stand here and listen to your prejudiced drivel. Say what you're going to say to the regional council members here and let's get on with it."

"Fine." The outsider turned to face the other group. "As it stands, we members of the Charleston witches council believe that Honeysuckle's council be put in review while our district absorbs it under out leadership."

Nana held up her hand. "Before you make any decisions, understand that I will file an immediate injunction on the proposition and appeal it."

"On what basis?" one of Calhoun's fellow council members asked.

"Is idiocy an okay answer?" Clint piped up.

Light flooded the room when the door opened again. Matt walked in, surveyed his surroundings, and met our grandmother's gaze. Instead of concern spreading on his face, he smiled with great amusement.

"Hey, y'all. Looks like I've come at the perfect time." My brother stood next to Nana, posturing opposite our aunt and the rest of the various council members.

"Matthew, I'm sure whatever you have to say can wait until

the regional council gives us its ruling." Aunt Nora cast an icy glance and sniffed again.

Although I'd made peace and started a burgeoning friendship with her daughter, my cousin Clementine, I still had no desire to renew any connection with my aunt. I'd have to settle on the idea that she and my mother shared very little DNA. That or, as Nana always said, blood doesn't make a family. Love does. And I felt quite the opposite of that emotion for the treacherous woman standing on the wrong side.

"What did they promise you, Leonora, for your loyalty to them and your betrayal of us?" Nana asked.

Aunt Nora smirked. "You'll find out soon enough, Vivian."

Matt sighed in relief. "Before anybody says anything else, I think it's my duty as a warden to inform all of you that we've let Earl, Cleetus, and the rest of the drunken fools go home."

Horatio stepped into view and held up his hand. When Nana called on him, he said, "Perhaps I misunderstood you, but are you implying that the ones who committed an assault upon my person as well as Miss Charli's during our ventures in winged competition have been released from their imprisonment?"

Most of the council members murmured in shock at my verbose friend's intellect. No doubt some of them had to concentrate hard to understand what he asked to begin with. Maybe I should conjure up a dictionary for them to use.

Matt held up a finger. "I said we let them go. I did not, however, say they went completely scot-free. Once they sobered up, they struck a deal that allowed them to be let off with time served and the whole list of incidents placed on their permanent records."

I'd have to ask my brother later if the wardens had made a similar offer to Owen and his crew.

"What deal is that?" Nana asked, setting my brother up.

Matt did his best to sound like Horatio. "In exchange for lesser charges, the cluster of scoundrels hereto forthwith and such, captured and imprisoned at the warden station, doth offered us the names of the persons currently present who lined their pockets with coin to create such chaos as to cause embarrassment and misfortunes for Honeysuckle and its leadership."

"In other words?" I pressed, holding back a giggle.

Matt wasn't as successful as me. He laughed as he explained, "It means they gave us the names of pretty much all of y'all from the Charleston council. You paid them to cause trouble. They were already prejudiced idiots to begin with, but you paid them double to take everything up a notch, didn't you?"

Calhoun Ravenel lost a little of his composure and confidence. "You can't prove any of those foul accusations."

Big Willie's large frame took up most of the door when he entered. "Oh, I think we can. We've already got someone checking their bank accounts. And one of them might not be as stupid as you took them for. Turns out, he recorded one of you giving the group directions on exactly what to do. Maybe we should take you down to the station and compare the recording to your voices?"

The contingency from Charleston panicked and whispered among themselves. Calhoun turned his back on Aunt Nora, leaving her standing on her own.

When he finished trying to control his group, he nodded once at the regional council members. "We withdraw our petition with immediacy." Without waiting for anything else to happen, he headed for the door.

"Wait, Cal, what about me? You said you would make sure I took control here," my aunt wailed, waving her hand.

"I have no idea what you're talking about," Calhoun Ravenel dismissed without even looking at her. He disappeared into the afternoon sun and, I hoped, out of our town forever.

Aunt Nora's supposed friends abandoned her, leaving her to pick up the pieces of her poor choices. She glanced around the room at all of us staring at her with pity mixed with loathing. "What are y'all looking at?"

"A loser," Sam Ayden said, earning himself a few laughs and slaps on his back.

She stormed out of the bar with her head still held high. But my aunt had nowhere to go where her traitorous acts wouldn't follow. And in a small town like ours, Aunt Nora might pay the price for her actions a very, very long time.

The small group of outsiders still left in the bar murmured to each other. Their leader, a shorter man than the rest, stepped forward. "Miss Vivi, I know I should be more formal about this, but if I told you that Honeysuckle Hollow remains a sanctuary city under its own leadership, can we have some of that delectable barbecue?"

Today would be full of celebrations for lots of reasons. Everyone cheered, and Raif escorted the council members from the Southeast region over to the table of food while Lucky got behind the bar to pour drinks. I chuckled to myself at the irony that after everything that happened, we all were left partying at The End.

"That was a little too close," Matt exclaimed, wiping his hand across his forehead for dramatic effect.

Nana wrapped her arms around both of us. "Well, Cal thought he had me, but he doesn't do his homework. The lead council member there is Bartholomew Keene. He's half gnome and half witch. If anyone appreciated what kind of community we've built here, he did. Leonora, Calhoun, and his cronies never had a chance. But I'm glad we took care of things on our own anyway."

All of a sudden, my stomach dropped, and I lost my appetite for food or partying. There was one person who hadn't made it out fully intact.

Dash brought over a glass of sweet tea. He handed it to me despite my protests. "Drink it down. You're gonna need the energy."

Because of his tone and my general exhaustion, I did as I was told for once. When I was finished, he took the glass back.

"I got a text from Georgia. They need you to come to

Doc's right now." The wolf shifter wouldn't look me in the eyes, and I knew something bad waited for me there.

Matt squeezed my hand three times and handed me off to Nana. All of the hugs she could give couldn't chase away the fear that consumed me.

"Chin up, Charli Bird. I think the time to choose whether or not you want to fight is here." She cradled my chin. "Be strong like the Goodwin woman I know you to be."

I nodded, unable to tell her that if I lost the man I now knew I would choose, that it would weaken me forever.

Chapter Twenty-Three

D ash gave me a ride on the back of his motorcycle to Doc Andrew's office. Once upon a time, feeling the wind whip through my hair while zipping around on the back of his bike would have made me happy. The closer we got, the more guilt burdened me.

We entered the examination room and found Mimsy talking with Lily and Lavender as well as Georgia and Ginny. All of them wore grim expressions.

Doc acknowledged Dash with a handshake and approached me. "These fine ladies have assisted me as much as they can to assess how much damage Rita inflicted before you stopped her. As of now, we're at a loss."

"Then why am I here?" I uttered, garnering the silent attention from the group of psychic witches.

"Because you have the deepest connection to him," Dash

said. "I suggested that you might be the only one to truly help him."

My heart ached, knowing that things could have been so different if he'd never returned to Red Ridge. But the fact that he did made him a man I admired. And it brought us new friends who wanted to help.

I drew in a shaky breath. "What do you want me to do?"

"Come here, child." Mimsy held out her hand for me to take and drew me closer to the head of the bed where Mason lay asleep. "I'm going to wake him up, and then we'll see what happens when he lays eyes on you."

"If y'all don't mind, I'll wait outside." Dash left the room with quick steps.

Georgia touched my arm. "What happened with Rita combined with the stress of what he's already been through, it messed with him." She touched her temple to let me know that Dash couldn't take much more.

I wanted to tell her I couldn't either, but Mason had already suffered from my cowardice before. For him, I would be brave and stay.

Mimsy placed her hand over Mason's forehead. "I'm waking him up. Now."

The detective blinked his eyes open and shut several times. "Where am I?"

Doc answered first, "You're in my office, Detective."

"Am I hurt?" Mason attempted to sit up, but the doctor pushed him back on the bed. "I don't feel injured."

Mimsy pushed her body against mine, keeping me from

running from the truth. "We've brought Charli to come visit you."

I offered a weak smile and wave. "Hey, Mason."

His eyes widened a little. "Hey."

Relief rushed through me, and I attempted to hold his hand. "You had us worried."

"That's nice." Mason smiled. "But why would you worry for me? You don't even know me."

All of the air got sucked out of the room and the bottom fell out underneath me. My greatest fear came true. Rita had been successful at stripping his memories of me away. I let go of my grip on him and stepped back.

"I don't know why," he continued. "But when I look at you, I feel...sad."

Mimsy laid her hand on his forehead again, and he slipped into a peaceful sleep.

Turning around, I grabbed Lily in desperation. "When I stopped Rita, I pushed my magic into her, like Mason and I had swapped powers. Did any of her psychic magic flow into me? Do I have the power to save him?"

Mimsy forced me to let go of her granddaughter. "Give me your hands, child." She bent her head and mumbled some words.

Lily and Lavender touched her shoulders, and Georgia and Ginny touched the cousins to give Ms. Blackwood a boost. All of them closed their eyes, letting their magic flow through each other.

"I'm sorry," said Mimsy. "But I don't feel any psychic

talents in you at all." She cast a sideways glance at her granddaughters.

Lavender's lower lip quivered. "Oh, Charli," she whispered.

"What? What did you see?" None of them would answer, and I yelled, "tell me now!"

Lily cleared her throat. "Your grandmother warned us that in using the kind of spell that you did, you might have given up your own magic."

I remembered pushing my powers into Rita to empty hers. But when Mason gave me his magical flying skills, he absorbed my magic. When the spell ran its course, my talents reappeared again.

"Rita must possess it," I exclaimed. "We need to go to the warden station and get it back."

Doc Andrews ushered us out of the room, and Dash joined us. The doctor did his best to calm me. "Big Willie had me do a medical examination on Rita. Other than a broken nose and a black eye, she was fine. When I specifically searched for her magic skills, I didn't find any. Not even yours."

I waved my hands in the air. "Then take me to another exam room and search me."

Doc scratched his bald head. "I could, but I trust Ms. Mimsy and her assessment. It could be that after all that you did to save Lucky's life, you may have lost your special talents. Or they may return to you."

"That's not very specific, Doc," complained Dash.

"I'm a healer not a miracle worker." The doctor hugged his clipboard to his chest. "Listen, the only thing that's going to give us more definitive answers is time. Time for Mason's brain to heal. Time for your powers to renew. Or time for both of you to adjust to how your life will be in the long run." He squeezed my shoulder and left.

"We'll keep working with him, Charli. I promise," Lily uttered, holding her grandmother's hand. "Granny's already coming up with ways to try and increase Lav's and my skills."

"And you shouldn't let this make you doubt how you feel about Mason," insisted Lavender. "His aura is wobbly, but I don't think all is lost for the two of you. Not yet." My friends followed their grandmother outside.

Georgia stayed behind and handed me the spell phone she borrowed. "Give this back to that guy for us, please."

I waved her off. "Henry can get himself a new one. Keep that one for you, and before you leave town, have Dash make Lee put together a stash of them for y'all to try when you get home."

Ginny snatched the phone out of her sister's hand, playing with it. Dash told the sisters that his brother was waiting for them back at the campsite. Making sure one of the cousins would take me home, he left without saying anything to me. His motorcycle roared to life and thundered away in the distance.

Georgia held me back as we walked outside together. "Dash told us that the leprechaun's okay thanks to you. Now I understand a lot of the stories he told us. You know, he's still trying to find a way out of his blood pact and his engagement. There may still be a chance for the two of you if things don't work out." She glanced at the door to the examination room where Mason rested. "I don't envy your life right now."

I kept my eyes on the barrier separating me from the detective. "When you were in there, did you see...were there any...?"

Georgia nodded. "He has a very friendly spirit that hovers near him. She says she's doing her best to bring back her boy."

For the first time since I got to the doctor's office, I smiled in genuine relief. "That must be Marian, the social worker who found him when he was in the foster system. She was the biggest mother-figure in his life. He was engaged to her daughter at one point."

Memories of our dinner together that one night where he tore down all the walls between us haunted me. Maybe I should have taken Rita up on her offer to strip away all my experiences with both men. Then my life would be much simpler, right?

"Don't give up on love, Charli. It's the most powerful thing in this universe, and it can create miracles. Hold on tight to it." Georgia embraced me in a warm hug.

"You sound like my Nana," I said.

"That's because my Meemaw used to say it to us when I was knee high to a grasshopper." She patted my back.

I parted in friendship with the two sisters, inviting them to return to Honeysuckle anytime they wanted to, with or without Dash, and accepting their returned invite to visit their mountains.

Lily drove me home in silence. I watched the world go by outside the window, wondering how much time was necessary to get back to normal. I should be back at Lucky's dancing, drinking, and celebrating the big win of stopping Rita from hurting anybody else. Instead, I was heading home to lick my wounds.

I'd waited too long to make a clear choice, and now, I no longer had any options. The universe had a perverted sense of humor throwing that kind of karma my way.

But I was a Goodwin woman, and we never gave up, even when every molecule in me thought that the best idea today. If Mason truly didn't remember me, then I would do everything I could to win him over. I was sixty percent confident I could rekindle his love for me again. Maybe fifty-seven. Okay, I had a fifty-fifty shot, but that was better than none at all. We could find new ways to enjoy spending time together or we could retrace our steps and use our former experiences as a trigger. Either way, one thing was for certain.

Brooms would be used for sweeping and our feet would stay planted on the ground.

Epilogue

Although the girls wanted to stay with me one more night, I sent them all home. I knew how bad things must be when Nana brought me a chocolate chess pie. She only made me those when she knew I needed some serious cheering up. I assured her I'd be okay and reminded her that Beau would be coming home tonight so I wouldn't be alone. When she left, I texted my vampire roommate and asked him to stay with one of his many lady friends.

Sadness smothered me like a wet blanket I couldn't shake off. Grabbing a fork and the pie tin, I shuffled out my front door and sat down on the top step of my porch, listening to the cicadas chirping away.

Peaches popped her head up from the rocking chair she napped in and stretched. Hopping down, she trotted over to me and rubbed her orange furry head on my elbow. I picked her up with one hand and plopped her into my lap. She turned a couple of circles and settled down while I scooped a bite of the pie into my mouth.

"It's just me and you, Peachy Poo," I crooned, stroking her little head and soaking in her comforting purr.

A dark shadow crossed the light of the moon, and a faint caw echoed nearby. Biddy flapped her wings and landed on the porch railing. She cocked her head back and forth, squawking like she always did. I picked off a bit of pie crust and tossed it on the porch for her to nibble on. If both my cat and my crow felt like I needed them, my life must be deep in the pits.

A thundering motor approached in the distance. It stopped at the edge of the property and cut off. I'd wondered if Dash would say a proper goodbye when he jetted from the doctor's office without another word. My heart raced and my mood lifted a bit at the chance to talk to him alone, but then it sank when I remembered the circumstances. I wasn't ready to have him leave my life.

"Looks like you're keeping good company," he rumbled from the shadows.

I would never get used to his stealthy ways. "They're the only ones I allowed to stay."

"Oh." He stepped into the porch light and ran a finger through his longer locks. "Do you want me to go?"

I would have jumped up and held on to him to prevent

just that, but I didn't want to desert Peaches, who nuzzled deeper into my lap.

I pointed at her. "I'm kinda stuck right now."

"Then if you don't mind," he bounded up the steps and sat down next to me, "I'll come to you."

His warm body crowded mine, and I resisted the urge to lean into him. Only an inch or less kept us apart, and it would take nothing but a neck tilt and a lean to lay my head on his shoulder. And yet again, I found myself conflicted between the guy with me and another that seemed to be slipping away.

"Wanna bite?" I asked without thinking. "Of pie. Do you want a bite of pie?" I stupidly clarified, holding the tin and the fork for him to take.

Dash chuckled. "Sure." He groaned with pleasure while chewing. "So good. I like a good chess pie. Mom used to make them."

Oh my heart. It was all too much to digest—Dash's engagement and Mason's lost memory. I plucked Peaches off my lap and stood up, grabbing onto the painted wooden railing for stability. The song of the cicadas filled my ears, and I breathed in and out to their rhythm.

"What are you thinking?" Dash asked in a quiet tone.

I swallowed the lump in my throat. "Uh, I was just thinking that I'm the one who makes the best chess pies."

"Did you make this one?"

Clearing my throat and wiping away the tears threatening to spill, I turned around with a phony smile. "No. That one Nana brought over."

"Hmm. Comfort food. I can understand why you would need it tonight of all nights." The shifter's kind gaze burned a hole right through me.

"Listen, Dash," I started.

He lifted his nose in the air, sniffing, and his smile dissolved. "Hold on." Standing up, he followed whatever scent drew him in. When he stopped at my screen door, he held up a finger. "Wait here and don't come in until I tell you to."

"You're freaking me out," I whispered, unsure of why I had to obey while at my own home.

Dash opened the door, wincing at its creaks and groans. "Good. Use that fear to stay outside." He stepped over the threshold and carefully let the door close behind him.

When I lost sight of him, I couldn't wait around. I approached on tiptoe and gazed through the screen. "Dash," I called out in a whispered yell. "What's going on?"

He didn't reply, so I took that as a clear sign I should walk inside. The door slammed against the frame with a loud *thwack*. All right, I wasn't a shifter with the ability to move around without being heard.

A hand covered my mouth and my whole body lifted off the floor. I flailed and screamed, managing to kick my heel into the groin of the person holding me. I landed on my butt when he let me go.

"Ow," grunted Dash, bending over. "Why'd you kick me there?"

"Why'd you put your hand over my mouth and pick me

up?" I shouted, getting back up and rubbing my behind. "You nearly gave me a heart attack."

He couldn't stand up straight and continued to moan. "I knew you wouldn't listen to me, so I was trying to play a joke on you. Seriously, you didn't have to catch me in that particular spot."

I tried to pat him on the back, but he pushed me away. When he regained a little composure, he stood up straight and blew out a big breath.

"Then there wasn't anything to be afraid of in here in the first place?" I asked.

He cast me some serious side eye, but answered, "I think there was. Someone has left their scent all over the place."

I waved him off. "You're probably detecting one of the girls. Alison Kate, Lily, Lavender, and Blythe were all over here. Plus, Beau and Mason moved around the house, too." At the mention of the detective's name, my guilt rose back to life and I second-guessed standing there alone with Dash.

The shifter scented the air again. "It's strongest in there." He pointed to the more formal living room where some of Uncle Tipper's old collections remained on display.

"I hardly ever use the room. It's always felt like my great-uncle's instead of mine. And I want him to feel at home if he ever comes to haunt me," I teased.

"Hmph, if you invite Georgia over, she could probably tell you whether or not he has. Hold on." He picked up a flask sitting in the middle of a small decorative table with inlaid decoration from Italy that depicted a scene from the Bay of

Naples using different species of wood. "Was this always there?"

"No, all the flasks usually go in the glass curio over there," I pointed at the far wall. "Hey, there was a folded piece of paper underneath it."

Dash picked the paper up and sniffed it. "Yeah, whoever came into the house wrote this." He took another deep whiff.

I wiggled my fingers. "Give it."

"Are you sure? Maybe we should get your brother involved," he suggested, holding the paper away from me.

"Whoever left it meant for it to be found, and it must be for me because this is my house now." I snatched the thin vellum from his fingers and opened it up.

In a scrawl I didn't recognize, I read the message addressed to me.

"*Dear Charli, I'm sorry to intrude without your permission, but I didn't want to disturb you this weekend as you seemed to be very busy. Please know that I have waited a long time to get in touch with you, but I guess I'll have to wait a little longer. I'll leave you my cell phone number for you to call if you want to talk. I think we have a lot of things we could share with each other. Until then, know that our family has been looking for you for a long time, and I hope we do get to meet soon. Sincerely, Abigail Wilson, your cousin.*"

I read through the words twice before I let Dash take a look. When Fate chose to mess with me, she didn't mess around.

"My cousin, Abigail. I have a cousin named Abigail." I

tugged on Dash's shirt. "She must be my blood cousin. I mean, biologically related to me."

He tossed the letter on the table. "And she broke into your house."

I picked it back up and pressed it to my chest. "So? She gives a good reason right here." I pointed to the middle part. "She says she knew I was busy."

"And how did she know that was true? She must have been spying on you, which, you have to admit, is a little creepy," Dash said.

I smacked his arm. "Hey, don't call my almost-cousin creepy."

"Almost-cousin?" Dash rubbed the spot I hit.

"Yeah, just because she says she is doesn't mean I'm gonna believe it one hundred percent until I check her out. Still, this is the first connection I've ever found to my biological family. Ooh, wait, there's a P.S.," I squealed, reading it out loud.

"*P.S. My friends call me Abby. Only my grandmother insists I be called Abigail. You can choose which one fits when we meet. Which, again, I hope will be soon.*"

"Abigail Wilson," Dash mumbled. "Doesn't even sound like a real name. She could be using a fake one and be lying about being related to you. I'd be really careful if I were you. Make sure Mason and the wardens..." he trailed off.

My face crumbled, and Dash reached out to rub my shoulder. "I'm sorry, Charli. I forgot he's not okay."

"He will be okay," I responded in a loud voice. "He has to be."

The mood between us sank like an anchor in the ocean. I folded the note and stuffed it in my pocket, wanting to read it a few more times, keeping it to myself until I figured out how to enlist the family members I'd known all my life for help.

"Hey, you didn't even tell me if you liked your gift," Dash said, trying to switch the subject.

I furrowed my brow. "You didn't bring me a gift."

"Not when I came. I dropped it off earlier. You mean you didn't see it? Come on." He grasped my hand and pulled me back outside.

We rounded the corner of my house, and he used his spell phone to shine a light on a metallic object parked by the side of my porch.

"Old Joe," I exclaimed, my hands reaching out to stroke down the worn leather of the seat.

My dad's old motorcycle looked better than it did when he was alive. I petted it like it was Peaches, excited to hear its engine purr. I found the key in the ignition and couldn't help myself. Throwing a leg over, I straddled the machine, my hands falling into place. I kick-started it, and the engine thundered to life louder than before.

I didn't have the heart to ride in the dark, so I killed it after letting Old Joe idle and vibrate underneath me for a couple of minutes. "You finally fixed him."

Dash flashed a toothy grin, very pleased with himself. "It took a long time to find all the parts. You'll have to take it to Lee's garage to have him do whatever he does to make sure it runs without failing here in Honeysuckle. But now you don't have to use your bicycle anymore."

"I like my magic bike," I defended. "But it will be nice to motor around on Old Joe again. Although now Matt will probably want to have his turn since technically Dad left it to him."

Dash chuckled. "Maybe you should have Lee cast a spell so Old Joe only responds to you."

I snapped my fingers, "Now there's an idea."

He shuddered at the sound, and I hated myself for doing it. I scrambled off the motorcycle and hugged him tight, knowing how it triggered him. "I'm so sorry. I shouldn't have done that."

"No, I shouldn't feel like this." His body trembled underneath mine. I stroked my hand on his back, wanting my touch to bring him back to the here and now.

Dash settled his chin on top of my head and stroked my hair. "She really did a number on all of us."

I squeezed my eyes tight, trying not to hear Rita's voice screeching in my head. "She did. And we weren't the ones she hurt the most."

Rita had said that exact phrase to me when she reached into Mason's mind and scrambled parts of it. I knew in my heart that although he was still under Doc Andrew's care, the retired racer had succeeded in causing me a great deal of misery.

"Mason will be okay. You'll get him through it all." Dash stopped petting my head. "Your strength could save the world. You do know that it was you who stopped her today. You flew on a broom, you survived her sabotage, and it was you who ultimately took away her powers."

"And lost mine in the process." The truth tasted bitter. "But yeah. Go me," I snorted.

He stepped back so he could look me in the face. Our eyes had adjusted to the little light the moon gave off, and I knew he wanted me to see and feel his sincerity.

"You are a wonderful woman." He squeezed my hand to make sure I heard him. "Never ever doubt that or I will have to return and kick your butt around until you do," he teased.

"Don't joke. Not about leaving." A tear ran down my face, and I didn't care. Goodbyes were terrible, and I knew we were living in that moment.

"This isn't the end, Charli. It's just a pause while I go back and fix my pack." He wiped the tear away, but another one fell in its place.

"And marry another girl," I whispered.

Dash cupped my face in his hands. "Don't think that I don't regret the day I left you standing in the park. Every damn day, I question what would have happened if I stayed. Whether or not you and I would—"

I placed my finger over his lips. "Please don't finish that," I begged.

Dash pressed a light kiss on the tip of the digit. "I know." Clearing his throat, he let go of me and backed away. "Instead of goodbye, let's just say see you later."

"That's what two buddies say to each other. That or peace out," I snorted, wanting the joke to fix my aching heart.

"Nobody says peace out. How about, I'll be back." He sounded just like the actor in the old movies.

"Too cheesy." A sudden wave of grief hit me, and I rushed to Dash, holding onto him with all my strength. "Don't go."

"I have to." He kissed the top of my head. "The pack needs me and there are things I want to do to...I have a list of stuff...shit." Dash threw his arms around me and hugged me tight against his chest, rocking me back and forth.

It wasn't a heated embrace. This time, we were telling each other everything we needed to say but couldn't. I didn't know if and when I would see him again, but something told me that Dash would never be completely out of my life. Until that time, he would remain a friend I cared for deeply, wanting him to live the best life possible.

When we released each other, we didn't have to say goodbye. Dash put his hand over his heart before turning around and taking long strides toward the road. I couldn't watch him walk away, so I ran to my porch and up the steps.

"Hey, Charli," he called out, stopping me.

"Yeah?"

"Don't worry about Mason. You saved Lucky, you saved me, and you kind of saved all of Honeysuckle. Again," he chuckled. "It's just gonna take a little longer for you to save him." With one last wave, he disappeared into the darkness of the night.

I plopped down on the steps and gave into my sobs. I

cried for Dash leaving, for Mason losing a part of what belonged to both of us, for the loss of my magic. My life was changing, and I had nothing to navigate which way I needed to go.

When the night air blew cool across my tear-stained cheeks and I had nothing left inside me to cry out, I pushed myself up and sat on the top step again. Peaches took back her spot in my lap, and I tried not to dump her out while pulling the note out of my pocket. I read it over and over until I'd memorized it.

Despite my current state, I wasn't alone in this world. I'd never really been alone because I had so many people that loved and cared about me in my life. But now, a new door opened, and whoever was on the other side of it beckoned me to step through.

Fate was definitely a witch with a capital *B*. And I loved witches.

❦

DEAR READER -

Thanks so much for reading *Barbecue & Brooms*! If you enjoyed the book (as much as I did writing it), I hope you'll consider leaving a review!

Collards & Cauldrons: Book 5 is ready to be one-clicked!

NEWSLETTER ONLY - If you want to be notified when the next story is released and to get access to exclusive content, sign up for my newsletter! https://www.subscribepage.com/t4v5z6

NEWSLETTER & FREE PREQUEL - to gain exclusive access to the prequel *Chess Pie & Choices*, go here! https://dl.bookfunnel.com/opbg5ghpyb

Southern Charms Cozy Mystery Series

Magic and mystery are only part of the Southern Charms of Honeysuckle Hollow...

Suggested reading order:

Chess Pie & Choices: Prequel

Moonshine & Magic: Book 1

Lemonade & Love Potions: A Cozy Short

Fried Chicken & Fangs: Book 2

Sweet Tea & Spells: Book 3

Barbecue & Brooms: Book 4

Collards & Cauldrons: Book 5

Cornbread & Crossroads: Book 6 (Coming Soon)

Join my reader group:

www.facebook.com/groups/southerncharmscozycompanions/

Acknowledgments

The phrase "it takes a village" doesn't even begin to cover how many of my friends and family helped bring Book 4 to life. Thanking them at the end of a book seems small compared to the love and encouragement that brought me to The End.

If it weren't for my coffee coven of fellow paranormal cozy writers Danielle Garrett, Cate Lawley, and Tegan Maher, I wouldn't have gotten in so many words. Thanks for keeping me accountable. I owe you all a latte when we meet up with our bigger coven with Amanda M. Lee, Amy Boyles, Leighann Dobbs, and Annabel Chase.

I seem to thank author Melanie Summers in every book I write, but that's because without her, I would never nail down my story plots. Thanks for listening, my friend from the fairyland of Canadia.

My family has always taught me that blood doesn't make a

family, love does. I'm so glad our travels have finally brought us home and closer to each other.

And finally, I have to thank my husband who lets me disappear into the writing cave but always makes sure I'm taken care of. Thanks for believing in my dream.

About the Author

Bella Falls grew up on the magic of sweet tea, barbecue, and hot and humid Southern days. She met her husband at college over an argument of how to properly pronounce the word *pecan* (for the record, it should be *pea-cawn,* and they taste amazing in a pie). Although she's had the privilege of living all over the States and the world, her heart still beats to the rhythm of the cicadas on a hot summer's evening.

Now, she's taken her love of the South and woven it into a world where magic and mystery aren't the only Charms.

bellafallsbooks.com
contact@bellafallsbooks.com
Bella Falls' Newsletter
Southern Charms Cozy Companions

 facebook.com/bellafallsbooks

 twitter.com/bellafallsbooks

 instagram.com/bellafallsbooks

 amazon.com/author/bellafalls

Made in the USA
Coppell, TX
12 July 2021